SUNG PORCELAIN AND STONEWARE

THE FABER MONOGRAPHS ON POTTERY AND PORCELAIN

Present Editors: R.J. CHARLESTON *and* MARGARET MEDLEY
Former Editors: W.B. HONEY, ARTHUR LANE
and SIR HARRY GARNER

BOW PORCELAIN *by* Elizabeth Adams *and* David Redstone
WORCESTER PORCELAIN AND LUND'S BRISTOL *by* Franklin A. Barrett
ROCKINGHAM POTTERY AND PORCELAIN 1745–1842 *by* Alwyn *and* Angela Cox
APOTHECARY JARS *by* Rudolf E.A. Drey
ENGLISH DELFTWARE *by* F.H. Garner *and* Michael Archer
ORIENTAL BLUE AND WHITE *by* Sir Harry Garner
CHINESE CELADON WARES *by* G. St. G.M. Gompertz
SUNG PORCELAIN AND STONEWARE *by* Basil Gray
MASON PORCELAIN AND IRONSTONE *by* Reginald Haggar *and* Elizabeth Adams
LATER CHINESE PORCELAIN *by* Soame Jenyns
JAPANESE POTTERY *by* Soame Jenyns
JAPANESE PORCELAIN *by* Soame Jenyns
ENGLISH PORCELAIN FIGURES OF THE EIGHTEENTH CENTURY *by* Arthur Lane
FRENCH FAÏENCE *by* Arthur Lane
GREEK POTTERY *by* Arthur Lane
YÜAN PORCELAIN AND STONEWARE *by* Margaret Medley
T'ANG POTTERY AND PORCELAIN *by* Margaret Medley
ENGLISH BROWN STONEWARE *by* Adrian Oswald, R.J.C. Hildyard
and R.G. Hughes
CREAMWARE *by* Donald Towner
ENGLISH BLUE AND WHITE PORCELAIN OF THE EIGHTEENTH CENTURY
by Bernard Watney
LONGTON HALL PORCELAIN *by* Bernard Watney
ENGLISH TRANSFER-PRINTED POTTERY AND PORCELAIN
by Cyril Williams-Wood

other books by Basil Gray

Early Chinese Pottery and Porcelain
Japanese Screen-Paintings
Buddhist Cave-Paintings at Tun-Huang
Persian Painting
Painting of India
The World History of Rashid al-Din

SUNG PORCELAIN
AND STONEWARE

BASIL GRAY

faber and faber
LONDON·BOSTON

First published in 1984
by Faber and Faber Limited
3 Queen Square London WC1N 3AU
Printed in Great Britain by
BAS Printers Ltd Over Wallop Hampshire

British Library Cataloguing in Publication Data

Gray, Basil
Sung porcelain and stoneware.—(Faber monographs
on pottery and porcelain)
1. Porcelain, Chinese—Sung dynasties, 960–1280—
Collectors and collecting
I. Title
738.2′0951   NK4565.5

ISBN 0-571-13048-8

FOREWORD

When in 1953 Basil Gray's *Early Chinese Pottery and Porcelain* appeared, the period covered ranged from the late Chou dynasty in about the fifth century BC to the end of the Sung period in the late thirteenth century AD. A time-span as great can no longer be seriously considered for a monograph series such as this. Even as long ago as 1965 a decision was taken to confine the subject of Chinese ceramics to much briefer, mainly dynastic periods. This was chiefly on account of our enormously increased knowledge of Chinese culture as a whole, together with the results of archaeological work carried out by the Chinese since 1949, upon which most of our new understanding of pottery depends.

Perhaps no period has been more affected by the advances of the last thirty years than that encompassed by Mr Gray's review of the wares of the Sung period. He has seen more of the changes that have taken place than most people working in the field, and he now gives us a clear picture of the Sung tradition in ceramics based on all the recent archaeological work. He discusses this, and in some cases earlier conclusions have been modified. In presenting much of the new material he has also been able to identify certain types in public and private collections which have formerly been puzzling. By limiting the time-span to the period from the tenth to the end of the thirteenth century, he has been able to enlarge on the historical and social background in a way not possible in his earlier volume, and show that the Sung was much more innovative than has generally been believed.

MARGARET MEDLEY

CONTENTS

ILLUSTRATIONS

For an artificer produces a determinate form in matter by reason of the exemplar before him, whether it be the exemplar beheld externally, or the exemplar interiorly conceived in the mind.

St Thomas Aquinas, *Summa Theologica*, Q.44, art. 3

There are plenty of craftsmen who can copy all details of form, but the inner nature can be understood only by the highest spirits.

Su T'ung-po (1036–1101)

ABBREVIATIONS

Basil Gray, *Early Chinese Pottery and Porcelain*	ECPP
Far Eastern Ceramic Bulletin	FECB
P. Hughes Stanton and R. Kerr, *Kiln Sites of Ancient China*	*Kiln Sites*
Percival David Foundation	PDF
Sekai Tōji Zenshū	STZ
Transactions of the of the Oriental Ceramic Society	TOCS

KILN SITES

1	TA-T'UNG	26	YÜ-YAO
2	HU-YÜAN	27	YIN-HSIEN
3	HUI JÊN	28	NING-PO
4	CHIEH-HSIU	29	LI-SHUI
5	HOU-CHOU	30	HUANG-YEN
6	YAO-CHOU	31	WÊN-CHOU
7	HSÜN-YI	32	LUNG-CH'ÜAN
8	TING	33	CH'I-K'OU
9	HSING	34	TA-YAO
10	KUAN-T'AI	35	CHIEN
11	TZ'U CHOU	36	LIEN CHIANG
12	HO-PI-CHI	37	TÊ-HUA
13	HSIU-WU	38	YUNG-CH'UN
14	KUNG HSIEN	39	NAN-AN
15	TÊNG-FÊNG	40	AN-HSI
16	MI-HSIEN	41	T'UNG-AN
17	LIN-JU	42	CH'ÜAN-CHOU
18	PAO-FÊNG	43	CHAO-CHOU
19	YÜ-HSIEN	44	HSI-TS'UN
20	LU-SHAN	45	CHING-TÊ-CHEN
21	YÜ-HANG	46	NAN-CH'ÊNG
21A	TZ'U-PO	47	CHI-CHOU
22	HANGCHOU	48	KAN-CHOU
23	HSIAO-SHAN	49	HSIANG-YIN (YO-CHOU)
24	SHANG-YÜ	50	CHANG-SHA
25	SHANG-LIN-HU		

Kiln sites of the Sung Period

PREFACE

It is thirty years since I wrote for this series a volume entitled *Early Chinese Pottery and Porcelain*. Meanwhile the whole study of the subject has been transformed, especially by the archaeological work carried out in the People's Republic of China. We now know far more about the development of the main kiln centres and about the techniques employed in them.

For me personally, also, horizons have greatly expanded: above all through three tours in Japan under particularly favourable conditions; through my month in mainland China as guest of the government; and through seven visits to the United States, which I had previously only visited once, in 1937.

When I was writing my earlier book, most of the fine collections of Chinese ceramics formed in Britain over the previous forty years were still in private hands, and I owed a deep debt to the generosity with which the early members of the Oriental Ceramic Society allowed me free access to their collections and the handling of their pots. Through participating in the preparation of many of the Society's exhibitions during the subsequent twenty years, I was able to enjoy a continuation of that privilege. It is natural therefore that not one word should survive from that first book. But I am not ashamed of the choice of illustrations for it and would gladly have included most of those of the Sung period in this new book had I not preferred generally to choose fresh examples. I regret not being able to include more illustrations from the now large collections in the museums of China; but the representation of the Japanese collections is now much greater.

As to chronology, I have sought greater refinement than is still general in either China or Japan, feeling that the time is ripe for an attempt at precision, through the growth of dated or datable material. I have been guided by the fact that this volume is part of a series and falls between two books in it—both by the editor, Margaret Medley—one on *Yüan Porcelain and Stoneware* and the other on *T'ang Pottery and Porcelain*, published in 1974 and 1981 respectively. Where these books have fully covered a subject, such as the Liao wares or the enamelled Tz'ŭ-chou type, I have decided against repetition.

17

On the other hand, I have regarded it as essential to an understanding of Sung ceramics to look first at the production of the green and white wares of the tenth century on the eve of the Sung dynasty. My book however, is not limited to the Sung dynasty but extends to the products of the Sung period in both north and south China. Sung in this sense represents the high point in Chinese ceramic achievement: a period of technical mastery without loss of the quality of craftsmanship. The stage in industrial growth of the industry had not yet destroyed the tradition of personal touch. With the introduction of moulds that was threatened, not only in the reduction of the potter's participation in each piece but also because their use encouraged over-elaboration of design.

I am especially indebted to Professor Grahame Clark and M. W. Ingram for access to their private collections and for help in obtaining photographs of pieces in their possession; and to Sir John Figgess for advice and help in securing photographs from Japan. Grateful thanks are also due to Yasuhiko Mayuyama for providing many photographic prints from the archives of his firm and some from his personal file; and to Julian Thompson for the supply of photographs of items that have passed through the sale-room of Messrs Sotheby's.

I have not appealed in vain for help in the search for the best possible photographs of pieces in their charge to my colleagues in museums in this country, so rich in the works of my period: John Ayers, Robin Crighton, Jessica Rawson, Rosemary Scott, Laurence Smith, John Sweetman and Mary Tregear. I am duly grateful to them and also to their governing bodies for permission to use this material for illustration. In the United States I thank Henry Trubner in Seattle, Marc W. Wilson in Kansas City and James Watt in Boston for their personal attention; and in Japan I acknowledge invaluable assistance from Masao Ishizawa, Director of Yamato Bunkakan, Haruo Igaki, Shuzo Yokoi of Kochukyo; and from Heibonsha Ltd and the Zauho Press for the loan of negatives.

My greatest debt is, however, to Margaret Medley, editor of this series of monographs, for constant help and encouragement and for her patience through the final stages of the completion of the book.

Long Wittenham, October 1982   Basil Gray

Chapter 1

HISTORICAL BACKGROUND

The first Sung emperor T'ai-tsu (960–76), a man of great energy as soldier and administrator, accessible and not a personal braggart, but above all a Confucian, abolished the governorships on the frontiers and so consolidated the authority of the central government and increased the power of the civil bureaucracy. Such tendencies towards imperial absolutism, supported by the power of a professional and well-trained bureaucracy, reached fulfilment in the reforms of Wang An-shih (1021–86) with resulting centralization and conformity to the interests of the state.[1] Although the conservatives reacted against these tendencies, the reformers prevailed till the end of the Northern Sung in 1126, when the Chin over-ran northern China, captured K'aifêng and the emperor Hui-tsung. Under the Southern Sung, with the capital transferred to Hangchou and its domain restricted to the south, moral control took the place of legal restraint by the central government, thus weakening the position of the state.[2]

These changes in the theory and practice of government did not however produce a static social or commercial situation. The Sung period was in fact a period of expansion, though this might have been greater and more securely based if it had not been for the superior attitude of the Confucian governing class towards the merchants, who were prevented from pressing home the technological revolution and great increase of trade.[3] The period is notable above all for the growth of agricultural production,[4] based on a rotation of crops, the acclimatization of early ripening rice—making double cropping the rule—and the use of iron agricultural tools. It provided surplus food and made possible the development of town life and its industries; and that in turn made for increased export trade. The basis of industrial growth lay in the spectacular

[1] J. T. C. Liu, *Reform in Sung China*, Lexington, 1959, p. 85.
[2] Ibid.
[3] E. Balazs, *Chinese Civilization and Bureaucracy*, London, 1964.
[4] M. Elvin, *The Pattern of the Chinese Past*, London, 1973, Ch. 9, pp. 113–21.

upsurge in iron and coal production. It is said that, under Northern Sung, China had an annual production of iron of about 150,000 tons, equal to that of all Western Europe in the early eighteenth century: it increased twelve-fold between AD 850 and 1050.[5] The demand for fuel led to the exhaustion of the timber supply;[6] by 1017 charcoal was rationed and by the end of the eleventh century it had been completely supplanted as fuel by coal. At the same time there were notable improvements in communications, including shipping; navigation profited from the introduction of the magnetic compass at a date earlier than 1119.[7]

Socially these changes encouraged urban growth and the vitality of commerce, with a corresponding increase in the role of the merchant class, not only as tax payers but also as influential citizens. The development of book-printing widened the basis of the educated classes and increased the catchment area for recruitment to the bureaucracy by the examination system. The old aristocracy had virtually disappeared during the disturbances following the fall of the T'ang empire and was replaced by the gentry-official or literati class, constantly renewed by increased social mobility,[8] but with its ambition always restrained by the prevailing Confucian emphasis on loyalty to the state and on public order. Education was improved and extended, bringing greater diversity of culture and a highly sophisticated period in which reaction against conformity was inspired by men like Su Shih (Su T'ung-po) (see page 23), who led a kind of cult of the rights of the individual in society.

All in all, these developments produced a society that was in every sense expansionist, not, as it has sometimes been represented, introvert or static. In particular, the government encouraged overseas trade and welcomed foreign merchants to the ports. Canton had already been designated for foreign trade in 971, and it was followed by Ch'üan-chou in 1087, a city which had by 1120 a population of half a million.[9] Foreign quarters were provided in these cities with their own elected chiefs who were recognized by the Chinese as competent administrators of their own affairs, their own law and schools.[10] The cutting of westward overland communication by the Khitan and Hsi Hsia led to rapid expansion of the role of shipping. Such needs were first met by the initiative of Muslim merchant fleets, but quickly led also to the growth of a Chinese navy. Larger ships were built and in increased numbers, while navigation improved and the use of the monsoon winds was mastered.[11] Chinese exports even reached the coast of East Africa, and trading missions

[5] R. Hartwell, 'A revolution in the Chinese iron and coal industries during the Northern Sung 960–1126 AD', *Journal of Asian Studies*, XXII, 1962; quoted by Elvin.
[6] Elvin, op. cit., p. 85.
[7] Ibid., p. 137.
[8] L. J. C. Ma, *Commercial Development and Urban Change in Sung China*, Michigan Geographical Publication No. 6, 1971, pp. 7, 79, 145.
[9] Ibid., pp. 33–5.
[10] Ibid., p. 39.
[11] Ibid., p. 29.

were received regularly from the Islamic world from 987 onwards, twenty of them being recorded in Sung sources.[12]

The growth of foreign trade and the import of many luxury goods such as ivory and pepper led to loss of coinage and the consequent introduction of paper currency from the early eleventh century[13] which was, however, a necessary step in the development of a credit system. The increase in coastal shipping combined with the agricultural revolution, already noted, shifted the centre of population and wealth to the south, where the provinces of Kiangsu and Chekiang became main centres of rice production. By late Sung the south represented at least two-thirds of the population and wealth of the whole of China.[14] Fukien had the largest ocean fleet, and the mining of silver, copper and lead in the province increased its importance. Even under Northern Sung it was a leading centre of book production, creating a great demand for paper, brushes, ink-slabs and sticks.[15]

The Sung government relied on the export of silk and porcelain to meet the cost of imports and encouraged their production. By the end of the period, Ching-tê-chên had more than three hundred kilns and employed between a quarter and half a million people[16] in an organized industry with a clear division of labour. Under Northern Sung it is clear that the Ting-yao kilns were very active, as can be judged from the vast quantity of kiln waste at Chien-tz'ŭ Ts'un building up a mound which measures 1,400 metres from east to west and about 1,000 metres from north to south, and must represent an enormous output, mainly from non-official or commercial kilns. The production at T'ung-ch'üan in Shensi of the Yao-chou celadon was also on a large scale, and there were many kilns producing stoneware to which we give the generic title of Tz'ŭ-chou type, named after the principal area of production.

Sung taste has also been misrepresented as wholly conservative and revivalist of archaic shapes. It is now clear that the ceramic imitations of ancient ritual jade or bronze shapes do not begin until late in the Southern Sung period and continue into the Yüan period. In fact bronze vessels seem to have been scarce, simple in decoration and of poor quality under the Sung; and their shapes were far from giving inspiration to the ceramic industry, though they were occasionally themselves derived from pottery shapes. Only in the thirteenth century did there begin a renaissance of the elaborately decorated bronzes of the Warring States period, inlaid with gold and silver; and it is this revivalism which at the same time affected also porcelain shapes and designs.

[12] Ibid., p. 33.
[13] Elvin, op. cit., p. 157.
[14] Ibid., pp. 205–8.
[15] Wai-kam Ho, *Chinese Art under the Mongols,* Cleveland, 1968, p. 111, note 150, for the preeminence of Fukien in culture under the Sung.
[16] K'o Ch'ang-chi, *The Problem of Hired Labor,* by J. T. C. Liu and P. J. Golas, Sung China Innovation or Renovation, Lexington, 1969, pp. 47, 49–50 (quoting Chiang Ch'i, *T'ao-hi-lüeh*).

The Northern Sung ceramic shapes represent rather a continuation and gradual modification of the T'ang tradition as is most clearly seen in the white wares, where the crisp line and clear demarcation of foot and body continues, and the relation to T'ang silver forms is still observable, as for instance in the cusped or lobed bowls such as that excavated at Ting-hsien in 1969 and dated AD 977 (Plate 33), and the bottle-shaped vases.[17] It may already have been in the intermediate stage of development under the Five Dynasties that the modified shapes of Northern Sung began to appear, as in the vase from the Bernat collection in which this shape is modified by a more emphatic and slightly splayed foot and by the transition to the expanded mouth by means of a single curve from the body instead of the earlier flange.[18] If this shape is compared with that of the famous Ju-yao vase from the Alfred Clark collection (Plate 71), now in the British Museum, it will be seen how the shape of the Bernat vase finds its fulfilment in the subtle line of the Ju piece, where it follows an organic curve from foot to lip, shaped like a growing plant, as against the more incisive shape deriving from metalwork still found in the Bernat vase.

In both white and green-glazed wares the gentle lobing of the T'ang–Five-Dynasties small bowls is carried through into the early Northern Sung bowls of the Yao-chou kilns, as for instance in the Seligman bowl carved with a duck against a wave ground (Plate 41), or of Ting-yao as in the bowl carved with lotus flowers from the Malcolm collection (Plate 40). Sometimes even the decoration is preserved, as with the butterfly designs carried through from Yüeh-yao into the late tenth-century Ting-yao.[19] This Yüeh shard was included in the exhibition from the People's Republic of China shown in the British Museum and the Ashmolean Museum in 1980 under no. 55.

Sculptural form which had been so strongly emphasized under T'ang is also carried forward into early Northern Sung ceramics, as witness the Sedgwick Yao-chou stand carved with dwarf or wrestler supports, now in the Berlin-Dahlem Museum.[20] Dr Wirgin has cited for comparison with this piece a Ting-yao incense burner in the Kempe collection with curled dragon support, dating both pieces to the early Northern Sung period.[21] For the most part Northern Sung wares are undecorated; but carved and incised designs of flowers and birds are found on Yüeh-yao of the tenth century, on Ting-yao bowls and dishes, and on the Yao-chou wares on which peony and lotus are commonly found, as well as ducks and fish of slightly later date. It could be argued that such motifs as these correspond to the Northern Sung taste in bird and flower

[17] B. Gray, *Early Chinese Pottery and Porcelain*, London, 1953, Pl. 37; hereinafter quoted as ECPP.
[18] *The Ceramic Art of China*, TOCS, 38, 1972, Pls. 40 and 41.
[19] Compare the design incised inside the lobed bowl dated 977 cited above with the carved design on a Yüeh piece of Five Dynasties date, demonstrated in *Wen-wu*, 1972, No. 8, and reproduced in OCS *Translations*, No. 8, 1978, figs. 1–2.
[20] G. Gompertz, *Chinese Celadon Wares*, London, 1980, second edn., Pl. 55.
[21] J. Wirgin, *Sung Ceramic Designs*, Stockholm, 1970, Pl. 58a.

album-paintings which were favoured above all at the court of emperor Hui-tsung (1103–25).[22] But it should be remembered that such subjects were already established in T'ang art, as can be seen in chased and repoussé silver-ware,[23] the influence of which on ceramic production is emphatic. More boldly carved lotus flowers are found on the Five Dynasties Yüeh-yao vases[24] and on Chi-chou wares of the same period,[25] and this type of design reappears on the carved black-painted wares of Tz'ŭ-chou type, together with the peony, which lends itself to a rather freer treatment. A peony design is also to be seen incised on a fine Ting-yao dish in the Kansas City museum.[26] At Chi-chou this type of design continues into the Southern Sung period, especially in the type of wares on which bands of floral patterns are reserved in a brown glaze.[27]

Thus the taste exhibited by the Chinese potter of the Sung period follows, as would be expected, that shown in the paintings of the court tradition; but it should again be stressed that the ceramic wares most highly praised and supplied to the court itself were mainly undecorated. Two-thirds of the products of the Ting-yao kilns are plain; and so is the whole of the Chün-yao and its noble off-shoot the Ju-yao, except for the very discrete flower inside the Percival David Foundation brush-washer (Plate 72). These depend for their beauty on the thick half-opaque opalescent-blue glaze which is sometimes crackled, as well as on their form.

In 1124 the Nuchen people, having destroyed the Khitan empire of the Liao dynasty, over-ran north China. They even burned Hangchou, but they withdrew from the Yangtze valley. Pushed from the north-west by the rising tide of the Mongols, they established their capital at Peking, where they built a copy of the palace at Pien-ching (K'aifêng) of the captured emperor Hui-tsung. They ruled for a hundred years until they were themselves conquered by the Mongols in 1234. The Chin as their dynasty was named, were more sinicized than the Khitans had been, perhaps because they occupied more Chinese territory and had a large Chinese population as subjects – their architecture being richly decorated in carved wood and with painted ceilings in the larger temples and palace halls. The Chin accepted Confucianism as a good guide for social life and received Chinese culture as a whole.[28] Prominent in this tradition was the scholar-official, philospher and painter Su Shih (1036–1101), more widely known as Su T'ung-po, leader of the tradition of wên-jên-hua, with its stress on painting and calligraphy as expressive of

[22] See O. Sirén, *Chinese Painting*, London, 1956, Pls. 230–9; J. Cahill, *Chinese Painting* (Treasures of Asia), 1960, pp. 72–3.
[23] S. Jenyns and W. Watson, *Chinese Art*, London, 1963, Pls. 21, 26, 28, 29.
[24] M. Medley, *The Chinese Potter*, Oxford, 1976, Fig. 67.
[25] Ibid., Fig. 70.
[26] Wirgin, op. cit., Pl. 74.
[27] Feng Hsien-ming, 'Problems concerning the development of Chinese porcelain', translated from *Wen-wu*, 1973, No. 7 in OCS Translations, No. 8, 1978, figs. 5 and 7.
[28] S. Bush, 'Literati culture under the Chin (1122–1234)', *Oriental Art*, 15, 1969, pp. 103–12.

personality. Ink-play with the painter's brush characterized their work and the bamboo became a favourite subject because it lent itself to this kind of brushwork. An illustration of Su's poem on the Red Cliff on the Yangtze river by the Chin painter Wu Yüan-chih (*c.* 1195), executed in wet ink on a paper handscroll, 136 cm (4 ft 5½ in) long, is now crumpled but treasured in the Imperial collection in Taiwan.[29] It has the quality of immediacy of execution, especially prized by this school, and a largeness of composition inherited from the Northern Sung landscape painters like Kuo Hsi. An anonymous hanging scroll of 'Clearing Snow in the Min Mountains' is a rather self-conscious exercise in revivalist painting of this time, bearing witness to a great respect for tradition.

A similar attitude is to be detected in the products of the Ting-yao kilns under the Chin, but also more obviously in some of the wares of the Tz'ŭ-chou group of kilns. The Sung period as a whole was one of unparalleled prestige and ascendancy for the scholar-official class, which enjoyed great social and economic privileges. It is therefore not surprising that their taste prevailed in the top grades of ceramic production.

[29] *Chinese Art Treasures*, 1961, no. 46.

Chapter 2

THE YÜEH-YAO KILNS:
FIVE DYNASTIES TO EARLY SUNG

The old tradition of stoneware production in Chekiang province, where the earliest green-glazed high-fired ceramics were made, reached its height during the Five Dynasties period when these kilns were officially patronized by the Wu-Yüeh rulers until, after their acceptance of Sung overlordship in 978, they were finally extinguished in 990. The centres of production, which was on a large scale, were at Yü-yao hsien and at the kilns situated by the Shang-lin-hu Lake and further east at Ning-po. These kilns are all situated south of the Ch'ien-t'ang estuary, on the north bank of which stands the city of Hangchou. Earlier kilns producing green stoneware were found in the area of Tê-ch'ing and Yü-hang north of the estuary, but these had ceased production in the fifth century. Shang-yü, about a hundred miles south-east of Hangchou was also an area for production under the Han in the second to third centuries AD, and continued until the sixth century but probably no later. Thereafter the centres of kilns shifted still further eastwards and by the T'ang dynasty the main centres were at Yü-yao and Shang-yü and further east at Ning-po and in Yin-hsien. According to the Chinese archaeologists only incised decoration was used under T'ang, carving starting only in the Five Dynasties period. Moulding was used for the decoration of flat box-lids from the later T'ang and Five Dynasties.

The main kilns were discovered in 1931 and reports published by Ch'ên Wan-li in 1937 and 1946 and by Matsumura in 1938. A. D. Brankston visited the site in 1937[1] and recovered some shards now in the British Museum; but substantial information came only with investigation by the Chekiang provincial Bureau of Antiquities in 1957–8. Further exploration has continued, the most recent being of the Yin-hsien kilns, and a clear picture of distribution and range of techniques, and styles of decoration has emerged, but close dating is still not achieved for many of the types. A second group of kilns was

[1] A. D. Brankston, 'Yüeh ware of the Nine Rocks kiln', *Burlington Magazine*, LXXIII, 1938.

discovered near the southern coast of Chekiang in the neighbourhood of the
port of Wên-chou in 1954–61[2] which was also in production from the Han to
the Sung dynasty with some later extensions. The most important of these
kilns was at Hsi-shan where a tablet dated 971 has been unearthed; but under
Sung the production here was extended to white and brown wares and the
green ware gradually dropped. Although the shapes of the vessels produced
at these kilns were near to those from the Yüeh-yao area well to the north,
the decoration was much simpler though sometimes with quite bold carving,
as on a type of bowl on a high splayed foot carved with lotus or peony flowers
outside. The glaze is always rather pale and the body greyish white, due it
is said to the low iron content, compared with the wares from the northern
Chekiang kilns. Additional shapes are the cup-stand combined with saucer,
a shape perhaps following a lacquer prototype.

Contemporaneous with the Shang-lin-hu kilns is the group of kilns at
Shang-yü, some distance to the south-west, which produced some of the finest
Yüeh wares. Examples of the finest incised and carved wares from here may
be dated to the early Sung period around AD 1000. For instance, the funerary
vase in the Fitzwilliam Museum (Plate 1), with spouts to take incense sticks,[3]
may be given to this kiln. Other kilns of the same period have been located
at Yin-hsien near Ning-po and these also were very active in the tenth century,
producing carved bowls and jars, on which the lotus was a favourite motif,
as for instance on the funerary vase with cover formerly in the Malcolm collection (Plate 2). Here the cover, which fits neatly within the row of spouts, is
carved above with a fully open lotus bloom carrying a small jar in the calix.
Around the foot are carved lotus petals above which are peony flowers, more
freely designed than the stiffer type symmetrically displayed between the
compartmental ribs on the Fitzwilliam vase.

A number of pieces from the Shang-lin-hu kilns bear dates incised under
the foot before glazing. Sir John Addis reproduces a box with date equivalent
to AD 978, on the cover of which is incised a design of a pair of cranes with
outspread wings confronted within the circular frame. Eight spur-marks are
to be seen inside the footrim beyond which the glaze does not extend.[4] Similar
boxes but with floral designs are in the Ashmolean Museum[5] and the Shanghai
museum, also dated 978. The same date of 978 is incised on the base of a
bowl excavated in 1954 at the Shang-lin-hu kiln site and included in the 1980
exhibition of finds from kiln sites shown at the British Museum.[6] This has
a thin everted footrim.

Some shapes known from examples in Japanese and Western collections

[2] Wen-wu, 1965, No. 1, pp. 21–34; OCS Translations, No. 6.
[3] Reg. no. C. 50. 1946.
[4] J. M. Addis, Chinese Ceramics from Datable Tombs, London, 1978, p. 18, fig. 11.
[5] M. Tregear, Chinese Greenwares in the Ashmolean Museum, Oxford, 1976, nos. 148 and 151.
[6] P. Hughes Stanton and R. Kerr, Kiln Sites of Ancient China, London, 1980, no. 63 (Abb.
Kiln Sites).

1 FUNERARY VASE, Yüeh ware
   Height 35.5 cm (14 in). *c.* AD 1000
   Fitzwilliam Museum, Cambridge. See page 26
2 FUNERARY VASE, Yüeh ware
   Height 34.2 cm (13.5 in). Late 10th century
   Formerly Malcolm Collection. See page 26

cannot yet be paralleled among excavated pieces. Among these shapes is the
mei-p'ing or flower vase for display of plum-blossom, but this shape is already
found in Korean celadon in the tenth century and in *ch'ing-pai* at least as
early as 1027, the date of a tomb find at Nanking.[7] Since the Yüeh type ceased
to be made early in the Sung period, the beautiful *mei-p'ing* in the Ingram
collection at the Ashmolean Museum (Colour Plate A)[8] has been regarded
as belonging to the group of early Chekiang celadons of Northern Sung date,
lying stylistically between the Yüeh wares and the Lung-ch'üan, and it has
been attributed to kilns at Li-shui to the north-west of Wên-chou and north-
east of Lung-ch'üan.[9] This group of kilns has not been investigated archaeolo-
gically, but the type of ware does agree with the earliest type associated by
the Chinese with the Lung-ch'üan kilns. In the 1980 shard exhibition nos. 93–
4 were closely associated in technique of combing with lightly incised floral
and fish designs, and the connections with Yüeh ware seemed clear and close.
These shards are among the recent finds of 1979 and full reports of them
have not yet been published. Wirgin noted a resemblance to the Yao-chou
wares of the north, and this is, as we shall see, an area where the influence
from the Yüeh kilns is strong. Thus we cannot be far wrong in taking the
Ingram vase as an example of transition from Yüeh to the Lung-ch'üan wares.
A similar *mei-p'ing* vase in the Aso collection, but with more stylized peony
flowers and a frieze of petals round the shoulder, retains a cover. This also
must be an early Lung-ch'üan ware piece (Ht. 38.2 cm (15 in)).[10] The absence
of any footrim is also in line with the earliest Lung-ch'üan wares, as in the
small brush-washer also included in the 1980 shard exhibition[11] though it
was lent from the Ku Kung museum and not from archaeological excavation.
A vase in the Percival David Foundation (Plate 3) bears a date incised under
the glaze on the side equivalent to AD 1080. It has loop handles on the shoulder,
the body is segmented by vertical grooves and the mouth is dished, all three
features connecting it with another vase from the Ingram collection in the
Ashmolean Museum[12] which is also decorated with incised stylized lotus
flowers and is provided with a low lotus-leaf cover. This might be slightly
earlier than the vase dated 1080 but hardly before 1000. The dated vase is
simply described as 'Celadon type' in Miss Medley's 1977 catalogue of the
celadon wares in the Percival David Foundation (no. 16). In 1960 it was shown
among the Yüeh wares at the Sung exhibition of the Oriental Ceramic Society
and that is why it is brought into association with the Yüeh wares in this
chapter, although I am satisfied that it is actually a product of the earliest
kiln in the Lung-ch'üan group. Of this group of kilns on the Hsi river around

[7] *China's Beauty of 2000 Years*, Tokyo, 1965, Colour Plate 2, No. 31.
[8] ECPP, Pl. 19; and Gompertz, op. cit., second edn., 1980, Pl. 29.
[9] Chu Po-ch'ien in *Wen-wu*, 1963, No. 1; OCS *Translations*, No. 3, 1968.
[10] H. M. Garner and M. Medley, *Chinese Art in Three Dimensional Colour*, Asia Society, 1969,
Vol. 3, p. 87, Reel 11 no. 4.
[11] *Kiln Sites*, no. 95.
[12] ECPP, Pl. 18.

3 VASE, Lung-ch'üan ware
    Height 38.1 cm (15 in). Dated AD 1080
    Percival David Foundation of Chinese Art. See page 28
4 EWER, Yüeh ware
    Height 19.8 cm (7.8 in). Early 11th century
    Umezawa Gallery, Tokyo. See page 30

Lung-ch'üan, with kilns both above and below it in the river valleys, those
at Chin-ts'un and Ta-yao were already functioning in the tenth century,[13]
when they produced a squat form of ewer with curved spout and tall handle
above a sharply formed shoulder; an example from the Seligman collection,
now in the British Museum,[14] has both carved and combed floral decoration.
It is therefore datable to the tenth or early eleventh century. A more advanced
form of ewer is in the Umezawa Gallery, Tokyo,[15] where the body is rounded,
the carved peony design freer and the handle and spout extended (Plate 4);
it is supplied with a cover nearer to those on the funerary vases and perhaps
not belonging to this ewer. This is no doubt from the Yüeh kilns and it demon-
strates the close connection between them and the earliest Lung-ch'üan types.
The Lung-ch'üan version of the funerary vase is illustrated in the catalogue
of the 1965 exhibition in Tokyo from the People's Republic of China 'China's
Beauty of 2000 Years'.[16] The decoration is like that on the Seligman ewer.

The Yüeh kilns at Yü-yao and Shang-lin-hu undoubtedly reached their
peak in the tenth century when, under the Five Dynasties and Early Sung,
they enjoyed the direct patronage of the Wu-Yüeh rulers who were able to
surrender 50,000 pieces of these wares to the Sung in 978.[17] Characteristic
of these wares are the rings of firing clay supports of which clear traces remain
under the base. Precise dating is not easy but the tendency among Chinese
archaeologists now is to date the finer types to Five Dynasties rather than
T'ang. Thus the shards from bowls decorated in fine incised line with parrots
shown in the 1980 exhibition[18] were assigned to this later period. The well-
known and beautiful bowl in the Percival David Foundation (Plate 5) with
a pair of incised phoenixes inside and carved lotus petals on the outside is
here called tenth century and attributed to the period 950–75; its foot resembles that of the dated vase of 978. Under the base is incised the character
Yung (eternal); shard no. 53 in the 1980 kiln site exhibition bears the character
hsin (bitter) and has carved lotus petals also outside. Similarly the saucer-dish
in the Fitzwilliam Museum with foliated rim is here regarded as tenth century
rather than T'ang (Plate 6).

In the Shanghai Municipal Museum is a covered vase with trumpet mouth,
four double handles springing from just below the lip and a double row of
lotus petals carved above the footrim, assigned to Five Dynasties in the 1979
volume of select masterpieces in the museum collection.[19] A vase with a
smaller double pair of loop handles, this time attached to the shoulder at the
base of the trumpet mouth, was the most striking piece in a group of Yüeh

[13] Chu Po-ch'ien, op. cit.
[14] J. Ayers, *The Seligman Collection of Oriental Art*, Vol. 2, *Chinese and Korean Pottery and
Porcelain*, London, 1964, no. D 156, Pl. LIV.
[15] Mayuyama, *Mayuyama, Seventy Years*, Tokyo, 1976, Vol. 1, fig. 338.
[16] *China's Beauty of 2000 Years*, Tokyo, 1965, no. 18a.
[17] Gompertz, op. cit., citing *Sung shih* and *Sung Hui-yao*, p. 62.
[18] *Kiln Sites*, nos. 52–3.
[19] Shanghai Municipal Museum, *Select Catalogue of Ceramics*, Shanghai, 1979, Pl. 26.

5 BOWL with incised design of phoenixes, Yüeh ware
  Diameter 17.4 cm (6.8 in). Later 10th century
  Percival David Foundation of Chinese Art. See page 30
6 SAUCER-DISH, Yüeh ware
  Diameter 15.2 cm (6 in). Later 10th century
  Fitzwilliam Museum, Cambridge. See page 30

ware found in 1969 at Hangchou in Chekiang and shown in the 1973 exhibition in Paris and London of finds by the archaeologists of the People's Republic (Plate 7).[20] It has the unique feature of flower or cloud decoration carried out in iron oxide. The lip is pronounced and the foot small. Another piece from this find is a deep bowl with marked flange to the lip.[21] This feature is seen also in a bowl in the Victoria and Albert Museum, though here the lip is strongly inverted (Plate 8); but this piece also has a remarkably smooth glaze, like the piece found at Lin-an (Hangchou).

Other shapes which point to a tenth-century date and to the Yüeh kilns at Shang-lin-hu are a small dish from the Seligman collection (Plate 9)[22] carved with a design of folded lotus leaves which seems to be unique; and a ewer with long spout, trumpet mouth with dished lip and double-strand handle, found in two versions, one in the Ingram collection,[23] the other in the Brundage collection (Plate 10) with a squarer shoulder, but both with small loops at the base of the neck, splayed foot, and vertical grooves on the body. There is also a lobed bowl in the Percival David Foundation (Plate 11) with flared lip and remains of a ring support under the base but otherwise completely covered by a transparent olive-green glaze. Miss Medley has suggested[24] that this may have been one of the *pi-sê* wares offered by the princes of Wu-yüeh as tribute to the Sung court and also from the Shang-lin-hu kilns.

On the other hand, a fine vase in a Japanese collection (Plate 12) with dished mouth but of sturdier shape than the Fitzwilliam funerary vase, has applied decorative uprights rising from the shoulder, and a strongly carved stylized peony in a lobed medallion.[25] This feature appeared also on a shard from the Shang-yü kilns included in the 1980 exhibition of archaeological finds in China[26] and dated to the Northern Sung period. The vase was in fact dated in Japan to the first half of the eleventh century.[27]

The excavations at the Wên-chou kiln site on the southern coast of Chekiang have been mentioned above; a characteristic of these wares is the pale green of the glaze over a greyish-white body. An example of these wares seems to be the deep bowl in a Japanese private collection with six lobes lightly incised with a peony flower design and with a strongly splayed foot (Plate 13). For shape one might compare shard no. 85 in the 1980 exhibition of *Kiln Sites of Ancient China*, and for style of decoration no. 86. In Japan this bowl is attributed to the eleventh century[28] but I would incline to date it to the late

[20] W. Watson, *The Genius of China*, London, 1973, nos. 329–32.
[21] Ibid., no. 330.
[22] Ayers, op. cit., D 59, Pl. XXV, now British Museum 1973 7-26. 208.
[23] Tregear, op. cit., no. 188.
[24] M. Medley, *Illustrated Catalogue of Celadon Wares*, London, 1977, no. 15, Reg. no. 214, Pl. II.
[25] Cf. Plate 1.
[26] *Kiln Sites*, no. 72.
[27] *Sekai Tōji Zenshū*, New Edition, 1977, Vol. 12, Pl. 171.
[28] Ibid., Pl. 43.

7 VASE decorated in iron oxide under the glaze, Yüeh ware
Height 50.7 cm (19.5 in). From Lin-an, Chekiang. Later 10th century
People's Republic of China. See page 32
8 BOWL with inverted thickened lip, Yüeh ware
Diameter 19.7 cm (7.7 in). Late 10th century
Victoria and Albert Museum. See page 32

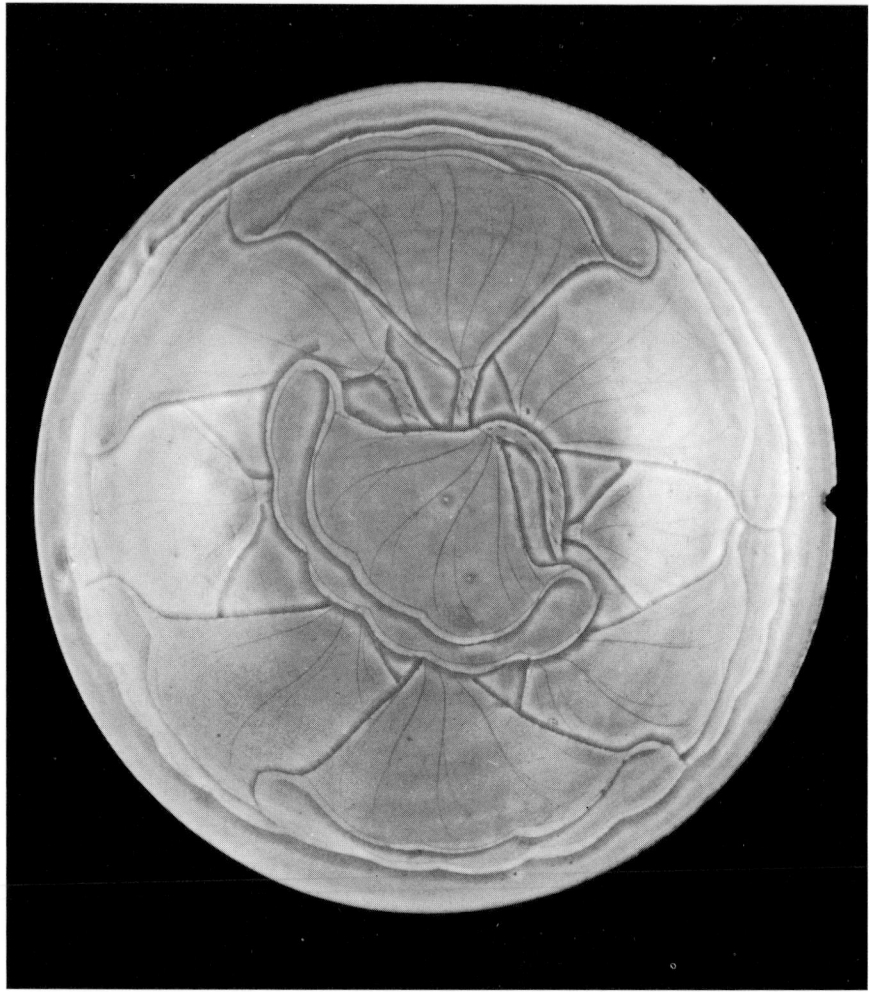

9 (*above*) DISH carved with a design of lotus, Yüeh ware
Diameter 14.7 cm (5.8 in). Late 10th century
British Museum, Seligman Collection. See page 32
10 (*above, right*) EWER, Yüeh ware
Height 17 cm (6.7 in). 10th century
Asian Art Museum of San Francisco, Avery Brundage Collection. See page 32
11 (*below, right*) Lobed BOWL, Yüeh ware
Diameter 13.5 cm (5.3 in). Shang-lin-hu kiln. Late 10th century
Percival David Foundation of Chinese Art. See page 32

12 VASE carved with a peony in a medallion, Yüeh ware
   Height 38.3 cm (15 in). Early 11th century
   Private Collection, Japan. See page 32
13 Lobed BOWL, Wên-chou ware, Chekiang
   Diameter 17.5 cm (6.8 in). Late 10th century
   Private Collection, Japan. See page 32

tenth century. In any case it is a distinguished piece and one that it is interesting to compare with the Percival David Foundation bowl,[29] also six-lobed and attributed to the Yüeh kiln of Shang-lin-hu.

To complete the survey of the Yüeh types it is only fair to include an example of moulding, as applied to the circular domed boxes. These may have a footrim or not; those without being probably slightly later in date, though still of the tenth century. A good example in the Ingram collection at the Ashmolean Museum[30] again has a body and glaze corresponding to the Wên-chou type; the mould carries a floral design of symmetrical scrolling and the foot is recessed. This box can be contrasted with a slightly larger box in the Freer Gallery with carved design of three scrolling peonies on the lid and splayed foot, which is from the Shang-lin-hu kilns and is attributed to the second half of the tenth century.[31]

By 1124, which is the date of the report by Hsü Ching on his visit to Korea, the Yüeh kilns were still remembered for their excellence but evidently no longer producing the ware which the Koryu celadons were reported to resemble. With the loss of the patronage of the princes of Wu-Yüeh the kilns rapidly declined. According to the report by Chu Po-ch'ien,[32] Emperor T'ai Tsung gave orders for the supervision of the ceramic industry in Yüeh-chou in 982,[33] but it is clear that shortly after this date production was concentrated in the kilns of the Lung-ch'üan area, where according to the Sung writer Chuang Chi-yu, the pi-sê ware continued to be made as tribute to the court. As we have seen, tenth-century wares from these kilns have now been identified by the Chinese archaeologists.

[29] Medley, op. cit., no. 15.
[30] Tregear, op. cit., no. 155.
[31] Freer Gallery of Art, *Masterpieces of Chinese and Japanese Art*, Washington, 1976, p. 66.
[32] Chu Po-ch'ien, op. cit.
[33] Chin Tsu-ming in *K'ao-ku Hsüeh-pao*, 1959, No. 3, pp. 107–15; OCS *Translations*, No. 6, 1976, p. 22 gives the date as 978.

Chapter 3

THE YAO-CHOU KILNS OF SHENSI:
AND THEIR IMITATIONS

The Yao-chou kilns, conveniently placed for access to the secondary or western capital Sian, and with abundant coal resources for firing and good communications and above all a source of china stone suitable for high firing with a high alumina content, were already established in the late T'ang period. But they began to specialize in the celadon green glaze only under Northern Sung. The site of the kilns has been thoroughly investigated by the Shensi Research Institute and much material is now available for study and comparison with pieces in Japanese and Western collections. It appears that the rapid development was favoured by contact with the Yüeh kilns, perhaps through migration of potters after the end of the rule of the princes of Wu-Yüeh in 978. At first the vessels, mainly at this time bowls and saucer-dishes, relied on the beauty of shape and glaze, crisp lobing being especially favoured. Carving of the decoration, especially floral or lotus or peony designs, soon became characteristic. This was boldly executed, as on a dish in Tokyo National Museum with a carved lotus design, or on a similar dish in the Victoria and Albert Museum (Plate 14). In the early phase under Northern Sung the design is exuberant and free, as on a dish with flaring lip in the Barlow collection, Sussex University (Plate 15); later with increased sophistication the design is tightened and more carefully organized, as on a dish in the British Museum, Seligman collection (Plate 16), on which two chrysanthemum flowers are displayed, and on a well-known saucer-dish in the Fitzwilliam Museum (Plate 17), on which the design has been developed symmetrically around the

14 DISH, Yao-chou
   Diameter 19 cm (7.5 in). Northern Sung, 11th century
   Victoria and Albert Museum. See page 38
15 DISH, Yao-chou
   Diameter 19.6 cm (7.7 in). Northern Sung, 11th century
   University of Sussex, Barlow Collection. See page 38

central interlace of the peony stems, instead of being more naturalistically laid out as on the Barlow bowl, where the flower nestles naturally among the foliage. Stylization is carried further in the masterly lay-out of the design on a box in the Percival David Foundation (Colour Plate B).

New shapes were now invented, especially different forms of vases and bottles, some with tapering neck, like one in the Michel Calmann collection now in the Musée Guimet, and a nearly identical vase in Japan, slightly smaller (Plate 18); others with wider mouth, as in the vase in the Victoria and Albert Museum, from the Eumorfopoulos collection (Plate 19). On all of them the peonies curl smoothly between stylized lotus petals or floral scrolls, thus beginning the practice of using the design to emphasize the shape of the vessel by dividing the field at points of change in direction of the profile.

With the achievement of complete mastery of kiln practice, more complex forms were produced, such as the ceramic reproduction of the traditional Buddhist water vessel the *kundika*, whose bronze ancestry is still clear in the tall undecorated tapering spout rising from elegant baluster-shaped body. The example in the Hoyt collection in the Boston Museum of Fine Arts (Plate 20) is covered with the same masterly design of floral scrolls as on the normal vases. Stands in a form developed in lacquer must have had a prototype in metal from which the Yao-chou version derives its shape, formed in three distinct sections, foot, stem and funnel-shaped bowl (Plate 21); both the lower sections are perforated, and the broad mouth-rim is carved with curling lotus. An especially beautiful shape is the cusped bowl with no foot. Two outstanding examples are the twelve-lobed bowl from the Sedgwick collection and the six-lobed bowl in the Tokyo National Museum (Plate 22),[1] both with carved floral designs, the former covering the whole surface both inside and out, the second divided into separate units by lobes.

Ewers and covered bowls are found under T'ang and Five Dynasties; but both these shapes were widely developed forms under Northern Sung, especially in the Ting and *ch'ing-pai* wares. At the Yao-chou kilns the ewer becomes slimmer and less bulbous than the Yüeh-yao shape, with longer and more decisively curved spout. In the British Museum a ewer from the Eumorfopoulos collection (Plate 23) has the spout terminating in a bird's head, resembling the early Yüeh-yao ewers with chicken spouts, but now more naturalistic. This ewer has a lobed body, while another example in the Baur Foundation[2]

---

[1] Tokyo National Museum, *Chinese Ceramics*, 1965, no. 203.
[2] J. Ayers, *The Baur Collection: Chinese Ceramics*, Geneva, 1968, Vol. 1, A24.

---

16 DISH, Yao-chou
    Diameter 19.6 cm (7.7 in). 12th century
    British Museum, Seligman Collection. See page 38
17 DISH, Yao-chou
    Diameter 18.75 cm (7.4 in). 12th century
    Fitzwilliam Museum, Cambridge. See page 38

18 BOTTLE, Yao-chou
Height 22.2 cm (8.7 in). 12th century
Private Collection, Japan. See page 40

19 BOTTLE, Yao-chou
Height 23.9 cm (9.4 in). 12th century
Victoria and Albert Museum. See page 40

has plain cylindrical body and spout; both however show the rather free design of carved peony flowers which suggests an early phase under Northern Sung. A more sophisticated shape of ewer and with more careful lay-out of the carved peony design is seen in the Avery Brundage collection in San Francisco (Plate 24), formerly in the Eumorfopoulos collection, which also has a double-strand handle and grooved neck; the handle and spout recall the Five Dynasties shape of ewer at the Yüeh-chou kilns.[3] A unique shape for a wine ewer

[3] Tregear, op. cit., nos. 138 and 182.

20 VASE of *kundika* shape, Yao–chou
   Height 21.8 cm (8.5 in). 11th–12th century
   Hoyt Collection, courtesy of the Museum of Fine Arts, Boston. See page 40

21 Tall STAND, Yao-chou
   Height 23 cm (9 in). 11th–12th century
   Asian Art Museum, San Francisco, Avery Brundage Collection. See page 40
22 Lobed BOWL, Yao-chou
   Diameter 15.7 cm (6.2 in). 11th–12th century
   Tokyo National Museum. See page 40

23 EWER, Yao-chou
Height 22 cm (8.7 in). 11th century
British Museum. See page 40

24 EWER carved with a peony design. Yao-chou
    Height 23 cm (9 in). *c*. AD 1100
    Asian Art Museum, San Francisco, Avery Brundage Collection. See page 42

25 WINE POT, Yao-chou
   Height 21 cm (8.2 in). *c.* AD 1100
   Metropolitan Museum of Art, New York, gift of Mrs Samuel T. Peters. See page 48

is in the Metropolitan Museum of Art, New York, with round body and triple lion feet, evidently deriving from a T'ang silver form (Plate 25), though no surviving piece shows this form of feet, common however in the T'ang pottery grave-goods. This ewer has a hoop handle of dragon shape on which a child riding provides a knop. The carved decoration admirably matches the shape of the body, the low relief peony scrolls and phoenixes emphasizing the curve of the profile. Only the small cover is missing from this outstanding product of the Yao-chou kiln at the height of its production.

A fine flask-shaped vase in the Palace Museum in Peking has a short straight neck and flat flanged lip above a swelling shoulder and is boldly carved with scrolling peony flowers above a faint frieze of petals.[4] A tall *mei-p'ing* vase in the Shanghai Museum[5] has similar carved designs to that illustrated in Plate 26. A small jar in the Musée Guimet is boldly carved with overlapping peony petals round the body (Plate 27), while a shallower pattern of similar petals in reverse direction spreads out from the well-formed lip. Rather less assertive is the peony carving found on the cover and cup of several small jars with lids, such as one in the Victoria and Albert Museum from the Alan Barlow collection (Plate 28), though the carving on the lid is slightly blundered. The style of decoration in low, almost flat relief resembles that on the phoenix ewer in the Metropolitan Museum. Perhaps the finest example (Plate 29), in the Seattle Art Museum, has a differently shaped cover, which, though obtained separately, fits perfectly. Here the loop handle is contained within a circle and the rim is everted. On both cover and jar the carving is flat and the glaze thin, giving increased contrast with the more heavily glazed parts.

Two new forms were introduced into the northern ceramic repertory at this time; the first is a squat form of vase called *tou-lou-p'ing* with small mouth like the *mei-p'ing* but without footring. Once more the Yao-chou version of this form is covered with floral carving of peonies between friezes of lotus petals, as in an example in the Ataka collection, Osaka.[6] This shape is much commoner in the Tz'ŭ-chou type wares, both in the kind with floral sgraffito decoration, more formal than in the Yao-chou wares, and in those with freely painted leaf sprays in black on white slip, vouched for at Kuan-t'ai-ts'un in Hopei, before the conquest of north China by the Chin.

The second is the kidney-shaped pillow, also frequent among the Tz'ŭ-chou wares of Northern Sung date, including one dated 1071 in the British Museum of rather squarer shape. The finest pillow is that from Yao-chou in the Seikadō collection in Tokyo (Plate 30), carved with peony blooms on the sides and a phoenix in flight over scrolling peonies on the top, enclosed within a cusped frame.

We know that the Yao-chou kilns supplied wares as 'tribute' to the Sung

---

[4] *Ku-kung Po-wu-yüan Ts'ang Tz'ŭ hsüan-chi*, Peking, 1962, Pl. 32.
[5] Shanghai Municipal Museum, op. cit., Pl. 40, Ht. 48.4 cm.
[6] *STZ*, 1977, Vol. 12, Pl. 48; and Gompertz, op. cit., Plate E facing p. 128.

A Yüeh celadon *mei-p'ing* VASE with incised and combed decoration
Height 27 cm (10.6 in). Northern Sung, 11th century
Ashmolean Museum. See page 28

B Yao-chou celadon BOX
with carved decoration
Diameter 17.7 cm (7 in).
Northern Sung, 11th
century
*Percival David Foundation
of Chinese Art. See page 40*

26 *Mei-p'ing* VASE, Yao-chou
  Height 43.2 cm (17 in). 11th–12th century
  Fitzwilliam Museum, Cambridge. See page 48

27 JAR with carved and incised decoration, Yao-chou
     Height 12 cm (4.7 in). 11th–12th century
     Musée Guimet, Calmann Collection. See page 48
28 Covered JAR, Yao-chou
     Height 10.5 cm (4.1 in). 11th–12th century
     Victoria and Albert Museum. See page 48

29 Covered BOWL, Yao-chou
Height 8 cm (3.1 in). *c.* AD 1100
Seattle Art Museum, Eugene Fuller Memorial Collection. See page 48

30 PILLOW, Yao-chou
Length 23.3 cm (9.2 in). Height 10.7 cm (4.2 in). 11th century
Seikadō Foundation. See page 48

court in the Ch'ung-ning reign (1102–6) and the vast hoard of shards found near Peking may represent the remains of a storehouse for tribute to the Chin conquerors in 1126.[7] Presumably the kilns were at their height at this period under Ch'ung-ning, and the *Sung-shih* confirms the arrival of tribute from Yao-chou under Hui-tsung and his predecessor for thirty years. But this is not to imply that these kilns were really 'official'; but rather that tax officers selected pieces for palace use as part of tax due. As early as 1085 there is a record of fifteen pieces being sent to the palace. It is clear however that the operation of the kilns was basically commercial. A tablet dated 1084 records the perfect control of potting at that time and the deliberate attempt to imitate the carving and colour of jade. The use of moulds begins to supplement carved decoration from the late Northern Sung period about 1085, as at the Ting-yao kilns. By the end of Northern Sung the moulds employed at the Yao-chou kilns surpassed in quality those from any other kilns. Designs with both dragons and phoenix against a wave background were special features of this period. Although the Chin conquest led to the devastation of the western capital of Sian and transfer to Peking of as many as a hundred thousand people, the activity of the Yao-chou kilns continued unabated; and production actually increased, thanks to the reduction of the incised designs to a sketchy decoration in which combing was used to supplement the rapid incised design, as in the small bowl in the British Museum with a duck among waves (Plate 31). The faint impress of combing is visible. In the moulded wares a common design was of boys vintaging, an example from the Seligman collection in the British Museum being paralleled by shards found in the Yao-chou excavations.[8] A more elaborately moulded piece is the incense vase excavated at Lan-tien in Shensi province in 1960 and included in the 1973 exhibition in Paris and London.[9] The shape and decoration recall the archaic bronze vessels of Western Chou period and thus illustrate the taste for archaizing copies which is now believed to have started in the very late Sung period; consequently this vessel is certainly of Chin date and probably not earlier than the late twelfth century. It is covered with a rather pale-green glaze which is characteristic of this period at the Yao-chou kilns. The main shape and decoration is from moulds but the *lei-wên* pattern round the shoulder and neck is impressed. The tendency

[7] This paragraph is based upon a lecture in the Ashmolean Museum, Oxford, in June 1980, by Fêng Hsien-ming of Academia Sinica, Peking.
[8] *K'ao-ku*, 1959, No. 12, Pl. 7/5.
[9] Watson, op. cit., no. 337.

---

31 SAUCER-DISH, Yao-chou
    Diameter 11.5 cm (4.5 in). Chin, 12th century
    British Museum, Seligman Collection. See page 52
32 SAUCER-DISH, Lin-ju ware, Honan
    Diameter 11 cm (4.3 in). 11th–12th century
    Grahame Clark Collection, Cambridge. See page 54

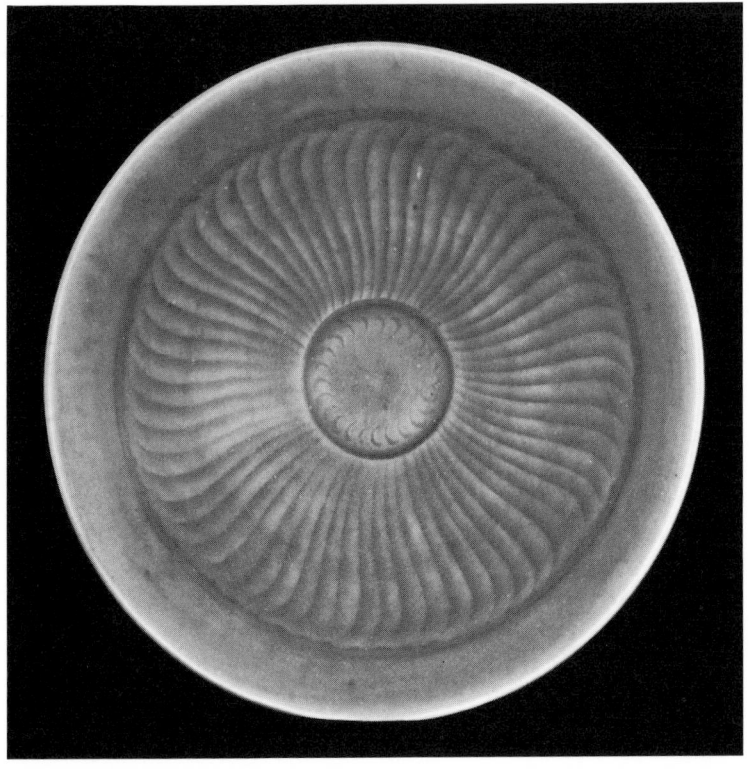

towards archaism arises only at the end of the Sung period when Chin taste in the north shared in this aspect of late Southern Sung taste.

Another tendency of this period towards sketchy design is well illustrated in a bowl with a Chin date equivalent to AD 1162 in the Los Angeles County Museum from the Heeramaneck collection.[10] Here we may see further evidence of hasty mass production in the ring bare of glaze inside the bowl, a result of the use of clay rings in stacking the bowls in the kiln, instead of the traditional use of stacked saggars which occupied more space and took longer to prepare. The incised and carved design of lotus floating on waves is nonetheless attractive. The thin glaze at the Yao-chou kilns allows the decoration to appear more clearly than in the products of the Lung-ch'üan or Koryu kilns. Chinese archaeologists have identified a kiln active under the Chin at Hsün-yi, seventy kilometres south-west of Yao-chou on shards from which a circle scraped clear of glaze shows where the ring support rested in the kiln.[11] In this period it is said that square frames are a feature of design of decoration, as on a bowl in the Ku Kung in Peking,[12] where a buffalo gazes at the moon carved within a decorative square.

Another group of kilns active in the Chin period in producing celadon-type wares was at Lin-ju hsien in Honan province; it was identified first in the early 1930s by Japanese archaeologists and was quickly assumed by Western as well as Japanese ceramic scholars and collectors to have been the main source of all 'Northern Celadons', as they were then called. In fact there is much in common between these two wares. However the Lin-ju kilns produced a much higher proportion of moulded pieces and the majority of its products were bowls and dishes. But carving was still employed, as on a bowl in the Grahame Clark collection (Plate 32), Cambridge, where the centre of the stylized chrysanthemum flower which fills the centre shows the corona incised, while the petals seem to be impressed from a mould. A clear use of an elaborate mould is seen on a saucer-dish excavated at the kiln site and exhibited in Japan in 1965.[13] Here there is a border pattern of a floral running scroll enclosing an almost arabesque lay-out of chrysanthemum flowers and foliage (diameter 19.3 cm (7.6 in), double that of the Clark bowl). A shallow bowl, of size midway between these, in the Neave-Hill collection in London,[14] has a moulded design of three shells agains a wave background in a symmetrical pattern. A shard with a similar design was found in the excavation at the Lin-ju kiln site of Yen-ho-tien by Fêng Hsien-ming.[15] Many of the finds there, however, were undecorated but not unattractive, as a jar with small

[10] Wirgin, *Sung Ceramic Designs*, op. cit., Pl. 3 i.
[11] *Kiln Sites*, nos. 493–500.
[12] Ibid., no. 493.
[13] *China's Beauty of 2000 Years*, no. 53.
[14] TOCS, 38, 1972, no. 72.
[15] *Wen-wu*, 1964, No. 8, p. 35.

mouth also shown in Japan in 1965.[16] This shape is found also in Koryu celadon of roughly contemporary twelfth-century date, and less surprisingly in the Chün ware from the same Lin-ju kilns, at neighbouring Yü-hsien.

More recently Chinese archaeologists have found another kiln in Honan, situated between Lin-ju and Yü-hsien at Pao-fêng, where a similar northern type of celadon was made, with other wares, under Northern Sung and Chin dynasties.[17] A shard shows a tall leaf pattern carved boldly under the glaze. This was evidently another kiln where the Yao-chou style was copied; and other imitations were made in the southern provinces of Kiangsi and Kuang-tung, and it is from these kilns that the wares were exported to the West and have been found in quantity at Fustat. I would regard it as improbable that the wares from the Yao-chou kilns could have made the distant sea voyage to the Red Sea.

[16] *China's Beauty of 2000 Years*, no. 55.
[17] *Kiln Sites*, nos. 380–1.

Chapter 4

TING-YAO AND THE WHITE WARES
OF NORTHERN SUNG AND CHIN

The kiln site of the Ting-yao, a ware famous in literature, was discovered in the 1930s at Chien-tz‘ǔ Ts‘un in Ch‘ü-yang hsien in Hopei province. The discovery was published by Fujio Koyama in 1941 and the site was investigated by Ch‘ên Wan-li in 1956 and by a team from the Hopei Province Bureau of Culture in 1961–2. Accounts were published in *Wen-wu* and *K‘ao-ku*,[1] and an abstract of this last report formed No. 4 of the *Chinese Translations* by the Oriental Ceramic Society in 1968. It is now clear that these kilns are in fact the primary source of the classic Ting ware.

Mrs Hin-cheung Lovell has pointed out how confusion over Chinese administrative nomenclature had delayed the discovery of the kilns in spite of the identification of the ware from descriptions in literary sources. She pointed out in 1964 that during the Northern Sung dynasty Ch‘ü-yang Hsien was a part of Ting Chou prefecture, which consequently gave its name to the products of these kilns.[2] Yeh Lin-chih observed this in 1934 and Koyama following this clue found the kiln site in 1941 and was astonished by the huge size of the mounds of kiln waste, as was Ch‘ên Wan-li in his turn. These remains cover an area of about 1,170,000 square metres. Although the waste heaps have been eroded during the centuries since the closure of the kilns, and thus the upper strata confused, it is clear that production started in the T‘ang period and continued through the Five Dynasties but reached a peak in quantity of output under Northern Sung. Pieces datable to the later tenth century have now been found; in 1969 a lobed saucer-dish was excavated in Ting-hsien with a dedication in ink under the foot to the second year of the T‘ai-ping period, equivalent to AD 977 (Plate 33). Under the glaze it was incised with the character *kuan* (official). This formed one of a group of finds under Buddhist pagodas where they had been deposited at the time of dedication. The date of this particular deposit was 995 and some of this group

[1] See *Wen-wu*, 1953, No. 9 and *K‘ao-ku*, 1965, No. 8.
[2] H-C. Lovell, *Illustrated Catalogue of Ting Yao and Related White Wares in the Percival David Foundation of Chinese Art*, London, 1964.

33 SAUCER-DISH marked *kuan*, Ting-yao
   Diameter 12.8 cm (5 in). Dated 977. Excavated in 1969 in Ting-hsien, Hopei
   People's Republic of China. See pages 22, 56
34 FLASK, Ting-yao
   Height 19.8 cm (7.7 in). From a Buddhist pagoda, dedicated in Ting-hsien in 995
   People's Republic of China. See page 58

were exhibited in Paris and London in 1973/4.[3] The significance here of the term *kuan* which is also found on a shard from the Ting-yao kiln site[4] is hard to assess, but it probably means 'as supplied for government service'; and it is not to be taken to mean that the kiln was a state factory. The find under the pagoda included also a piece of conch-shell shape and a flask originally with a silver lid (Plate 34), bottle neck and bulbous body, carved below the shoulder with a double frieze of lotus petals. This form of decoration is also found on the most striking piece from this find, a *kundika* or Buddhist pure-water ewer (Plate 35) of original metal shape with tall tapering spout above a grooved neck and short dragon-headed spout above the shoulder; between the lotus petal friezes are stylized chrysanthemum sprays and the height is over 60 cm.

The archaeologists state that the T'ang period products were always un-decorated, while those of the Five Dynasties sometimes have incised floral designs, but plain pieces still predominate and the use of moulds is unknown. The pre-Sung wares are thick and with unglazed foot. From the Northern Sung onwards stepped saggars were usually employed for the making of the most numerous shapes, bowls and dishes, which were fired resting on their rims. The bare lip seems generally to have been fitted afterwards with a narrow metal sheath to conceal the bare body and to protect it in use. This practice covered much the greater part of the production; it was not used for every piece but it was obviously essential to large production, for the side walls of the saggar were grooved in successive steps so as to take several vessels of increasing size inverted one above another.

Among early pieces fired on the footrim is a jar with ceramic lid (Plate 36) in the Percival David Foundation,[5] carved round the body and on the shoulder with a stylized leaf pattern. By analogy with datable finds in China this can be dated late in the tenth century, at the beginning of the Sung dynasty. The carved petals have been compared by Mrs Lovell with the de-coration of Yao-chou pieces and she even suggested that it might be a product from a Shensi or Honan kiln, where celadon was also made; but this seems improbable in the light of kiln evidence. It has in fact been accepted as Ting-yao by the most recent writers, Gakuji Hasebe and Margaret Medley, and attributed, surely correctly, to the early Northern Sung period *c*. AD 1000.

Indeed there is a good deal in common among several of the types of vessel fired on the footrim in the eleventh century. Double or treble rows of lotus petals rising from the foot are the main decoration of the *kundika* and a flask from the dedication of 995, and of a ewer in the Goto Art Museum, Tokyo (Plate 37); and of the beautiful cut-down *mei-p'ing* vase, formerly in the Alfred Clark collection and now in Japan;[6] but in this last the swelling body is filled

---

[3] Watson, op. cit., nos. 339–44.
[4] *Kiln Sites*, no. 341.
[5] M. Medley, *T'ang Pottery and Porcelain*, London, 1981, no. 6, Reg. no. 163.
[6] ECPP, Pl. 40, and STZ, 1977, Vol. 12, Pl. 4.

35 BOTTLE of *kundika* shape, Ting-yao
    Height 60.5 cm (23.8 in). Excavated in Ting-hsien, Hopei. Early 11th century
    People's Republic of China. See page 58

36 Covered JAR, Ting-yao
    Height 15.3 cm (6 in). Late 10th century
    Percival David Foundation of Chinese Art. See page 58
37 EWER, Ting-yao
    Height 19 cm (7.5 in). 11th century
    Goto Art Museum, Tokyo. See page 58

38 JAR with ear handles, Ting-yao
    Height 14 cm (5.5 in). 11th century
    Baur Foundation, Geneva. See page 62
39 BASIN with incised design of lotus flowers inside, Ting-yao
    Diameter 28.5 cm (11.2 in). Early 11th century
    Victoria and Albert Museum. See page 62

with deeply carved peony scrolls and with incised veins to the leaves, a more advanced technique which we shall meet again. Undecorated pieces were of course still produced, such as the jar in the Baur Foundation (Plate 38), with carefully formed footrim and loop handles on the shoulder. The lip is bare and may originally have been provided with a lid.

The greater part of the products of the Ting kilns must have been produced for the ordinary market and it represents therefore the taste of the increasingly wealthy citizen classes, merchants as well as officials, in the rapidly expanding society. They must have been for everyday use as dishes, tea-bowls, ewers or bottles and deep basins. These basins may have the sides formed with a mould into eight lobes, as examples in the Percival David Foundation[7] and the former Alfred Clark collection,[8] in the first case with a lotus scroll carved in the centre inside, in the second, peonies incised in each of the lobes as well as in the centre of the interior. Alternatively the basin may be larger and have either straight or curved sides; both types are represented in the Percival David Foundation[9] and there are also basins of the second type in the British and Victoria and Albert Museums (Plate 39). These all have rows of lotus petals outside, while incised over the inner surface are either fish among weeds or freely growing lotus scrolls. The straight-sided type has naturally a groove separating base from wall inside, and thus dividing the decoration into a field and border; but in the David basin both are filled with peony scrolls, as is also the outside. This design is more dense and brocade-like and is probably rather later than the rounded type and dates from later Northern Sung. The basin in the Victoria and Albert Museum (Plate 39), from the Eumorfopoulos collection, has a freely incised design of lotus flowers over the whole interior, among which a fish is disporting; the rim, which is without copper sheath, is slightly everted and thickened at the edge. It may be dated to the early eleventh century.

The commonest types and perhaps the most beautiful are, however, the bowls and dishes on which a rather limited range of designs appear, always incised or carved. Most frequent are the bowls with free lotus flowers or peonies incised over the whole surface without distinction of the central field. These bowls may be gently lobed, as in the example from the former Malcolm collection (Plate 40). This is probably the earlier type; later the design becomes

[7] Medley, *Ting*, nos. 24 and 22, Reg. nos. 102 and 154 respectively.
[8] ECPP, Pl. 39.
[9] Medley, *Ting*, no. 37, Reg. no. 113.

---

40 Six-lobed BOWL with an incised design of lotus, Ting-yao
    Diameter 21.5 cm (8.5 in). 11th century
    Formerly Malcolm Collection. See pages 22, 62
41 DISH with incised design of lotus flowers, Ting-yao
    Diameter 16.9 cm (6.6 in). 11th century
    British Museum, Seligman Collection. See pages 22, 64

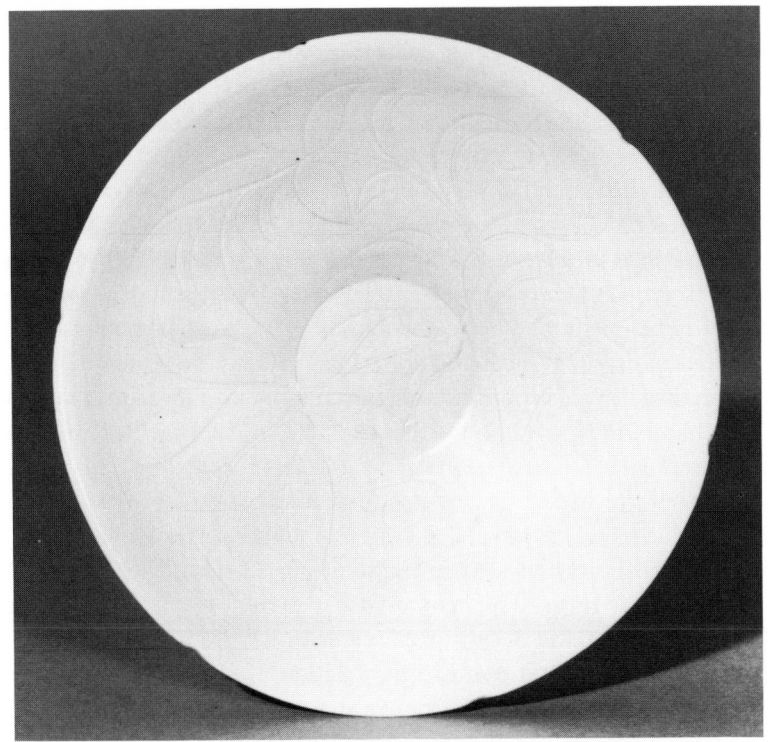

more carefully developed with a tendency to symmetry, as in the British Museum bowl from the Seligman collection (Plate 41), in which combing has been introduced to give texture to the lotus plants, here directly disposed on either side of the bowl, which is unlobed. Another favourite type of design on the bowls is of pairs of fish or ducks on a background of waves and with the addition of water-plants. A bowl in the Museum of Far Eastern Antiquities (Plate 42), Stockholm, is a fine example of this latter design and shows very natural lotus plant and rushes. The use of a comb is clearly apparent. Sometimes the underside of a bowl may also be incised with petals to complement the peony foliage inside as on a small bowl of very good quality from the Oppenheim collection in the British Museum.[10] Other bowls have only spirals from the centre towards the rim incised in double line to suggest vegetation, as in examples in the David Foundation (Plate 43)[11] and the British Museum. Such decoration seems perfectly adapted to the adornment of this ware, discreet, never interfering with the shape, but on the contrary gently enhancing it; free, uncluttered, organic. The taste it follows corresponds to the taste in painting of the Northern Sung Academy in its simplicity, restraint and feeling for natural form. The ground is never fully charged, as it is in the moulded pieces, nor the design enclosed within a framing pattern. In fact this represents the highest point in the relation of form and design in Sung ceramics, which is to say, in all ceramic history.

The dishes with flat rim provide variants on these types, to my mind not so perfect, though a dish in Kansas City Art Gallery (Plate 44) is worthy of esteem for the design of the peony spray and its proficient execution in the style associated with emperor Hui-tsung. It may however be correct with Jan Wirgin to attribute it to the Chin period. But, if so, that would help to indicate how little the Chin conquest affected the Ting kiln production. At this point it may be well to refer to the *obiter dictum* in the *Ko Ku Yao Lun* of 1388 that 'the best Ting wares were produced in the Hsüan-ho and Chêng-ho periods',[12] that is between 1111 and 1125. This is to be considered in relation to the judgement of the Hopei Archaeological Team that 'the decline of the Ting ware kilns was a result of disturbances caused by the invasion of the Tartars. The golden age of Ting ware came to an end with this political event. The only post-Northern Sung artifacts so far found are very few pieces of Chin and Yüan ceramics collected from the surface of area two (of the kiln waste).'[13] It must be stated, however, that this opinion is prejudiced or circular; for the dating of the finds at the kiln sites is on a basis of traditional dating, which assumes this decline under the Chin. In fact, as we shall see there is every reason to think that the very best moulded Ting wares were made under the Chin; and that there was no cessation in the production of

[10] BM, Reg. no. 1947, 7–12, 58.
[11] Medley, *Ting*, no. 37, Reg. no. 113.
[12] P. David, *Chinese Connoisseurship: the Ko Ku Yao Lun*, London, 1971, p. 141.
[13] *K'ao-ku*, 1965, no. 8.

C Chün-yao JAR
Height 9.5 cm (3.7 in). Northern
Sung, 12th century
British Museum. See page 84

D Chün-yao foliate DISH
Diameter 25.6 cm (10.1 in).
Northern Sung, 12th century
Percival David Foundation of
Chinese Art. See page 84

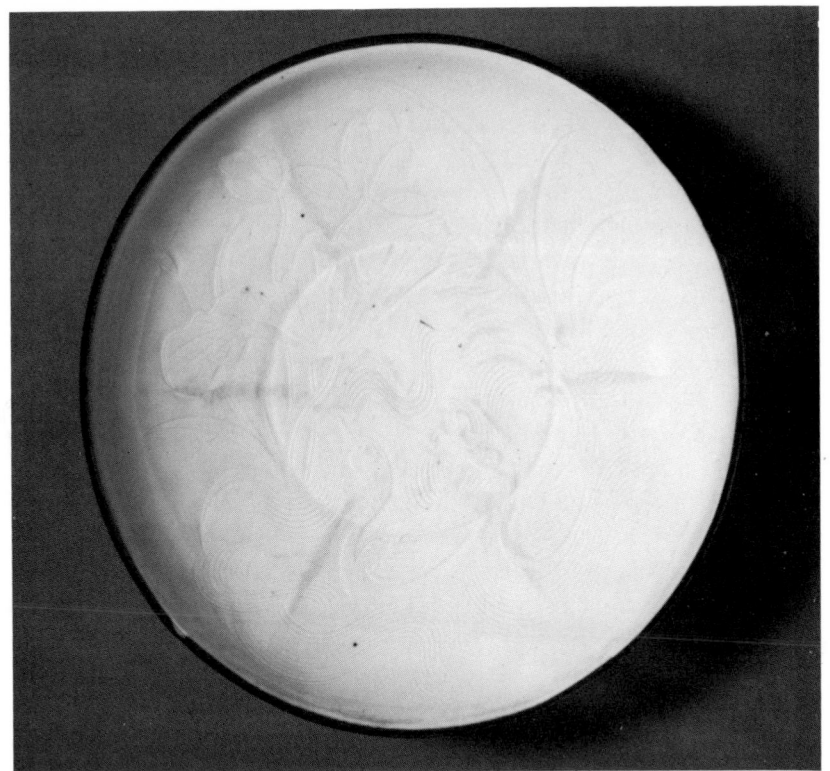

42 Lobed BOWL with incised design of ducks and water-plants, Ting-yao
Diameter 20.7 cm (8.1 in). 11th century
Museum of Far Eastern Antiquities, Stockholm. See page 64
43 BOWL with formal incised design, Ting-Yao
Diameter 12.7 cm (5 in). 11th century
Percival David Foundation of Chinese Art. See page 64

the plain or incised wares. The legend of the mass emigration of potters to the south on the fall of K'aifêng in 1126 is without foundation and there seems to have been no significant interruption of production at the Ting kilns nor abrupt changes in technique or design.

We must return meanwhile to the Northern Sung production of the kilns, which was not confined to the bowls and dishes but included some very distinguished shapes fired on the footrim. Foremost among these is a tall *mei-p'ing* type of vase, of which the best-known example is in the Percival David Foundation (Plate 45). This vase is remarkable for the beauty of the profile rising from a rather small foot to a swelling shoulder and contracting to a small well-formed flaring mouth. This curved outline has been achieved in spite of its having been thrown in three separate parts still distinguishable under the glaze just below the peony flower which is the central unit in the design, and where the neck joins the shoulder. The frieze of lotus petals above the foot is freely incised and with additional combing, which also appears less conspicuously in the detail of the peony blossom and foliage above. The design covers the ground and is developed in a highly sophisticated style; the date is therefore likely to be early in the twelfth century. For long this vase was believed to be of unique shape; but similar vases have since been discovered in tombs in China. A perfect example is now in the Ku Kung in Peking.[14] This vase was excavated from a tomb in Kiangsu province in 1956. A second even taller vase is also in the Ku Kung collection; it is damaged and came from a different tomb.

An apparently unique-shaped ewer in the Musée Guimet, Paris, has the body constructed to form a double gourd and the handle looped round to form a large oval. The glaze is white and the body is carved with a naturalistic rendering of peony flowers and foliage, the foot and mouth being encircled by friezes of lotus leaves (Plate 46). The treatment differs essentially from the conventionalized peony design on the *mei-p'ing* vase from the tomb of 1027 which is described below (page 144) in the account of the *ch'ing-pai* wares, to which this ewer was once ascribed.[15] In it a result is achieved of one of the happiest marriages of form and decoration. It is worth noting that

---

[14] *Ku-kung*, 1962, Pl. 15; height 37.5 cm (14.8 in) as against 36.3 cm (14.3 in) for the David Foundation example.

[15] Wirgin, *Sung Ceramic Designs*, op. cit., Pl. 23a, as *ch'ing-pai*, Southern Sung. Also reproduced by J. Mayuyama, *Chinese Ceramics in the West*, Tokyo, 1960, Pl. 55, where it is again attributed to Southern Sung, but with white, not a *ch'ing-pai* glaze.

---

44 DISH with incised design of flowers, Ting-yao
   Diameter 26.7 cm (10.5 in). Early 12th century
   William Rockhill Nelson Gallery of Art, Kansas City. See page 64

45 *Mei-p'ing* VASE, Ting-yao
   Height 36.3 cm (14.5 in). 11th century
   Percival David Foundation of Chinese Art. See page 66

46 EWER of double gourd shape, Northern white ware
Height 24.4 cm (9.6 in). 11th century
Musée Guimet. See page 66

47 VASE of paper-beater shape, Ting-yao
   Height 24.5 cm (9.6 in). 11th–12th century
   Percival David Foundation of Chinese Art. See page 70

48 BOTTLE carved with peony design, Ting-yao
   Height 27.4 cm (10.7 in). 11th–12th century
   University of Sussex, Barlow Collection. See page 70

the general shape of double-gourd ewer with loop handle is found in Ting ware of simpler design without decoration, as for instance in a ewer from the Eumorfopoulos collection now in the British Museum. The Guimet ewer is to be attributed to the eleventh century.

Another striking shape of strong form is the mallet or paper-beater vase (Plate 47), again in the David Foundation,[16] with which it is interesting to compare a vase in the Barlow collection of dumb-bell shape with tall flared neck and lip and high splayed foot (Plate 48). This also is of strikingly strong form, probably deriving from a silver prototype and apparently unique.[17] Both these vases have sketchy lotus flowers of large size as principal decoration carved on the body; indeed the Barlow vase has no other. The David example has a single shallow frieze of outward facing petals on the shoulder, its lip is sheathed in copper to conceal a break, though it was of course fired on the foot. It is, however, not likely to have been flared like the Barlow vase.

Ch'ên Wan-li told me in 1957 that he had found on the kiln waste mounds only one piece of 'red' Ting and two of spinach green, but many black Ting fragments. The so-called red Ting is in fact a glaze which may be described as reddish brown or rust brown; and because of the imprecision of Chinese colour terms, traditionally known as 'purple' Ting.[18] A shallow lobed bowl in the Ku Kung is labelled 'purple'. In view of its rarity at the kiln site it is not surprising that few whole pieces are found in Western collections. Probably the finest is the cup-stand in the Carl Kempe Foundation, Sweden (Plate 49), with lobed saucer and slightly splayed foot. A smaller and simpler example of this shape is in the Victoria and Albert Museum.[19] Both were evidently fired on the footrim. In the Seattle Art Museum is a tea-bowl of conical shape and bare footrim (Plate 50), on which to the reddish-brown glaze has been added gilt decoration inside, of which traces only now remain.[20] On two similar tea-bowls in Japan more extensive gilt floral patterns remain.[21] Such gilding is occasionally also found on white Ting pieces and one black piece.[22] The black Ting is represented here by a shallow bowl with flared sides (Plate 51), resting on a smaller foot than that of the red Ting bowl and wider spread.

One other technique of decoration is occasionally found at the Ting kilns: designs in iron-oxide slip carved and covered with a cream glaze. The iron oxide develops into a greenish-red-brown colour described by Jean Gordon

---

[16] Medley, *Ting*, no. 20, Reg. no. 103.

[17] An example in China has however been reproduced in 1981 in *Chūgoku Tōji Zenshū*, Kyoto, Vol. 9, the Ting monograph, Pl. 71.

[18] The term for the colour may be translated alternatively by brown, yellow or purple; it is used to describe the colour of monks' robes.

[19] TOCS, 38, 1972, Pl. 47, no. 70.

[20] H. Trubner, *Asiatic Art in the Seattle Art Museum*, 1973, Colour Plate 119.

[21] STZ, 1977, Vol. 12, Pls. 17–21.

[22] F. Koyama, *Chinese Ceramics*, Tokyo, 1960, nos. 50–2.

49 CUP-STAND with a red-brown glaze, Ting-yao
   Diameter 11 cm (4.3 in). 11th–12th century
   Carl Kempe Foundation, Ekolsund, Sweden. See page 70
50 TEA-BOWL with red-brown glaze, formerly with gilt decoration inside, Ting-yao
   Diameter 12.7 cm (5 in). 11th–12th century
   Seattle Art Museum, Thomas D. Stimson Collection. See page 70

Lee as 'kaki' (persimmon colour).[23] She fully described a pillow in the Phila-delphia Museum of Art (Plate 52) of which the top shows a phoenix flying over a peony plant; this is bordered by scrolling vegetation, which also appears on a larger scale round the sides of the pillow, giving it a very rich and elegant appearance of real painterly quality. She also published two other pillows in the USA with decoration in this technique and a *mei-p'ing* vase in the Freer Gallery of Art; but the most famous example of this shape and type of vase is in the Ataka collection in Osaka.[24] Koyama found shards at the kiln site on which peony scrolls densely cover the ground as on the Philadelphia pillow. There is also a dish in Japan with a lotus spray executed in the same technique (Plate 53).

Among finds of the Chinese investigators of the kilns are examples of carving through the white slip in the manner of the T'zŭ-chou type;[25] also a fragment with a dragon incised under an intense bottle-green,[26] presumably Ch'ên Wan-li's 'spinach-green'. No whole piece of this type is known at present.

We now turn to the use of moulds at the Ting kilns, a practice already adopted to some extent under Northern Sung but much more developed under the Chin dynasty and later under Yüan. Many mould fragments have been found in the kiln waste heaps.[27] The whole moulds preserved in Western collections bear dates only in the Chin dynasty,[28] e.g. David Foundation no. 181 dated 1184,[29] with phoenixes among chrysanthemums. Two are in the British Museum, one dated 1203 and the second 1189, both with floral designs.[30] An undated mould in the Freer Gallery of Art cannot be earlier than the thirteenth century.[31] Miss Medley discusses the moulded Ting wares in her *Yüan Porcelain and Stoneware* (1974) and distinguishes the later four-teenth-century types.[32] She believes that the kilns ceased production in the fourteenth century.[33] One innovation which appeared only in the moulded wares is the orientated or landscape scene. This step was certainly taken under the Chin and probably before the end of the twelfth century. A rough chrono-logy can be established by noting the gradual development of styles further and further removed from the carved and incised designs. At first, as on the mould of 1184 the phoenixes are displayed among stylized chrysanthemums with a central design clearly separate. A similar lay-out can be seen in a bowl in the Museum of Far Eastern Antiquities, Stockholm (Plate 54), where two

[23] *Far Eastern Ceramic Bulletin*, XII, 1960.
[24] STZ, 1977, Vol. 12, Pl. 14.
[25] *Kiln Sites*, nos. 339 and 414.
[26] Ibid., nos. 328 and 400.
[27] OCS *Translations*, No. 4, Pl. VI, no. 2: Fig. 12, no. 9: Fig. 13, nos. 1–3.
[28] Moulds excavated in China are also dated between 1184 and 1206. See *Chūgoku Tōji Zenshū*, Vol. 9, 1981, figs. 128–33.
[29] Medley, *The Chinese Potter*, fig. 73, and the same author's *Ting*, no. 46, Reg. no. 181.
[30] Wirgin, *Sung Ceramic Designs*, op. cit., fig. 23.
[31] Ibid., Pl. 93.
[32] pp. 96–104, and Pls. 89–91A.
[33] Ibid., p. 83.

51 TEA-BOWL with black glaze, Ting-yao
Diameter 18.3 cm (7.2 in). 11th–12th century
Private Collection, Japan. See page 70
52 PILLOW with iron-oxide design, Ting-yao
Diameter 23.2 cm (9.1 in). 11th–12th century
Philadelphia Museum of Art, gift of Mrs Carroll S. Tyson. See page 72

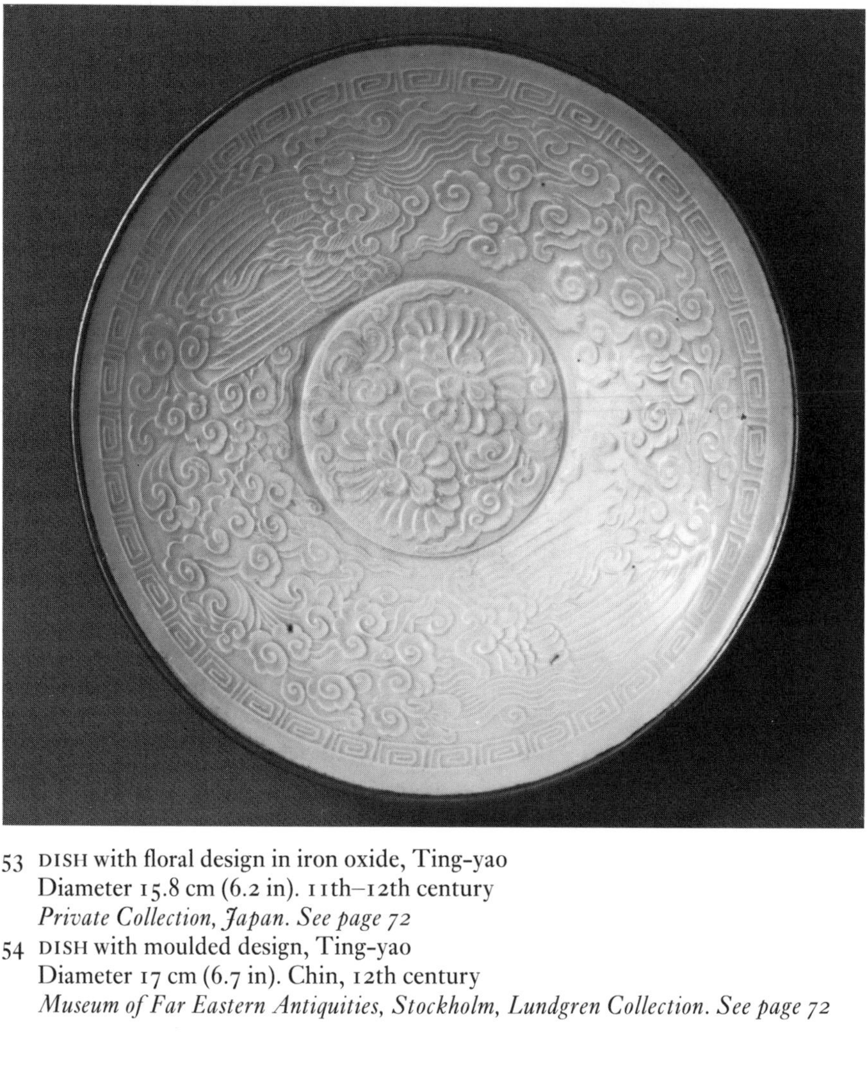

53 DISH with floral design in iron oxide, Ting-yao
    Diameter 15.8 cm (6.2 in). 11th–12th century
    Private Collection, Japan. See page 72
54 DISH with moulded design, Ting-yao
    Diameter 17 cm (6.7 in). Chin, 12th century
    Museum of Far Eastern Antiquities, Stockholm, Lundgren Collection. See page 72

55 BOWL with moulded design, Ting-yao
   Diameter 19 cm (7.5 in). 12th century
   Baur Foundation, Geneva. See page 76
56 DISH with moulded design, Ting-yao
   Diameter 21.3 cm (8.4 in). 12th century
   Victoria and Albert Museum. See page 76

phoenixes fly among stylized clouds while the central design shows stylized chrysanthemum blooms, all contained within a key-fret border. The tapestry effect is perhaps stronger in the mould than on the dish and this is probably earlier than 1184. Nearer to this date would be the bowl in the Baur Foundation (Plate 55), again showing phoenixes in flight, but this time more closely involved with the naturalistic lotus and chrysanthemum foliage and buds, while the central design is of a pair of fish over waves. Another moulded design obviously quite close to the incised Ting is on a dish in the Fitzwilliam Museum.[34] Here the four fish swim among waves and water-weeds almost as freely as the pair on an incised dish in the same collection.[35] On the conical bowls the central area is so reduced as to take only a floret, as on an example in the British Museum,[36] with yet another moulded design of phoenixes among flowers. Perhaps rather later but not much, may be a bowl of the same shape, also in the British Museum,[37] which shows small boys apparently swimming among melons and lotus flowers, a subject certainly connected with fertility.

The moulds with directional designs are only novelties so far as they depict landscape, for we have seen that the early carved and incised designs of ducks swimming are of course orientated. Now, however, the pictorial element begins to predominate, though at first it is rare. It has been convincingly suggested that a dish in the David Foundation[38] showing a duck and goose by a willow tree is an early use of such a scheme of pictorial illustration. This type never became popular, the overall rich tapestry effect being preferred. The two modes are combined on the Freer Gallery mould already mentioned[39] on which the central design of the rhinoceros gazing at the moon is surrounded by a rich complex cloud design on a textured ground, framed on each side by a running key-fret border. This dotted textured ground is also seen beneath the border design of lotus plants on an exceptionally fine dish in the Victoria and Albert Museum (Plate 56), on which the main field is filled with a luxuriant design of two stags running among rich vegetation. This background appears to break into cloud forms at the top; and this ambiguity appears also in a fine moulded dish in the former Malcolm collection (Plate 57), showing a pair

[34] ECPP, Pl. 44A.
[35] Ibid., Pl. 45.
[36] Ibid., Pl. 43.
[37] Medley, *Yüan Porcelain and Stoneware*, London, 1974, Pl. 88A.
[38] Medley, *Ting*, no. 28, Reg. no. 171.
[39] Wirgin, *Sung Ceramic Designs*, op. cit., Pl. 93.

---

57 DISH with moulded design, Ting-yao
    Diameter 17 cm (6.7 in). Chin, 12th century
    Formerly Malcolm Collection. See page 76
58 Eight-lobed PLATE, Ting-yao
    Diameter 21.5 cm (8.5 in). 12th century
    Asian Art Museum, San Francisco, Avery Brundage Collection. See page 78

of winged dragons disporting among scrolling clouds and with a border which may be intended for fungus or cloud. Once again there are double framing bands of key-fret. Close to this dish is one in the David Foundation[40] on which the main subject is a lion playing with a ball among floral scrolls.[41]

Another unusual piece is an eight-lobed dish in the Avery Brundage collection, San Francisco (Plate 58); the ribs are sharply defined through having been pressed into the mould, but the floral design which densely covers the ground of the centre is hard to decipher in detail, though its luxuriance is apparent. Although there is no metal sheath this dish was evidently fired on the rim and it is to be assigned to the twelfth century.

One other uncommon product of the Ting kilns must be mentioned; the fully sculptural pillow. In the Ku Kung in Peking is a pillow in the form of a sleeping child;[42] while the Brundage collection includes a small pillow in which a child holds a great fungus which serves as a head rest. This has a typical Ting floral pattern incised on the upper surface. These pillows are individual models, made without the use of moulds and highly sophisticated products of Sung small-scale sculpture. In the British Museum is a pillow supported by a stand representing the entrance to a tomb, while the leaf-shaped rest is incised with a floral design (Plate 59). This piece from the Eumorfopoulos collection has been attributed to the tenth century but is probably not earlier than the later eleventh. A closely similar pillow is in the Shanghai Municipal Museum, where it is attributed to the Five Dynasties period, no doubt correctly. Both pillows are not from the main Ting-yao kilns, but equally they are not from the southern kilns of Ching-tê-Chên but must come from some secondary northern kiln related to Ting.[43] Robert Paine cites a pillow from Chü-lu hsien dated 1103.[44] These sculptural pillows may all be Northern Sung. No. 338 in the 1980 kiln site exhibition seems to be part of a pillow, not a box as suggested in the catalogue; it shows the use of a mould and is therefore of later date, probably Chin.

Recently, a large dish in the Percival David Foundation,[45] with moulded central design of lotus, divided by a key-fret band from a border of scrolling peony, has been attributed to South China by Miss Medley who is thus reviving the claim to the existence of a kiln producing Ting-type wares in the south. Her reason is the similarity of this dish to two large dishes found among the great quantity of ceramics salvaged from the ship wrecked off Sinan, near Took-to island, on the southern coast of Korea. These appeared as nos. 204 and 202 in the catalogue of a special exhibition held in the National Museum

[40] Medley, *Ting*, no. 51, Reg. no. 115.
[41] Wirgin, *Sung Ceramic Designs*, op. cit., Pl. 86a.
[42] *Ku-kung*, 1962, Pl. 17.
[43] Shanghai, op. cit., Pl. 24.
[44] FECB, VII, 3, 1955, Pl. 29.
[45] Medley, *Ting*, no. 54, Reg. no. 164.

59 PILLOW on a stand representing the entrance to a house, the head-rest incised
     with floral design
     Height 13.5 cm (5.3 in). 11th century
     British Museum. See page 78
60 Covered JAR, from Chü-lu-hsien
     Height 11.5 cm (4.5 in). Early 12th century
     British Museum, Seligman Collection. See page 80

at Seoul in 1977, where they were described as of 'Ting ware style'. Unfortunately in the statistical chart of the different categories recovered from the wreck the *ch'ing-pai* wares are grouped with the white wares in a single group running to 2,281 pieces. But from the catalogue it is clear that much the greater number of them are *ch'ing-pai*, while the only other white pieces are specifically attributed to Ching-tê-Chên, including two bowls with moulded designs. These reappear in the reference section in groups of two and eight examples under nos. 343–4, where they are attributed to the first half of the fourteenth century.

The two large dishes nos. 204–5 do indeed resemble the group of Ting ware described by Wirgin[46] and illustrated by him on pls. 78–9, all about 30 cm (12 in) in diameter and with central design separated from that on the gently curved sides. He calls them Chin and more specifically, in his outline of a 'Tentative Chronology', dates them to the second part of Chin, that is to the period of the three dated moulds of 1118, 1189 and 1203.[47] Miss Medley writes that although tear-marks characteristic of Ting-yao appear on the David Foundation dish, the body material is slightly different from the accepted Ting and 'the decorative style appears to have little connection with that normally associated with the Ting vocabulary'.[48] Even granting the justice of these criteria, which lack precision, it is not at present possible to adduce any comparable piece from a southern kiln site. The possibility should not be excluded that this small group recovered from the Sinan wreck might already at the presumed date of the voyage *c.* 1310, like the Koryu celadons which were also part of the cargo, have been up to a hundred years old, whether or not they were loaded at a southern port or picked up *en route*. It must be recalled also how the reputation of the Ting kiln led to wide export of its products over a large area of China. Many pieces were found on the flooded site of Chü-lu-hsien submerged in 1107 by the change of course of the Yellow River (Plate 60). The evidence which they provide is surely insufficient to point to the existence of a southern kiln producing 'Ting-type' ware under the Yüan dynasty without confirmatory finds from kiln sites in Kiangsi.

In the north, however, kilns have been discovered in Shansi province near Chên-jun where a white ware of Ting type was made from the Chin dynasty onwards. The Chinese archaeologists have identified these kilns with the centre mentioned in the *Ko Ku Yao Lun* as Hou-chou, where a Yüan designer called P'êng Chun-pao is said to have imitated Ting ware especially in neat slender-waisted vessels. A stem-cup in the Ku Kung was exhibited in the 1980 exhibition of Kiln Sites of Ancient China[49] as a product of this kiln, with ribbed stem and everted lip to the wide mouth; and as of Yüan date. A small stem-cup from the Alfred Clark collection (Plate 61)[50] is quite close to this

[46] Wirgin, *Sung Ceramic Designs*, op. cit., pp. 144–5.
[47] Ibid., pp. 224–5.
[48] See note 45 above.
[49] Nos. 448 and 465.
[50] Sotheby Sale 25.3.75, lot 34.

E Ju-yao BOTTLE
Height 25 cm (9.7 in). Northern Sung, 12th century
Percival David Foundation of Chinese Art. See page 94

F Tz'ŭ-chou type PILLOW
with sgraffito decoration
under polychrome lead
glazes
Length 39 cm (15.4 in).
Chin, 12th century
Buffalo Museum of Science.
See page 106

61 STEM-CUP, Ting type
    Height 8 cm (3.2 in), Diameter 13.2 cm (5.2 in). 12th century
    Formerly Collection of Mr and Mrs Alfred Clark. See page 80

piece. It was described as Northern Sung, but it may be suggested that both
it and the Ku Kung piece are actually of Chin date. Miss Medley does not
mention this kiln; for it was discovered only in 1977. The general form of
the stem-cup does indeed approach that of the Shu-fu ware[51] and the earliest
blue and white,[52] especially in the grooving of the stem, but it is considerably
more squat and can well therefore be dated from the thirteenth rather than
the fourteenth century. It may well be that as with the Yao-chou ware, other
kilns may be found in the north at which imitations of this ware of so high
reputation may be found.

Many specimens of Ting ware have been found in Korea, and Hsü Ching
in his report on his mission to Korea in 1123 stated that the Koryu celadon
bowls, dishes, tea-bowls and flower vases made in recent years in superior
quality were all of shapes deriving from Ting-yao, thus assumed to be pre-
eminent at this date.

[51] S. E. Lee, and Wai-kam Ho, *Chinese Art under the Mongols: the Yüan Dynasty* (1279–1368),
Cleveland, 1968, no. 121.
[52] Ibid., nos. 131–2 and 136.

Chapter 5

CHÜN-YAO

Chün ware was another type of stoneware produced at the Lin-ju kilns in Honan. As recorded in *Wen-wu* (1964, No. 8), by Fêng Hsien-ming, eight kiln sites were found there; four to the north-east of Lin-ju hsien in the Ta-yu-tien district and four to the south in the Mang-ch'üan district. Of these the main centre, where the best wares were made, was at Shên-hou in Yü-hsien at the Tung-kou kilns, sixty kilometres north-east of Lin-ju. It is to be noted that the dating of the finds from these sites is on stylistic and not archaeological evidence. However some of the shards bore two characters incised in the base, *fêng-hua*, identified as the name of a Sung palace, from which it is argued that these pieces were part of an official commission for palace use. These characters are also incised on the base of a vase in the ex-Imperial collection in Taiwan.[1]

The Sung wares from these kilns are completely covered with glaze except for the inner side of the footring, by which they must have been held during the application of the glaze and before being placed in the saggar for firing in the kiln. A number of saggars have been found, including some with the vessels still adhering. A large number of wasters from the kiln sites are unglazed; and from this circumstance it is deduced that there must have been two firings, one at a low temperature before glazing and the second at a higher temperature after glazing. The commonest shapes found were bowls and dishes; but they also included foliated cups and flanged dishes and small jars (Plate 62).

When the firing is successful, the beautiful colour of the blue glaze is due to the de-oxidizing action of a reducing kiln, operating on a small quantity of iron in the glaze. Much thus depends on firing practice, the length and variation of the temperature in the firing. The special opalescence of the glaze is also due to the presence in it of phosphates. Traces from residual plant

[1] *Chinese Art Treasures*, 1961–2, no. 143.

62 JAR, with ear handles. Chün-yao
    Height 12 cm (4.7 in). 12th century
    Baur Foundation, Geneva. See page 82
63 Lobed BOWL, Chün-yao
    Diameter 17.3 cm (6.8 in). 11th–12th century
    Umezawa Gallery, Tokyo. See page 84

ash have been found in the glaze by analysis carried out by A. L. Hetherington
in the 1930s. The flambé effect of purple suffusion was achieved by the
addition to the body surface of small quantities of copper; but this was not
done until the twelfth or thirteenth century and at first with great restraint
(Colour Plate C); but later, under Yüan and early Ming with a freedom which
produced a rich but rather gawdy effect.

Chün-chou, from which the ware takes its name, was not far from the Sung
capital K'aifêng. In the Northern Sung period the wares were undecorated,
the potter relying on the beauty of the opalescent glaze and the distinguished
shapes. There is a lack of hard evidence for dating. Fêng Hsien-ming distinguished the Sung from the Yüan period wares by the complete glazing
of the foot in the earlier period and also by detecting lighter weight from
the Sung pieces. He argues against the criterion of glaze colour as an index
to dating, the varied shades of blue being due to fluctuations in the reducing
firing and even to the position of the individual piece in the kiln. A general
criterion for dating some of the shapes is the belief, already discussed, that
the influence of archaic bronze shapes can only be noticed in the late Southern
Sung period and becomes predominant under Yüan.

Chün wares are believed to have supplied the court in the later Northern
Sung period, as we have seen; and a class of Kuan-Chün, or official Chün,
has been identified, especially in Japan, where there has been great reluctance
to recognize the existence of the Ju ware first identified by Sir Percival David
in 1935. Undoubtedly once this ware, which is described below, has been
defined, it is clear that there is a class of Chün ware which approaches very
close to it. In 1960 Sir Harry Garner called attention to the resemblance of
the five-lobed dish (Colour Plate D) in the Percival David Foundation and
the so-called 'moon' bowl from the Oscar Raphael collection, now in the
British Museum, to Imperial Ju ware. The first piece is notable for the fine
crackle in the glaze, a feature usually occurring in Ju-yao also. Delicate
foliation is also characteristic of this superior category of Chün wares, as in
small bowls from the former Alfred Clark collection, and in the Umezawa
collection in Japan (Plate 63).[2]

Another Northern Sung shape is the incense burner with three small mask
feet, straight neck and small collar mouth.[3] In general it seems that the profile
of vases and bowls is more generously expansive than under Yüan, when forms
became more vertical or inverted. This can be illustrated by a comparison
of the tripod vase (Plate 64) in the Grahame Clark collection or the globular
jar from the Eumorfopoulos collection, now in the British Museum (Colour
Plate C), with such a piece as the jar in the Victoria and Albert Museum,
which was reproduced beside the last on pl. 54 of the Jubilee Catalogue of
the Oriental Ceramic Society in 1971. This jar is to be dated to the thirteenth

---

[2] *Mayuyama, Seventy Years*, Pl. 393.
[3] Ibid., Pl. 391.

64 Tripod JAR, Chün-yao
  Height 8.9 cm (3.5 in), Diameter 10.1 cm (4 in). 11th–12th century
  Grahame Clark Collection, Cambridge. See page 84
65 Bottle-shaped VASE, Chün-yao
  Height 26.4 cm (10.4 in). Northern Sung, 11th century
  Tokyo National Museum. See page 86

century, to which date it is assigned by Margaret Medley.[4]

Another shape in which the gradual transformation of profile can be observed is the tall bottle. The earliest example is in the Tokyo National Museum where it is attributed to Northern Sung. The pear-shaped body extends into the slightly expanding neck and finishes in a gently expanded lip (Plate 65). It is, incidentally, instructive to compare this shape with that of the famous Ju vase from the Clark collection. Here the profile forms a continuous double curve of great subtlety and the mouth is further expanded. In the Chün ware bottles the next stage sees the neck gain a funnel shape and the lip disappear, as it does in the example in the Ingram collection of about 1100 (Plate 66). Finally the body is depressed and the whole covered with an extensive flambé purple diffusion in a bottle in the Percival David Foundation (no. 92), exhibited in Tokyo in 1980 as twelfth century (no. 18). The Chün kilns seem to have continued in operation without a break through Northern Sung, Chin and Yüan dynasties so that it is naturally not easy to establish an absolute chronology. The uniform diffusion of copper in the glaze producing an all-over rich lavender-blue, as on a small but distinguished bowl from the Seligman collection in the British Museum (Plate 67), probably represents the beginning of the use of this effect and may be dated early in the twelfth century about the beginning of the Chin period. From the turn of the thirteenth century may come a bowl with lobed sides and bracketed rim in the Percival David Foundation (Plate 68); for this shows well-controlled purple splashes both inside and out.

Some examples of the superior or *kuan* type of Chün ware have spur-marks under the base, quite small and not far from the 'sesame seed' type of the Ju ware. An example is a brush-washer with flange and loop handle in the Barlow collection at Sussex University.[5] A similar, but probably rather later, example passed from the Blanco-White collection to that of Mrs Brodie Lodge.[6] This has three spur-marks on the base while the flange is longer and the bowl shallower.

The variant green Chün occurs by adjusting reduction period in the kiln, as regularly in the Northern celadons. It is to be considered therefore, at least initially, as an accidental effect in the Chün wares. It still naturally preserves the features of opacity with numerous bubbles characteristic of all Chün types. Since the green Chün pieces are generally fairly large, they probably date from the twelfth to thirteenth century and not earlier.

Another shape of cup which has been seen to come close to Ju ware in quality of glaze is the octagonal cup with dragon-head handle (Plate 69), also generally with a loop below it for suspension. The shape is evidently derived from silver and may be connected with several cups found in Central Asia

[4] Medley, *Yüan Porcelain and Stoneware*, p. 93.
[5] M. Sullivan, *Chinese Ceramics, Bronzes and Jades in the Collection of Sir Alan and Lady Barlow*, London, 1963, C 92, Pl. 34a.
[6] TOCS, 38, 1971, no. 80.

66 Bottle-shaped VASE, Chün-yao
   Height 29.4 cm (11.5 in). Northern Sung, *c.* 1100.
   M. W. Ingram Collection. See page 86
67 BOWL, Chün-yao
   Diameter 11.7 cm (4.6 in). Early 12th century
   British Museum, Seligman Collection. See page 86

or Siberia,[7] all with dragon handles, though none of octagonal shape. That is found only in silver in a differently shaped cup on a splayed foot.[8] It is also worth noting in this connection that numerous shallow cups with flanged handles are among these finds, one at least of which has a ring beneath the handle.[9] The sites from which these come are nearly all near the river system of Siberia by which they travelled in the Middle Ages. The dates suggested by Smirnov are within wide brackets, between the eleventh and thirteenth centuries. One of the octagonal cups appears in Orbeli and Trever,[10] with no suggestion of date. These silver cups are cited here not as direct ancestors of the Chün vessels but to suggest their silver ancestry. The dragon handles at least must be of Chinese origin.

The kiln sites in Yü-hsien in Honan, east of the Lin-ju group, were investigated in 1973 and numerous finds of Chün ware made at the Pa-hua-tung kiln. The excavators believe that these kilns were active from Northern Sung through the Chin period and into the Yüan dynasty. Nine shards from this kiln site were included in the 1980 exhibition shown in the British and Ashmolean Museums (nos. 394–402). Four of these were from the bulb bowls standing on three feet, a type of vessel well represented in Western collections. They are generously suffused with purple. The remaining shards exhibited were from flower pots with straight sides, also known in Western collections. All these forms were made with the use of moulds and all have dressed bases. On three of the excavated shards and on four of the flower pots numbers were impressed in the base before firing and this feature is common on similar pieces in the West and has been the subject of much controversy over the past fifty years. The excavations do not carry this question any further but they do reveal the source of this type of ware. It is to be remarked that no piece of this type was found at the kiln sites round Lin-ju.

The 1973 excavations are not yet fully published but the shards sent to England in 1980 were all attributed to the Sung dynasty. This would be in line with current opinion in the Ku Kung museum where all specimens of the types are labelled Sung; as indeed they were in Japan and the West thirty years ago. Even Fêng Hsien-ming believed that the principal Chün kilns were at Shên-hou in Yü-hsien and that the Lin-ju kilns were secondary. By 1960 however this type was excluded from the Oriental Ceramic Society's Sung exhibition, and in the catalogue of the Avery Brundage collection of Chinese ceramics of 1967 they are attributed to the thirteenth to fourteenth century, while John Ayers in 1964 put them as late as the fourteenth to fifteenth century.[11] Even in 1953 I suggested that the flower pots and bulb bowls might

[7] Y. Smirnov, *Atlas; Argenterie orientale en argent et en or, trouvée principalement en Russie*, St Petersburg, 1909, Pls. CXII, nos. 237–8, CV, nos. 231–2, CXVIII, no. 300.
[8] Ibid., Pl. LVII, nos. 115–16.
[9] Ibid., Pl. XCVIII, no. 228.
[10] J. Orbeli and C. Trever, *Orfèvrerie Sasanide*, Moscow/Leningrad, 1935, Pl. 56.
[11] Ayers, *Seligman Catalogue*, II, 1964, p. 58.

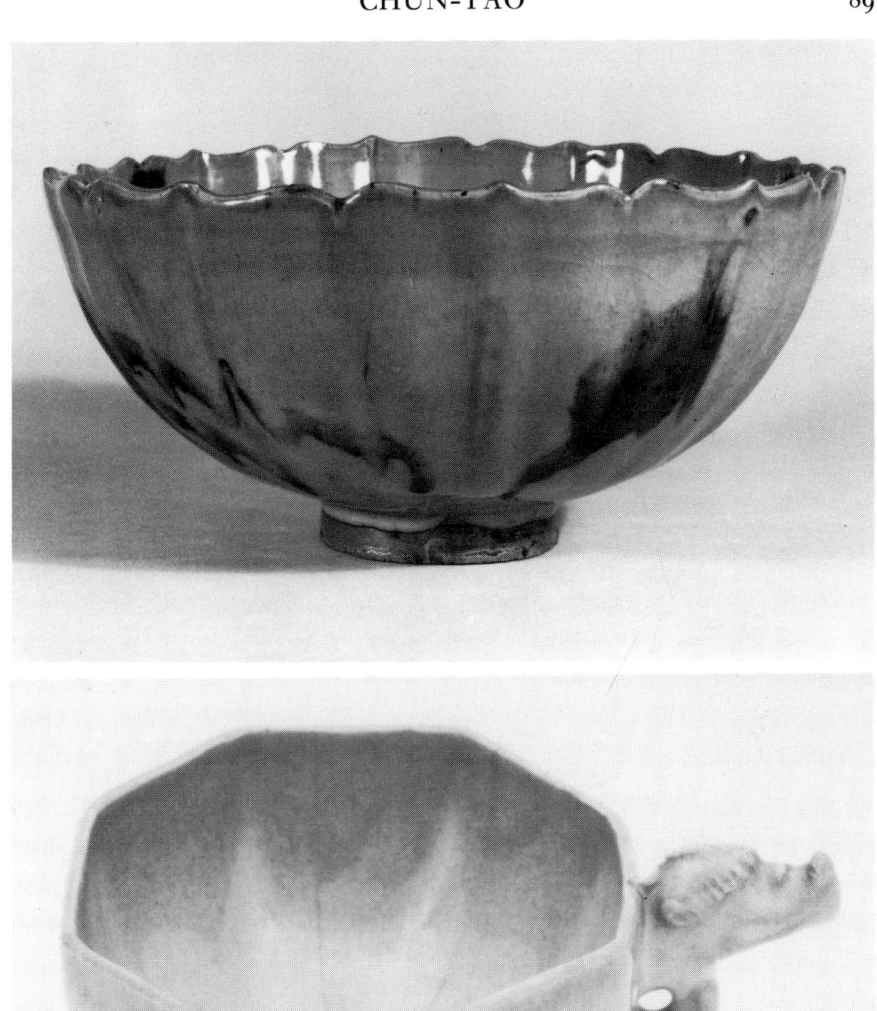

68 BOWL lobed with ten petals, in foliate form, Chün-yao
  Diameter 24.1 cm (9.5 in). Late 12th to 13th century
  Percival David Foundation of Chinese Art. See page 86
69 Octagonal CUP with dragon handle, Chün-yao
  Diameter 8.5 cm (3.4 in). 12th century
  Formerly Malcolm Collection. See page 86

be not very much earlier than the fifteenth century.[12]

Another product of the Yü-hsien kilns are stated to have been boxes but none of these has been reproduced; they too must have had moulded decoration as do the *ch'ing-pai* and celadon examples. The other types are well illustrated in Margaret Medley's volume *Yüan Porcelain and Stoneware*,[13] and they are not included here; and there is also, therefore, no need to go again into the elusive problem of the numbers of the bases.

JU-YAO

Closely allied to the Chün wares is the imperial Ju-yao, successfully identified by Sir Percival David in 1935[14] by confrontation of surviving pieces, mostly either still or formerly in the Imperial collection, with accounts in the literary sources. The most important of these was the reference to this ware 'from the new kiln of Ju-chou' as resembling the contemporary Korean celadon wares, contained in the report of Hsü Ching who visited the Korean court in 1123. And next, a reference to the kiln is in the first edition of the *Ko Ku Yao Lun* of 1388 among the northern wares of the Sung dynasty, as notable for its pale-blue glaze, for the crackle called 'crab's claw' (*hsien chao wên*) and for the thin paste of the body. Indicative of the Ju-yao potting is the presence under the foot of three or five elliptical spur-marks where the vessel had been supported in the kiln. The footrim is generally rather low and splayed outwards. As Sir Percival David and Sir Harry Garner[15] have pointed out, the crackle was induced by differentiation of the cohesion of body and glaze, so that the latter shrank sooner and was subject to tension which produced the all-over pattern of a network of crazing marks. In any case, the effect was greatly admired by Chinese connoisseurs and subsequently extensively imitated. The effect emphasizes the beauty of the glaze and was also perhaps admired as suggestive of antiquity, since a somewhat similar effect had been observed on excavated ceramics. As a matter of fact, this description of the crackle as like crab's claw is better suited to the Southern Kuan ware than to the Ju, on which the crazing is of the finest mesh. The glaze itself has a gemlike quality, not opalescent like Chün, nor unctuous like the Southern Kuan, but both clear and refractory, smooth to the touch and soft to the eye.

Ju ware was always rare; in 1388 it was already 'difficult to obtain', according to the *Ko Ku Yao Lun*; under Yung-chêng in 1729–32 two pieces, then believed to be Ju-yao, were sent from the palace to be copied for Imperial use under the superintendence of T'ang Ying. One of these was said to have had a fish-roe crackle, that is of the finer mesh; the other was said to be uncrack-

---

[12] ECPP, p. 31.
[13] Medley, *Yüan Porcelain and Stoneware*, Pl. 85a.
[14] TOCS, 14, 1936–7, pp. 23–47.
[15] H. Garner, 'Early Chinese crackled porcelain', TOCS, 32, 1959–60.

70 NARCISSUS BOWL, Ju-yao
   Length 23 cm (9 in). Early 12th century
   National Palace Museum, Taiwan. See pages 92, 94
71 VASE, Ju-yao
   Height 20.4 cm (8 in). Early 12th century
   British Museum, from the collection of Mr and Mrs Alfred Clark. See pages 22, 92

led and has been identified with the bulb bowl now in Taiwan (Plate 70), reproduced here.[16] There are now known to exist about fifty pieces, of which twenty are in Britain, all in public collections, eight in the Ku Kung in Peking, and about a dozen in the Imperial collection, now in Taiwan. Gompertz lists sixty-one[17] but some of the pieces in Taiwan would not be accepted by Western scholars as really correctly identified.

The number of different shapes in Ju-yao is limited; the most distinguished being the vase formerly in the Alfred Clark collection and now in the British Museum (Plate 71). Only 20 cm in height, this achieves a beauty independent of scale, in form and glaze colour, which is so subtle as to defy successful reproduction in colour, as may be seen by comparing the colour plates in Koyama's *100 Masterpieces of Chinese Ceramics*[18] with M. and C. Beurdeley's *Chinese Ceramics*.[19] Also exceptionally beautiful is the elliptical brush-water in the Percival David Foundation (Plate 72), almost boat-shaped and with three spur-marks in the slightly recessed base. It is further remarkable for the faint and subtle incised design of two sesamum flowers under the glaze inside. The only other instance of carved decoration on a Ju vessel is the design of lotus petals on a cup-stand, of which there are two examples in London, one again in the David Foundation, the second, finer in form and colour, in the British Museum, given by Sir Harry and Lady Garner (Plate 73). This cup-stand, although based on a lacquer prototype, has been subtly reshaped to ceramic form by the reduction of the cusps from eight to five, the more emphatic upturn of the lip of the saucer and the spread of the splayed foot. A lacquer cup in the Victoria and Albert Museum bears a date equivalent to AD 1094, a decade or more earlier than the Ju pieces. This shape is also found in Chün ware in an example, perhaps slightly earlier and with less-modulated saucer profile, also in the British Museum as a gift from Sir Alan and Lady Barlow. In a version in Koryu celadon the form, while clearly de-rived from the Ju ware, is further formalized, the lobed sides straightened and more deeply carved. This cup-stand, from the Gompertz collection, was shown at the Fitzwilliam Museum in 1975 beside the David Foundation cup-stand.[20] Michael Sullivan has suggested that this cup-stand shape may have originated in metal as early as the Five Dynasties; the shape is represented in early paintings of palace scenes like the famous 'Night Revels' by the tenth-century painter Ku Hung-chung.[21] A silver cup-stand of this shape was among the finds in the tomb of the Liao prince of Wei who died in 959 at Ch'ih-fêng, Liao-ning.[22] It is incised and not carved. Another shape which may have

[16] *Chinese Art Treasures*, 1961–2, no. 145.
[17] Gompertz, op. cit., 1980, p. 94.
[18] F. Koyama, *Chinese Ceramics*, Tokyo, 1960, Pl. 7.
[19] M. and C. Beurdeley, *Chinese Ceramics*, Translated by K. Watson, 1974, p. 25.
[20] Medley, *Chinese and Korean Ceramics*, 1975, nos. 24–5.
[21] O. Sirén, *Chinese Painting*, Vol. 3, 1956, Pl. 122.
[22] Watson, op. cit., no. 355.

72 Oval DISH with impressed design of sesamum flowers, Ju-yao
   Length 14.3 cm (5.6 in). Early 12th century
   Percival David Foundation of Chinese Art. See pages 23, 92
73 CUP-STAND, Ju-yao
   Diameter 16.5 cm (6.5 in). Early 12th century
   British Museum, gift of Sir Harry and Lady Garner. See page 92

derived from metalwork is the globular vase in the David Foundation[23] with splayed foot and slightly expanded mouth now sheathed in copper. This has a pale-lavender glaze covered with a fine network of crackle which certainly enhances the form. This may be compared with a bottle vase from the silver treasure from Pei-huang in the British Museum, though on this piece repoussé decoration has been added.[24] This treasure is now attributed to the ninth to tenth centuries.

A narcissus bowl on four flanged feet is preserved in the Imperial collection in Taiwan (Plate 70). A poem by emperor Ch'ien-lung inscribed under the base, in which it is described as Kuan-yao, correctly identifies it as of official status but is surprisingly imprecise as compared with poems incised on a pair of saucer-dishes excluded from the palace after fire damage, now in the Percival David Foundation[25] and the British Museum,[26] attributing them to the 'factory of *ch'ing* (blue-green) ware of the Chao Sung family founded at Ju-chou'. This bowl has six spur-marks on the base revealing the standard Ju-yao buff body but it is exceptional in being uncrackled. It is believed to be one of the two examples of Ju ware sent from the palace for copying at Ching-tê-chên in 1729, as mentioned above.

Another piece of distinguished shape bearing a Ch'ien-lung poem is the paper-beater-shaped vase (Plate 74) which was lent from the Imperial collection to the great 1935–6 exhibition at the Royal Academy in London (no. 957) and was shown again in the United States in 1961–2 (no. 144). As usual with this shape there is no footrim and the mouth is sheathed in copper, but it is likely to have had a narrow flange like the Ting-yao vase from the Barlow collection—though this is nearer in shape to the David Foundation piece (Colour Plate E), having a flanged foot—rather than the Koryu vase in the Gompertz collection[27] which has a fully dished mouth. The vase in Taiwan has in addition to the Imperial poem the two characters *fêng-hua* incised in the base; as explained above, this is the name of one of the Northern Sung palace pavilions. The inscription may, however, not be of Sung date. In any case this vase has a beautiful crackled glaze of typical Ju-yao type. The shape was already established in the Northern Sung Ting-yao (Plate 47), and it was to be continued in the Southern Sung Kuan and Lung-ch'üan wares; but in these the delicate curve of the body is lost in the more sharply cut angles between neck and body and the more vertical line above the foot. It is worth noting that the Yung-chêng version of the Ju vase[28] shows no flange at the lip and is much more globular or depressed.

[23] S. Yorke Hardy, *Catalogue of Tung, Ju, Kuan, Chün etc.*, London, 1953, no. 61.
[24] R. L. Hobson, 'A T'ang silver hoard', *British Museum Quarterly*, 1, 1926–7, pp. 18–20; BM Reg. no. 1926. 3–19. 1.
[25] Yorke Hardy, op. cit., no. A58.
[26] R. L. Hobson, *Handbook of Pottery and Porcelain in the Far East*, London, 1937, fig. 31.
[27] Medley, *Chinese and Korean Ceramics*, no. 56.
[28] Yorke Hardy, op. cit., no. 66.

74 VASE of paper-beater shape, Ju-yao
Height 22.5 cm (8.8 in). Early 12th century
National Palace Museum, Taiwan. See page 94

75 BOWL fitted with a copper rim, Ju-yao
    Diameter 16.7 cm (6.6 in). Early 12th century
    Percival David Foundation of Chinese Art. See page 97
76 INCENSE BURNER, Ju-yao
    Diameter 14.3 cm (5.6 in). Early 12th century
    Percival David Foundation of Chinese Art. See page 97

G Tz'ŭ-chou *mei-p'ing* VASE with black and white slip decoration
Height 29 cm (11.4 in). Chin, 12th–13th century
Fitzwilliam Museum. See page 116

H Honan brown ware JAR
　 Height 20.1 cm (7.9 in). Chin, 12th century
　 Glasgow City Art Museum, Burrell Collection. See page 122

Another piece of fine quality is a bowl with slightly everted lip, now sheathed in copper (Plate 75), presumably to conceal some slight damage, and with the usual five elliptical studs on which it was fired showing inside the footrim. This piece now in the Percival David Foundation[29] was also once in the Chinese Imperial collection, for it is engraved with a poem by Ch'ien-lung referring to it as Chün ware. However, it bears again the typical crackle, though in this case the faint close mesh is overlaid by a wide irregular crazing, perhaps due to burial. A bowl of similar shape is now in the Ku Kung in Peking.[30] Here is also an incense burner on three feet[31] like one in the David Foundation (Plate 76).[32] This shape too has its counterpart in Chün ware, as in an example formerly in the Bruce collection and included in the Oriental Ceramic Society's Sung exhibition of 1952,[33] as well as in Lung-ch'üan, from the Southern Sung period[34] into the Yüan, when it seems to have enjoyed considerable popularity, judging from the nine variant versions of this shape included among the finds from the Sinan wreck and in several sizes.[35]

To sum up, Ju-yao appears to be an experimental ware intended to improve upon and refine the products of the Chün-yao kilns by modification of existing shapes, by perfecting the opalescent glaze and controlling the suffused copper colour, and by taking note of the effects of crazing through the adjustment of air-flow in the kiln during the reduction process. These experiments must have been carried out by care with each piece in potting and firing at a level which could only have been supported by court patronage. What is strange is that where the maintenance of so high a standard of perfection was being achieved and where consequently so many pieces must have been rejected with an accumulation of wasters, it should still not have been possible to locate the kiln where the Ju-yao was made, though we know the area. Until it is found, it will not be possible to draw a hard and fast line between the finest Chün-yao and the Ju. At present we must be content to give, as has been done here, to some intermediate products the title of Kuan-Chün or Chün with official status, though some of them may have been made before the Ju kiln began to operate.

[29] Ibid., no. 3.
[30] *Ku Kung Po-wu-yüan ts'ang Tz'ŭ hsüan-chi*, 1962, Pl. 20.
[31] Ibid., Pl. 18.
[32] Yorke Hardy, op. cit., no. A44.
[33] TOCS, 28, 1953–4, no. 10 in catalogue.
[34] Gompertz, op. cit., Pl. 75B.
[35] 'Special exhibition of cultural relics found off Sinan coast', National Museum of Korea, Seoul, 1977, Pls. 79–87.

Chapter 6

TZ'Ŭ-CHOU WARES

As Li Hui-ping pointed out in his report in *Wen-wu* (1964, No. 8), the term
Tz'ŭ-chou ware has been used very loosely to cover the products of many
kilns distributed over the provinces of Honan as well as Hopei in which Tz'ŭ-
hsien is situated. Now with the thorough investigation of a number of the
more important kiln sites, it is beginning to be possible to assign groups of
these wares to specific kilns. But inasmuch as the name Tz'ŭ-chou has been
given currency ever since the publication of the first edition of the *Ko Ku
Yao Lun* in 1388, it has seemed best to retain it as a generic title for the
whole group and to refer to these wares as of Tz'ŭ-chou type.

It must be recognized that we have thus to do with a wide range of quality,
but it must also be emphasized that the best of these products are of the finest
quality both in form and decoration. This was evidently recognized in 1388
or they would not have been compared with Ting-yao, even though the prices
were then stated to be lower and they lacked the tear-marks of the Ting. Indeed, subsequent reference to 'popular wares made for common use' is clearly
wide of the mark. It is true that the fact that these are stonewares fired at
about 1200°C means that they do not have the sensuous appeal of the fully
fused porcelain and are not for handling; but visually, in form and decoration,
they are second to none at their best. Moreover, some of the techniques used
in the decoration are more elaborate and sophisticated than on any of the
classic wares and there is greater variety of shape and decoration than in any
other of the major groups of kilns. One explanation for this low esteem may
be the Chinese depreciation of the northern kilns after the withdrawal of the
Sung court to the south and during the two hundred and fifty years when
these kilns were under so-called 'barbarian' rule. In fact nowhere in ceramics
was the ethos of the new freedom of expression favoured by the literati so
well fulfilled as in the Tz'ŭ-chou painted and sgraffito wares. The brushwork
on the painted wares under Northern Sung and Chin is usually lively and

98

77 PILLOW with incised design. Tz'ŭ-chou type
Height 7.9 cm (3.1 in), Length 16.9 cm (6.6 in). Late 10th century
British Museum, Seligman Collection. See page 100

78 PILLOW with painted design, Tz'ŭ-chou type
Length 28.8 cm (11.4 in). 11th century
People's Republic of China. See pages 102, 108

sometimes masterly, as on a tall *mei-p'ing* in the Tokyo National Museum[1]
or on one in the Goto Museum;[2] or on a pillow like that in the Yamato Bunkakan, Nara with leaf-shaped head-rest painted with fish among weeds
(Plate 94);[3] or again, of a peony spray, on a vase in a Japanese private collection.[4] The Japanese have long appreciated and collected this ware and so own
many of the finest surviving pieces, but now the Chinese are beginning to
show their appreciation: three pieces are included in the 1962 volume of
selected ceramics in the Ku Kung,[5] Peking, and five in the similar volume
on the Shanghai museum.[6]

The Chinese archaeologists have investigated kiln sites in both Hopei and
Honan. They consider that the kilns south of the Yellow River in Honan are
earlier than those in Hopei. These kilns are in two groups, one centred on
Mi-hsien and the second on Têng-fêng. Next they place the group in Tz'ŭ-
hsien in Hopei, of which the most important are one near Kuan-t'ai and
another at Tung-ai-k'ou. Thirdly there are groups at Ho-pi-chi and Pa-ts'un
just across the border from Hopei in Honan.

Fêng Hsien-ming, one of the best ceramic experts in China today, in *Wen-
wu* (1964, No. 3) has attributed a type of Tz'ŭ-chou ware found at Mi-hsien,
in which the background is stippled with rings made by repeated impressions
from a hollow rod or bamboo, to the T'ang period.[7] He calls this type 'the
ware with the pearl background' and sees in it a close resemblance to the
decorative treatment of T'ang dynasty gold and silverware. This 'pearl' background is found on a fragment of a pillow from Mi-hsien showing a bird,
quail or partridge and not a parrot, shown in the 1980 exhibition of shards[8]
and illustrated in *Chinese Translations*, No. 5.[9] A closely similar pillow
(Plate 77) is in the British Museum from the Seligman collection.[10] Pillows
of the same type are in the Ku Kung, Peking, and the Ashmolean Museum,
Oxford.[11]

While admitting some resemblance to the decoration of T'ang silverware,
one must observe that the background there is punched all over with a much
closer pattern of dots or circles, and that this silverware is often difficult to
date closely. A dish in the Carl Kempe Foundation with floral designs on
a punched ground has been attributed to the Sung period, while a bowl from

[1] Tokyo National Museum, *Chinese Ceramics*, 1965, no. 285.
[2] STZ, 1977, Vol. 12, Pl. 119.
[3] Yamato Bunkakan, *Chūgoku Tōji*, 1977, no. 59.
[4] *Mayuyama, Seventy Years*, Pl. 523.
[5] Ku Kung, op. cit., Pls. 36–8.
[6] Shanghai Municipal Museum, op. cit., Pls. 50–5; the last two, though labelled 'Sung', are
no doubt of Yüan date.
[7] OCS *Translations*, No. 5, fig. 7.
[8] *Kiln Sites*, nos. 338 and 377.
[9] OCS *Translations*, No. 5, fig. 7.
[10] Ayers, op. cit., D104, Pl. XXXVI.
[11] Mino, *Freedom of Clay and Brush through Seven Centuries in Northern China: Tz'ŭ-chou
Type Wares*, Indianapolis, 1980, fig. 34.

79 EWER with design carved through slip, Tz'ŭ-chou type
  Height 20.4 cm (8 in). Late 10th century
  Tokyo National Museum. See page 104
80 Truncated VASE with design carved through slip, Tz'ŭ-chou type
  Height 19.2 cm (7.6 in). Early 11th century
  Aso Collection, Tokyo. See page 104

the collection of the late F. Mayer on which partridges and other birds appear against a natural floral setting but with a punched background was attributed to T'ang. In the Ho-chia find in 1970 at Sian,[12] of silverware dated to the mid-eighth century, the ground is stippled with small discs, not rings, as it is on some late Sassanian silver vessels, on at least one of which this type of background serves as shading to stylized floral and animal designs.[13] Sassanian influence was notoriously long-lived, and I see no reason to attribute the Mi-hsien pillow and its fellows to a date earlier than the tenth or even the eleventh century.

This conclusion has now been reached independently by Yutaka Mino in his survey of the Tz'ŭ-chou type ware decorated with incised patterns on a stamped 'fish-roe' ground.[14] He argues for a date for the Mi-hsien pillow in early Sung, the late tenth century, because of the resemblance of the Ku Kung pillow, its sides filled with a star pattern similar to that on a pagoda, with lead glaze excavated from the foundation deposit of a pagoda datable to 998.[15] He has described a group of Tz'ŭ-chou pillows and vessels, especially *mei-p'ing* vases, all with ring punch-marks, which he confidently attributes to the first period of Northern Sung rule, while showing that this background treatment continued in use for a hundred and fifty years in all, until about 1125, though latterly less carefully executed. A firm point for dating the middle style in this sequence is the pillow in the British Museum dated 1070,[16] on which the main decoration of four characters is placed against a stippled background of this type.

The pillow provided the finest surface for the painter to show this skill and invention, not necessarily confined to flowers, birds and fishes. Even figural subjects are not rare and show a delightful reticence and restrained humour, as on a pillow excavated at a Hsing-t'ai tomb in Hopei in 1955 (Plate 78),[17] where a small boy is depicted fishing from a river bank. Similar fragments of painted pillows with cranes and bamboo were excavated at the Tung-ai-k'ou kiln site in Hopei.[18]

A more complex technique was involved in the production of the sgraffito wares, in which areas of slip are carved or incised to reveal a lower level, either the clay body or a primary slip beneath the secondary. The dark colour is usually black or a dense brown, the light white, and the piece is then covered with a translucent glaze, generally colourless but sometimes green. The technique is used for both vessels and pillows, and the designs are very varied but tend to be more geometric than on the painted wares. This type starts

[12] Watson, op. cit., no. 305.
[13] Orbeli and Trever, op. cit., Pl. 51.
[14] 'Tz'ŭ-chou type ware decorated with incised patterns on a stamped "fish-roe" ground', *Archives of Asian Art*, Vol. XXXII, 1979, pp. 55–71.
[15] *Wen-wu*, 1972, No. 10, Pl. 8.
[16] ECPP, Pl. 55B.
[17] Watson, op. cit., no. 338.
[18] OCS *Translations*, No. 5, Pl. 1, fig. 4; *Kiln Sites*, no. 429.

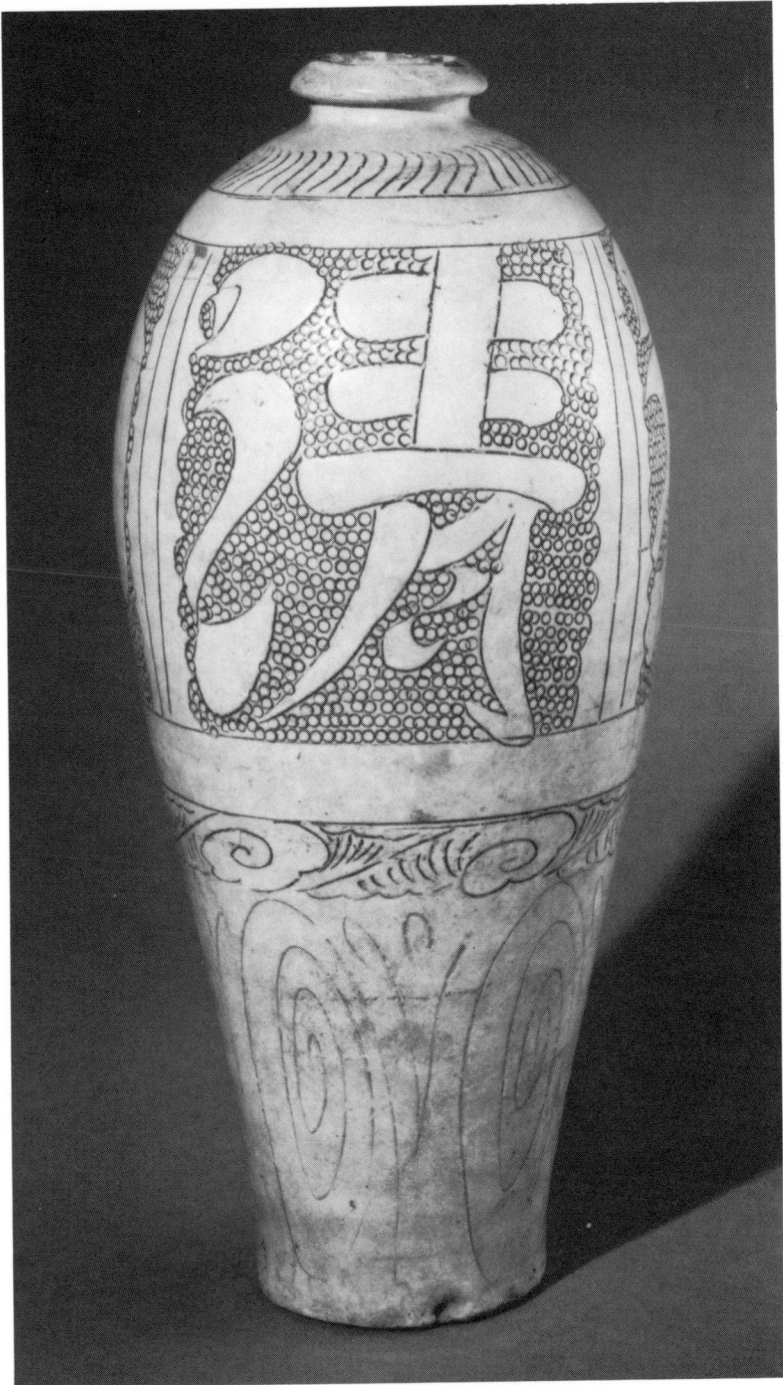

81 *Mei-p'ing* VASE with characters carved through slip and with stamped pattern, Tz'ŭ-chou type, from the Kuan-t'ai kiln, Honan
Height 37.5 cm (14.7 in). 11th century
British Museum, Seligman Collection. See page 104

from the very beginning of Sung and may be descended from the T'ang and Liao incised wares; but these are really quite different technically, the incisions on them being used only to separate different colours. Some of the early sgraffito wares are deeply carved, as in a group of wine ewers with globular bodies, well-marked shoulder, short spout and tall neck, originally supplied with a cover, and loop handle, all following the shape of a silver original. The bold foliage design is carved through white slip to reveal a dark body beneath it, as in a well-preserved example in the Tokyo National Museum (Plate 79), to be dated late tenth century. A more formal style of floral design is seen on a truncated bottle-shaped vessel (Plate 80) in a Japanese private collection, on which the white slip is carved through with a design of peony sprays set in diamond-shaped frames and with interlaced foliage in the resulting triangular lappets. The background colour of the body revealed beneath the carving is light brown. This piece is to be dated eleventh century. A tall *mei-p'ing* vase (Plate 81) provides the surface for striking designs such as the three characters for purity, clarity and endurance (*ch'ing, ch'ung, jên*), each carved against a ground stippled with the same impressed pearl pattern as the pillows mentioned above. Round the foot is a summary petal pattern; here can be seen how, in this technique also, freedom and vitality of line can be achieved.

The design can be much more formal, as in the three registers of stylized flowers which encircle a more barrel-shaped *mei-p'ing* formerly in the Malcolm collection (Plate 82), to be attributed to the twelfth century. The dotted background is here much more random and less carefully controlled; it belongs to a group attributed by Mino to the early twelfth century.[19]

A different effect, softer and more painterly, was achieved by a skilful use of the sgraffito technique. Here the ground was covered with a white slip which was then carved through to the body, details were incised and the whole covered with a nearly colourless glaze. A bottle from the Eumorfopoulos collection (Plate 83) now in the British Museum shows how delicate an effect can be achieved by this means, in which the peony design appears against a pale-grey ground.

Naturally a richer effect is achieved in the use of two slips, black over white. The black slip has an intensity and consistency like lacquer and could be crisply carved.[20] This technique was certainly in use at the Kuan-t'ai-chên kilns in the Tz'ŭ-chou area and also at Tung-ai-k'ou Ts'un in the same group.[21] It probably dates only from the twelfth century, that is from the end of Northern Sung and into the Chin period. A similar technique was also used at Hsiu-wu in Honan, also known as T'ang-yang-yü. A pillow from Hsiu-wu in Honan is in the Shanghai Municipal Museum.[22] The shape is

[19] Mino, *Freedom of Clay*, p. 15, Group 5 and pp. 76–9.
[20] Ibid., p. 16, Mino believes that the technique was to cover the white slip with a layer of black slip which was scraped away to reveal the white slip; see also ibid., p. 102.
[21] These kilns are in Han-tan-shih in Hopei: *Wen-wu*, 1964, No. 8; OCS *Translations*, No. 5, pp. 8–9, Pl. 1. i.
[22] Mino, *Freedom of Clay*, p. 96, fig. 89. Shanghai Municipal Museum, op. cit., Pl. 53.

82 *Mei-p'ing* VASE with design incised through slip and with stamped pattern
Height 34 cm (13.4 in). 12th century
Formerly Malcolm Collection. See page 104

paralleled at the T'ang-yang-yü kiln[23] and the technique at the Lu-shan kiln, also in Honan.[24] They date from the late Northern Sung into the Chin period of the twelfth century. The technique is used most frequently and successfully on *mei-p'ing* vases, all decorated with large-scale sprays of peony flowers on the body and with friezes of petals round the foot and below the mouth. Several of these are in Japanese collections, but there are also two in Britain, from the Sedgwick collection in the British Museum and in the Fitzwilliam Museum, Cambridge.[25] These are likely to be from the Kuan-t'ai kiln in Hopei. But probably from Hsiu-wu is a type of small bowl with a regular pattern of conventional flowers in the same technique and of about the same date, of which we illustrate an example from the Seligman collection (Plate 84), now in the British Museum.

Occasionally a more complex process was used in which the white slip was carved away and the background painted with black slip, as on some pillows, of which a fine example is in the Avery Brundage collection, now in the Asian Art Museum of San Francisco, on which a peony spray fits the top surface of an octagonal kidney-shaped head-rest (Plate 85). A similar technique is used on a series of bean-shaped pillows, of which the finest seems to be one in the Buffalo Museum of Science (Colour Plate F). This is unusual in having a patterned scroll as background to the central design of lotus flower and leaves. A pillow of this shape in the Tokyo National Museum is dated 1156, and this is likely to be the approximate date for this group with its advanced technique, though the use of coloured lead glazes revived a technique common under the Liao about one hundred years earlier. The Chin designs are much freer in drawing and more substantial in execution. Here the sides are undecorated, but it is more usual to leave the dark ground unpainted, as on a pillow formerly in the Malcolm collection, this time with rounded ends (Plate 86). The sides are decorated with peony scrolls on a larger scale than that in a bracketed field on the upper surface, more carefully executed in a tighter spiral. Another pillow, rectangular and with overlapping flange, in the Seattle Art Museum (Plate 87), has even more elaborate decoration in the same technique of white sgraffito on a dark ground. Here, while the top carries a bold peony design, the back side shows two stags back to back with space-filling foliage. Examples of this technique were found among shards from the Kuan-t'ai-chên

[23] Ibid., p. 97, Pl. 36; Museum für Ostasiatische Kunst, Cologne.
[24] *Kiln Sites*, no. 412.
[25] Mino, *Freedom of Clay*, Pl. 39, figs. 97–100: TOCS, 32, 1960, Pl. 39, nos. 92 and 103.

---

83 BOTTLE with design in sgraffito technique, Tz'ŭ-chou type
  Height 32 cm (12.6 in). 12th century
  British Museum. See page 104
84 Deep BOWL with design carved through black slip to white slip, Tz'ŭ-chou type, probably from Hsiu-wu, Honan
  Height 15.6 cm (6.1 in). *c.* 1100
  British Museum, Seligman Collection. See page 106

kiln site, but 'relatively few' states the report by Li Hui-ping.[26] This again is to be dated to the twelfth century.

A word must be added about the extensive series of pillows on which is a stamped escutcheon with the name of the Chang company (*Chang-chia tsao*) as makers. Fragments of this type have been found in the Tung-ai-k'ou group of kiln sites in considerable numbers,[27] all with black-painted decoration on a white-slip ground. An example is the bean-shaped pillow already mentioned (Plate 78) painted with a boy fishing, found in a tomb at Hsing-t'ai, which carries this stamp.[28] A similar pillow with a boy on a hobby horse is in the Metropolitan Museum.[29] Varieties of the Chang stamp are reproduced in the article by Li Hui-ping already referred to.[30] They correspond with similar marks discussed by earlier writers before the discovery of this kiln site and summarized by John Ayers.[31] Subsequent to the identification is the article by Roderick Whitfield[32] which shows the insecurity of the Northern Sung date given as starting point for this firm of Chang; and it must be added that even a provenance from Chü-lu-hsien is not conclusive owing to the unsatisfactory evidence about pieces supposed to be from the site flooded in 1108. There appear in fact to be no reliably dated pillows with the Chang family mark. In his recent study of the Tz'ŭ-chou wares Mino places this whole group in the Chin (1124–1234) and Yüan dynasties; the earliest, a pillow in the Montreal Museum, being assigned to the late twelfth century.[33] This pillow has a projecting flange round the upper surface, a feature also of the Hsing-t'ai pillow; and according to Mino antedating the type with smooth rounded edge. The Chinese official date for this pillow was twelfth century, but Mino calls it early thirteenth century.

There is, however, a pillow in a Japanese collection with a calligraphic inscription dated 1133 complaining of the invasion of the area by the Chin army,[34] suggesting that the kiln was already in operation before the date of the Chin invasion in 1126, as shown by the finds made at the site of Chü-lu-hsien flooded in 1108. In any case, we should not be wrong in believing the period of the activity of the firm to have started in the twelfth century, but it is clear that it continued beyond the end of Chin into the Yüan period, and even apparently into Ming. True landscape scenes may not have been painted on the Chang pillows before the thirteenth century. Whitfield suggests very plausibly that these may derive from illustrated woodcut books, such as one dated 1242, where the double-page spread of the open book produces

[26] *Wen-wu*, 1964, No. 8, Type No. 4, Pl. 1 no. 3. OCS *Translations*, No. 5, p. 16, fig. 11.
[27] OCS *Translations*, No. 5, p. 17.
[28] *Wen-wu*, 1965, No. 2, p. 40, fig. 4: Mino, *Freedom of Clay*, Pl. 53, fig. 138.
[29] S. G. Valenstein, *A Handbook of Chinese Ceramics*, New York, 1975, Pl. 47.
[30] *Wen-Wu*, 1964, No. 8; OCS *Translations*, No. 5, figs, 16 and 24.
[31] Ayers, op. cit., pp. 67–8.
[32] R. Whitfield, 'Tz'ŭ-chou pillows with painted decoration', *Percival David Foundation Colloquies of the Art and Archaeology of Asia*, No. 5, 1970.
[33] Mino, *Freedom of Clay*, p. 116 et seq., and Pl. 46.
[34] Whitfield, op. cit., p. 75.

85 PILLOW with sgraffito decoration, Tz'ŭ-chou type
Height 10.5 cm (4.1 in), Length 43.5 cm (17.1 in). 11th century
Asian Art Museum, San Francisco, Avery Brundage Collection. See page 106

86 PILLOW decorated in sgraffito technique, Tz'ŭ-chou type
Length 33 cm (13 in). 11th century
Formerly Malcolm Collection, courtesy M. Medley. See page 106

a shape of design not far removed from that of the top surface of a rectangular pillow.[35] Most of the pillows with framed landscape designs painted on them are however clearly of Yüan dynasty date.

An extensive production of brush-painted wares has been characteristic of the Tz'ŭ-chou group of kilns from the Sung period until recent times. Quality naturally varies greatly, from the work of master painters to rapid repetition of conventional design. Close dating is difficult; we have already mentioned the problem even for the pillows with Chang family marks. For other types it is even more difficult still to construct reliable chronology. The earliest example bearing a date is a vase with foliate mouth in the Barlow collection at Sussex University; it is of the 11th year of the Ch'un-yen era, equivalent to AD 1251, after the Mongol conquest of the Chin empire.[36] A finer example of this unusual shape, painted with peony scrolls, is in the British Museum (Plate 88) from the Eumorfopoulos collection,[37] which I would attribute to the Chin period. This form later developed into the rather heavy almost dumbbell shape on a high conical foot, a type vouched for at the Yü-hsien kiln of Pa-ts'un.[38] Another example, in the Shanghai Museum,[39] is there given a Sung dynasty date, but is surely also of the Yüan period. Both these vases are densely decorated with complex floral designs. In general the more restrained and painterly style of decoration may be regarded as an indication of Chin date in the twelfth or very early thirteenth century.

A covered jar in the Avery Brundage collection seems to be of a type made in the Tung-ai-k'ou kilns in Hopei (Plate 89); and the very free and dashing brushwork would point to a date in the eleventh century.[40] A vase in Japan is more difficult to place (Plate 90), though the shape again points to the eleventh century; but here the painting is more subtle and complex, for the peony bloom is shaded by incising through the black to the white-slip ground. A similar vase with the addition of butterflies to the painted design is in the Hakone Museum.[41] Both vases are attributed by Mino to the Chin dynasty. The same date would apply to the tall slender *mei-p'ing* vases painted with elegant peony foliage on very slender stalks. A refinement of this type of brush-

[35] Ibid., p. 83, Pl. 5.
[36] Sullivan, op. cit., p. 68, C 176, Pl. 62a.
[37] Hobson, *Handbook*, 1948, fig. 56.
[38] Medley, *Yüan Porcelain and Stoneware*, Pl. 97; Mino, *Freedom of Clay*, p. 179, Pl. 77 and fig. 205.
[39] Shanghai Municipal Museum, op. cit., Pl. 54.
[40] *Wen-wu*, 1964, No. 8, fig. 23.
[41] Mino, *Freedom of Clay*, p. 199, Pl. 87.

---

87 PILLOW decorated in sgraffito technique, Tz'ŭ-chou type
   Height 12.5 cm (4.9 in), Width 22 cm (8.6 in). Early 12th century
   Seattle Art Museum, Eugene Fuller Memorial Collection. See page 106
88 VASE with foliate mouth and painted design, Tz'ŭ-chou type
   Height 37.8 cm (14.8 in). Chin, *c.* 1200
   British Museum. See page 110

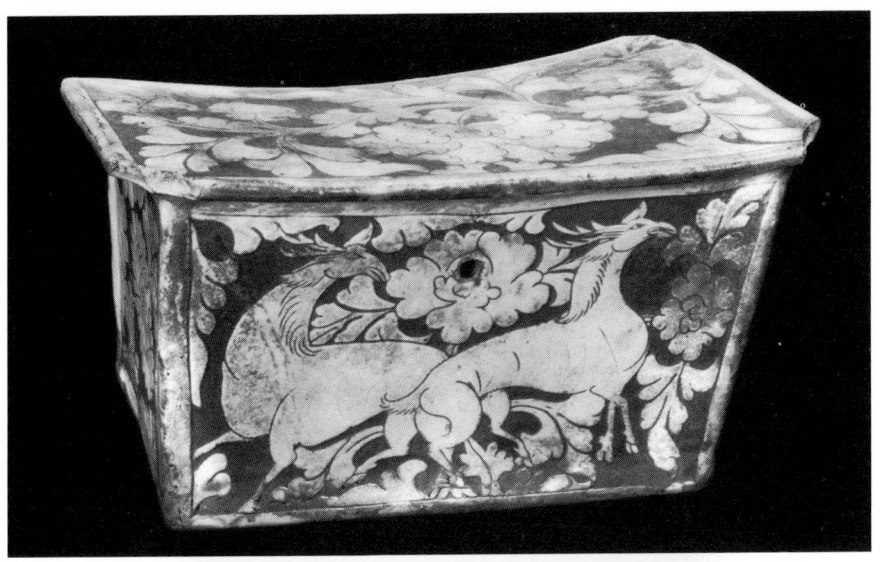

89 Covered JAR with painted design. Tung-ai-k'ou kiln, Hopei, Tz'ŭ-chou type
Height 15.9 cm (6.2 in). 11th century
Asian Art Museum, San Francisco, Avery Brundage Collection. See page 110
90 JAR with painted flower spray, Tz'ŭ-chou type
Height 25.5 cm (10 in). Chin, *c.* 1200
Private Collection, Japan. See page 110

I Oil-spot TEA-BOWL, Northern
black ware
Diameter 10.8 cm (4.25 in).
Northern Sung, 12th century
Fitzwilliam Museum.
See page 124

J Leaf *Temmoku* TEA-BOWL
from Chi-chou
Diameter 14.9 cm (5.9 in).
Southern Sung,
12th–13th century
Fitzwilliam Museum.
See page 126

91 *Mei-p'ing* VASE painted with foliage, Tz'ŭ-chou type
   Height 43 cm (17 in). Chin, *c.* 1200
   Seattle Art Museum, Eugene Fuller Memorial Collection. See page 116

92 *Mei-p'ing* VASE painted with a peony design, Tz'ŭ-chou type
    Height 35.4 cm (14 in). Chin, 12th century
    Victoria and Albert Museum. See page 116

93 *Mei-p'ing* VASE painted in white slip under a translucent brown glaze, Tz'ŭ-chou
type
Height 34.5 cm (13.5 in). Chin, 12th century
British Museum. See page 116

work is by the addition of incised shading on flowers and leaves to the black brush-drawing, a technique of which there are several examples in Japanese collections, and one in the Seattle Art Museum which is illustrated here (Plate 91). This advanced technique is unlikely to have been introduced before 1200. A more robust form of *mei-p'ing* with wider shoulders and with the painting of the peony foliage more substantially realized is in the Victoria and Albert Museum (Plate 92). An apparently unique effect is achieved on a vase of similar shape in the British Museum (Plate 93) by the painting of the peony spray in white slip on a brown ground under the translucent light-brown glaze. Here the foliage is carefully modelled and the whole execution is very superior.[42] Another *mei-p'ing* vase, in the Fitzwilliam Museum, shows a more sketchy treatment of chrysanthemum sprays in brown under a greenish glaze (Colour Plate G).

A head-rest of leaf shape in the Yamato Bunkakan, has already been mentioned for its beautiful brushwork depicting fish among water-plants (Plate 94). This shape of pillow is regarded by Mino as being of the Northern Sung period;[43] and this example shares with those that he reproduces the use of incised line, here on the fins and tail of the fish. Mino compares with this type a shard from the Kuan-t'ai site on which the same technique of incised detail appears; but it may be added that the seaweed motif was popular at the Pa-ts'un kilns at Yü-hsien, Honan.[44]

Under the Chin dynasty we find also a revival of the use of coloured glazes which may probably be related to a survival from the Liao dynasty *san-ts'ai* and now used especially for the decoration of pillows. The colouring is however limited to yellow, green and white glazes controlled by incised outlines. A pillow from the Malcolm collection shows mandarin ducks with yellow beaks swimming among lotus plants on a green ground.[45] A pillow of similar shape with square ends, in the British Museum, is decorated only with lotus plants.[46]

A more important Chin innovation, introduced apparently only after 1200, is the use of two or three colours (red, green and yellow) in overglaze enamel painting which would have required a second firing in a muffle kiln. At this time the technique was used only on small bowls of open shape, and the designs, limited to flower, bird and fish subjects, are always enclosed within a frame of multiple rings. Several of these bowls bear dates written in ink on the body under the foot and partly under the glaze, most unusual on wares of this period. A fine example painted with a great bursting peony bloom was exhibited in the Oriental Ceramic Society's jubilee exhibition in 1971.[47]

[42] For comparable pieces see Mino, *Freedom of Clay*, Pl. 71 from the Indianapolis Museum of Art; and Wirgin, *Sung Ceramic Designs*, op. cit., p. 115, Type Tc 36, Pls. 54 d-f.

[43] Mino, *Freedom of Clay*, pp. 104–7, Pls. 40–1.

[44] *Wen-wu*, 1964, No. 8, pp. 27–33.

[45] See coloured frontispiece in TOCS, 1954–5.

[46] Wirgin, *Sung Ceramic Designs*, op. cit., Pl. 52b.

[47] OCS, *Ceramic Art of China*, 1971, no. 93, Pl. 63.

94 Leaf-shaped PILLOW painted with a design of two cat-fish, Tz'ǔ-chou type
Height 19.5 cm (7.7 in). Northern Sung, 11th century
Yamato Bunkakan, Nara, Japan. See pages 100, 116

The best examples are however in Japan, including the two bowls dated 1201
and 1230 in the Tokyo National Museum, the latter with a sketchy drawing
of an orchid. One, in the Ataka collection[48] shows a more carefully executed
design of a single and a double peony flower. The type continues into the
Yüan period when some larger shapes are introduced and with less simple
designs; and of these some excellent examples are reproduced by Margaret
Medley in her *Yüan Porcelain and Stoneware* volume in this series.[49] Production of wares with this enamelled technique ceased, however, before 1300 and
it can never have been extensive. There seems to be no continuity with enamelled wares of the Ming dynasty produced in the Ching-tê-chên kilns or in
the Tê-hua group.

[48] *Mayuyama, Seventy Years*, Pl. 638.
[49] Medley, op. cit., Pls. 101c and 103a.

Chapter 7

THE BROWN WARES OF NORTH
AND SOUTH CHINA

The brown-glazed stoneware tea-bowl has achieved so high a reputation not only in Japan as *Temmoku* but also in the West that it seems best to treat together the quite distinct wares from Honan and Fukien, though fortunately there is no difficulty in distinguishing between the products of these two different areas. It is evident, moreover, that there was some interchange of expertise in kiln practice between the two, since such special effects as the hare's-fur and the oil-spot glaze is common to both. It is also clear that production from both kiln centres was large, to meet a wide and continuing demand. There is, however, one fundamental difference: the Fukien kilns produced only tea-bowls and no other shape, whereas the Honan kilns formed part of an extensive ceramic industry producing not only a variety of shapes but also other wares at the same time. Indeed contemporary Chinese practice would treat these northern brown wares as a part of the general Tz'ŭ-chou grouping. Similar effects were also obtained at the productive kilns at Chi-chou in Kiangsi province, but here decoration was generally more developed and techniques more varied, as was revealed by excavation of kiln sites in 1979. The peak of production here was under Southern Sung.

THE NORTHERN KILNS

The earliest of the brown wares were those produced at the Têng-fêng kilns in Honan at Ch'ü-ho, conveniently placed for transport by the Ying river to the not far-distant capital K'aifêng.[1] According to a Northern Sung Gazetteer by Wang Ts'un dating from the reign of emperor Yüan-fêng (1078–85), tribute from this area of Honan at that time included annual shipment of two hundred pieces of ceramics.[2] But the principal market for their products

[1] Fêng Hsien-Ming, *Wen-wu*, 1964, No. 3; OCS *Translations*, No. 5, pp. 13–19.
[2] OCS *Translations*, No. 5, p. 16.

95 *Mei-p'ing* VASE with applied clay ribs. From Ch'ing-ho, Hopei, Tz'ŭ-chou type
Height 25.5 cm (10 in). 12th century
Formerly Mr and Mrs Alfred Clark Collection. See page 120

was for the opulent restaurants of the city frequented by well-to-do merchants.[3] There they would have been seen in the company of paintings by well-known contemporary masters, hanging on the walls. These tea-bowls were then used and appreciated by connoisseurs. Consequently the Japanese tea-masters were not the first to show their appreciation of the products of the Têng-fêng bowls. The kiln also produced a brown-painted ware and a moulded ware under a green glaze. A range of shards from tea-bowls from this site was exhibited in Japan in 1965.[4] A drawing of the profile of a typical bowl showing the everted lip is illustrated by Fêng Hsien-ming.[5] Some bowls have a nearly vertical lip with a ridge about an inch below it to avoid spilling the tea (Plate 98).[6] Two types are illustrated: one with a hare's-fur marking, the other with a ring of white slip round the lip. This latter type seems to be of a coarser ware. Both types are represented by whole pieces in Japanese and Western collections, for instance in the Umezawa[7] and the Barlow[8] collections. The report also mentions that some bowls had been stacked in the kilns on ring supports leaving a circle bare of glaze round the centre of the interior; evidently therefore a poorer quality type.

Other kilns in Honan at which brown wares were made have been located at Ho-pi-chi in T'ang-yü hsien south of Anyang and not far from the Hopei border,[9] where also Tz'ŭ-chou type painted wares were made. Another source for these northern brown wares was at Ch'ing-ho[10] in Hopei itself. At Tuan-tien, Lu-shan and Pao-fêng in Honan shards were found[11] of a type well represented in Western collections[12] on which applied vertical ribs of clay remain white under a very thin translucent glaze. A vase of this shape was in the Alfred Clark collection (Plate 95) and this was actually stated to have come from the Ch'ing-ho site.[13] This vase of mei-p'ing shape has a brown dressing on the foot where the glaze stops short as it frequently does on this type of ware. From Palmgren's exploration of the site came other shapes, including a vase with a funnel mouth of a kind represented in the British Museum,[14] a globular jar and a type of vase with a contracted mouth, as in the Umezawa collection.[15] But the finest example of the type in a Japanese collection is a ewer with flat foot, ribbed sides and tall neck with a cover and a loop handle.[16]

[3] Ibid., p. 18.
[4] China's Beauty of 2000 Years, 1965, nos. 475, 478–9.
[5] Wen-wu, 1964, No. 3, p. 54, fig. 14.
[6] China's Beauty of 2000 Years, no. 467.
[7] Mayuyama, Seventy Years, Vol. 1, Pls. 673–4; STZ, 1955, Vol. 10, Pl. 105; F. Koyama, Tem-moku (Tōki Zenshū 26), Pl. 10.
[8] Sotheby Sale 26.3.75, lot. 23, cf. Barlow collection, TOCS, 1971, no. 95.
[9] Wen-wu, 1964, No. 8, Pl. 1, no. 7; OCS Translations, No. 5, pp. 1–14.
[10] China's Beauty of 2000 Years, nos. 486–90.
[11] Kiln Sites, nos. 413 and 419.
[12] Wirgin, Sung Ceramic Designs, op. cit., Pls. 53j–l and 54a–c.
[13] Sotheby Sale 25.3.75, lot 22, illustrated in colour p. 35.
[14] ECPP, Pl. 65.
[15] Mayuyama, Seventy Years, Pl. 525.
[16] G. Hasebe, Jishū-yo 'Tz'ŭ-chou Ware' (Tōki Zenshū 13), Pl. 54.

96 JAR with suffused-iron design of birds, Honan brown ware
   Height 19 cm (7.5 in). *c.* 1200
   Victoria and Albert Museum. See page 122
97 BOWL with streaked brown glaze, Honan brown ware
   Diameter 23.5 cm (9.2 in). *c.* 1200
   Victoria and Albert Museum. See page 122

Other effects achieved by the northern potters represent real achievements in kiln control, which reached its peak in the Chin period about 1200. In these iron oxide has been precipitated in the reducing atmosphere of the kiln to produce rusty-brown suffused patterns in the glaze. At first this effect was almost random, streaks or splashes as exemplified in Japanese collections and reproduced by Mayuyama.[17] These depend for their effect on the quality of the interchange between the deep brown and the rusty red, as on the covered jar in the Neave-Hill collection.[18] But soon the potters learnt to control the effect so as to produce a design in the glaze, generally floral, as on a bottle with a screw mouth in the Burrell collection in Glasgow (Colour Plate H) or the well-known vase in the British Museum from the Oppenheim collection,[19] which has been several times reproduced. A very distinct bird is represented on a jar in the Victoria and Albert Museum (Plate 96). The larger vases, such as one from the Seilern collection with wide bulbous body and bottle mouth,[20] or a vase with wide mouth from the Eumorfopoulos collection in the British Museum,[21] are no doubt of Yüan date in the later thirteenth century. Miss Medley reproduces a fine example from Japan with well-developed peony flowers and 43 cm (17 in) in height.[22] A bowl with regular rusty streaking is in the Victoria and Albert Museum (Plate 97), a gift in 1975 from Sir John Addis. The glaze surface is slightly pitted as with the oil-spot pieces; and the shaping of the body on the wheel can be distinguished on the exterior.

Another effect, related to the iron-splashed wares, is that already referred to, the oil-spot, produced by the bursting of bubbles of salts imprisoned in the glaze and released during the reduction in the kiln. The rusty-brown ferruginous spots sometimes resemble the silvery bubbles of the oil-spot, as can be seen by comparing two bowls in the Metropolitan Museum.[23] The oil-spot wares are rare and most are tea-bowls, often of great distinction. One piece, at present unique, is the small ewer in the Stockholm Eastern Antiquities Museum from the collection of the late King Gustaf Adolf.[24] Only 12 cm (4.7 in) in height and with the glaze stopping well short of the foot, the glaze is here completely covered with a fine spread of silver stars of different magnitude. At present the only tea-bowls of which wasters have been found on the Honan kiln sites are those with a white slip round the lip, which Margaret Medley believes to have been applied to the biscuit after cutting away a first application of the black slip glaze. These are not comparable in quality with the oil-spot bowls, like examples in the Barlow collection at Sussex Univer-

[17] Op. cit., Pls. 3, 6 and 8.
[18] TOCS, 1971, no. 97, Colour Plate H.
[19] ECPP, Pl. 62, also the pear-shaped vase from the same collection, TOCS, 1971, no. 98.
[20] Christie Sale 17.6.82, Lot 95, p. 74, illustrated in colour.
[21] Reg. no. 1936 10–12.15.
[22] Medley, Yüan Porcelain and Stoneware, Colour Plate H.
[23] Valenstein, op. cit., Pls. 49, 50.
[24] Exhibited in 1971, Ceramic Art of China, TOCS, 33, 1971, no. 96; British Museum, 1972, no. 132.

98 TEA-BOWL with oil-spot glaze, Honan
    Diameter 19.3 cm (7.6 in). 12th century
    British Museum. See pages 120, 124
99 Covered JAR with oil-spot glaze, Honan brown ware
    Height 26.8 cm (10.5 in). 12th century
    British Museum. See page 124

sity[25] or in the Fitzwilliam Museum from the Raphael collection (Colour Plate I). However, in one single example in Japan the two effects are combined; this is in the Fujita Art Museum in Osaka.[26] A damaged specimen was in the Alfred Clark collection.[27] In both these bowls the oil-spots are small and sparse.

Much fuller development of the burst bubbles is to be seen on a bowl in the British Museum (Plate 98) from the Eumorfopoulos collection, but parted into separate constellations in the interior. This bowl has a straight lip slightly everted at the rim and the ridges caused during the throwing on the wheel are conspicuous outside. Another important example in the British Museum, from the Oppenheim collection, is a jar with domed cover (Plate 99), both covered with a fine mesh of oil-spots. The flanged footring is unglazed.

THE SOUTHERN KILNS

CHI-CHOU IN KIANGSI

In the area round the city of Yung-ho in Kiangsi province have been found great heaps of ceramic waste. They are generally referred to by the name of the provincial capital, Chi-chou, which lies about 32 kilometres south on the Kan river. Both Palmgren and Brankston brought back shards from this site in the 1930s and it was not difficult to identify the kilns with those mentioned in the first edition of the *Ko Ku Yao Lun* of 1388 as 'producing brown ware similar to brown Ting'.[28] This account adds that the body 'is thick and the paste coarse'. In the second edition of 1462, which has little reliability for events of the Sung dynasty, it is added that there were five kilns, in which Shu Kung produced the most commendable pieces in white and brown. 'The big pieces are worth several taels of silver; smaller ones were decorated with delightful designs.' It also produced good crackled ware. The site of the kiln 'was still to be seen, though dwelling houses have been built on it'. We may deduce from this account that by the fifteenth century the kilns were no longer operating; but we do not know when they ceased. Production was evidently continuous from Southern Sung into the Yüan dynasty.

The only precise date is provided by a tomb find at Nan-ch'ang dated 1209 in which were two pieces with painted decoration in brown on a white-slip ground. These are reproduced by John Addis,[29] who repeats the suggestion by Fêng Hsien-ming,[30] shortly after it was discovered, that the kiln was influenced by the Tz'ŭ-chou kilns through potters moving south with the Sung

[25] Sullivan, op. cit., C115 Pl. 52c.
[26] STZ, 1977, Vol. 12, Pl. 260.
[27] ECPP, Pl. 61, and Sotheby Sale 25.3.75, lot 23.
[28] David, op. cit., p. 141.
[29] J. Addis, *Chinese Ceramics from Datable Tombs*, p. 32, Pls. 22a and b.
[30] *Wen-wu*, 1973, No. 7; OCS *Translations*, No. 8, 1978, p. 18, figs. 4, 5.

refugee court. But for this there is no literary evidence. The style is, however, different from the northern wares and Addis remarks that the design on both pieces is an astonishing anticipation of the blue and white style of Ching-tê-chên more than a century later. Yet shards have been found at Chi-chou precisely in this style, which is thus shown to be that of the early thirteenth century under Southern Sung. On one piece, a flower pot, a naturalistic lotus is reserved on a white ground between rows of key-fret pattern. On the other, a covered jar, a leaping deer is depicted in rapid brushwork in a sketchy landscape inscribed within a lobed medallion, while round the neck is a highly stylized floral scroll. Shards from the kiln site show fishes among weeds within a similar border of lotus flowers reserved in a brown ground.[31]

The tea-bowls vouched for by the site finds are all decorated in one way or another, the simplest being a hare's-fur pattern, which is a clear development of the Honan type of iron-patterned glaze. Two new techniques were introduced at Chi-chou. A unique practice at these kilns involves the use of cut-out paper patterns covering parts of the vessel during the application of the glaze, thus providing resist, analagous to the use of wax resist in textile (*batik*) design. Examples of vessels produced with the aid of this process were found by the Kiangsi Provincial team of excavators in 1979 and shards were included in the 1980 loan exhibition to London and Oxford with a diaper pattern of flowers.[32] These were attributed by the excavators to the Southern Sung period. The outsides of these bowls generally show a tortoiseshell effect in the glaze.[33]

Long before the official excavations took place, many examples of tea-bowls of this type had reached Japan and the West; of the former four are reproduced by Hasebe,[34] including the best known, from the Tokyo National Museum, on which flowers were stylized into a geometric pattern, each containing four characters of lucky omen. A similar bowl reached the British Museum as long ago as 1922 (Plate 100). Other designs in this cut-out technique include a pair of phoenixes[35] and of dragons.[36] Among the shards brought back from Chi-chou by Brankston and now in the British Museum are two with delicate floral designs cut into the white slip; in the excavations at the kiln site fragments were found carved through black slip into floral designs.[37] An example of a whole vase of this type is in the Barlow collection.[38]

Yet another effect was achieved at these kilns by the use of actual tree leaves to make their imprint in the brown glaze. There are examples in the Baur

[31] *Kiln Sites*, no. 255.
[32] Ibid., nos. 227–8, 273–4.
[33] Medley, *Yüan Porcelain and Stoneware*, Pls. 110b and 111b.
[34] STZ, 1977, Vol. 12, Pls. 99–105.
[35] Clark collection example, see Sotheby Sale 25.3.75, lot 26; Bristol City Art Gallery, *The Schiller Collection*, 1948, Pl. 5, no. N2589; *Mayuyama, Seventy Years*, Pl. 680.
[36] STZ, 1977, Vol. 12, Pl. 99.
[37] *Kiln Sites*, nos. 277–9.
[38] TOCS, 32, 1960, no. 194, Pl. 70; Medley, *Yüan Porcelain and Stoneware*, 112a.

Foundation (A67), the Seligman collection[39] and the Fitzwilliam Museum (Colour Plate J); but the finest examples are no doubt in Japan where they have been especially appreciated, that in the Goto Art Museum being registered as 'an important art object'.[40]

Also represented among the kiln site finds is a ware painted in white slip on the brown ground with rather free designs of plants.[41] A bowl of this type is in the Brundage collection in San Francisco.[42] In the 1967 catalogue d'Argencé quotes Chiang Hsüan-t'ai as calling this design 'plum blossom in moonlight'. There are also a number of bowls with gold-painted patterns on the brown glaze and these have been discussed by John Figgess and others, including John Ayers in the Seligman catalogue, which includes a bowl inscribed with four characters (Plate 101): 'May you endure as long as the hills and your contentment be as the sea.'[43] The same four characters are inscribed on a bowl in the Tokyo National Museum[44] and on another in the Barlow collection.[45] These were both described as of Chien ware, but the body is not that of the typical Chien bowl and they may be from the more sophisticated Chi-chou kilns. These were superintended by an official in Chi-chou, a sign of their importance to the bureaucracy, at least as a source of taxation.

THE CHIEN WARES OF FUKIEN

The bowls and cups of Chien-yao are mentioned in the first edition of the *Ko Ku Yao Lun* (1388) as 'black in colour and unctuous with spots like the yellow fur of the hare' and mostly with flaring mouth and as coming from Fukien province. 'Genuine examples have large pearl drops', referring to the thick runnels of glaze which overlap the exposed body below the shoulder. The bowls must have been dipped in the glaze by the potter holding them by the footrim. They were then placed in the saggar ready for insertion in the kiln; to avoid the risk of the glaze sticking to the saggar, which nonetheless frequently happened, the glaze was controlled well short of the foot. In the light of this information it was not difficult to identify the Chien tea-bowls which had survived, especially in Japan, where they had long been treasured because of their association with the tea-ceremony. There they were known as *Temmoku*, the Sino-Japanese form of *T'ien-mu*, 'heavenly eye', the name of the highest peak in the Chekiang mountain chain, on which was a Ch'an (Zen) monastery, from which the practice of tea drinking is said to have been

[39] Medley, ibid., Pls. 110, 111.
[40] *Mayuyama, Seventy Years*, Pl. 668.
[41] *Kiln Sites*, no. 278.
[42] R. Y. L. d'Argencé, *Chinese Ceramics in the Avery Brundage Collection*, San Francisco, 1967, B60 P.176, Pl. XLVII.
[43] Ayers, op. cit., p. 70, with line drawing to show the characters.
[44] Tokyo National Museum, op. cit., no. 354.
[45] Sullivan, op. cit., C157, p. 122, Pl. 125b.

100 TEA-BOWL with resist decoration, Chi-chou ware, Kiangsi
   Diameter 11.5 cm (4.5 in). Southern Sung, early 13th century
   British Museum. See page 125
101 TEA-BOWL with four characters in gold over the glaze, Chi-chou ware
   Diameter 10.8 cm (4.2 in). Early 13th century
   British Museum, Seligman Collection. See page 126

introduced into Japan, traditionally about the year 1200.

Actually this mountain is some 320 kilometres from the kilns at which the Chien-yao was produced. These were first identified in 1935 by an American sinologist then in the Chinese Maritime Customs, James Marshall Plumer (1899–1960), afterwards professor, who revealed his discovery in an article published in the *Illustrated London News* later in that year. He had noted the arrival in antique shops in Fu-chou, the port at the mouth of the Min river, of tea-bowls of this type; and elicited that they had arrived by boat from far up the river. It was not until 1935 that he was able to travel from Hangchou over the pass between Chekiang and Fukien to Shui-chi on its upper course and then to find kiln debris some three kilometres south of the town in the wooded hills above the Min river between there and the prefectural capital of Chien-ning, which had given its name to the ware. Plumer found great mounds, at least eighteen metres thick, of kiln waste and identified three kiln sites. It was not, however, until 1972 that his full account of his finds and of the wares was published posthumously in a monograph in Japan.[46]

Meanwhile Chinese government archaeologists had investigated some of the kiln sites in 1955 and identified eleven kilns in this same area.[47] Plumer found that in his time these kiln wasters were being systematically quarried by local farmers and the vessels that they could salvage taken downstream to market. He himself was able to collect a large series of wasters and saggars and so to give a circumstantial account of the ware, including references to many pieces in Western collections which could be identified, without question, as products of these kilns. He could also establish the kiln practice of these Sung potters, and demonstrate by experiment how the glaze effects were achieved.

Plumer concluded that the only products of the Chien kilns were bowls intended for the drinking of tea, for the cultivation of which this district was famed. He charted seven distinctive profiles for the bowls of which three,[48] and those the most frequent, have the out-turned lip mentioned in the *Ko Ku Yao Lun*, but he pointed out that there were no rigidly defined shapes but an infinite variety within these types. The sizes, though not uniform, varied little, except for the making of a very small number of larger bowls, less than three per cent of the products, of diameter between 18 and 30 cm (7 and 12 in). This is in contrast to the Chi-chou kilns where the range of types is much greater and small jars and tripod incense vases were made,[49] in the floral decoration of both of which the cut-out technique was used.

The body of the Chien-yao bowls is a rather dark-grey coarse clay fired at a temperature high enough for stoneware, and was designed by its porosity when combined with the thickness of body and glaze to retain the heat during

[46] J. M. Plumer, *Temmoku: a Study of the Wares of Chien*, Tokyo, 1972.

[47] *Wen-wu*, 1955, No. 3.

[48] Plumer, op. cit., fig. 38.

[49] OCS, *Chün and Brown Wares*, 1952, no. 123: BM Reg. no. 1926.4–14.1.

K Chien-yao hare's-
fur TEA-BOWL
Diameter 20.5 cm
(8 in). Sung,
12th century
British Museum.
See page 130

L Kuan-yao VASE
Height 23.2 cm (9.1 in). Southern Sung, early 13th century
Freer Gallery of Art. See page 134

102 a, b TEA-BOWL known as 'Inaba Temmoku', with iridescent markings in the glaze, Chien ware, Fukien
Diameter 12.2 cm (4.8 in). 12th–13th century
Seikadō Foundation, Tokyo. See page 130

the slow drinking of the tea.[50] The varied range of dark-brown glaze is due to the presence of iron oxide. As Plumer puts it 'the many gradations of colour and surfaces, streaking and mottling, sheen and texture, are due to the concerted action of a variety of kiln conditions.' Clearly the potters knew what to expect and exploited the variation due to positions in the kiln and control of the draught. They were thus able to achieve the glaze effects, such as hare's-fur, singled out in the *Ko Ku Yao Lun* account. The glaze tended to collect at the base of the bowl and thus form a pool, generally very dark in colour. The hare's-fur also occurs on the outside of some bowls, but less markedly. As with the northern brown wares a so-called 'oil-spot' effect is occasionally achieved. An American professor, Charles Harder,[51] reported on an experiment for making Chien-type bowls in New York, to the effect that the clay used in the glaze would contain traces of twenty or more chemical elements that are released seriatim during firing and then crystalize out during cooling into the glassy glaze cover of the bowl. The results are predictable only within general categories; but the potters would have acquired empirical knowledge of the positions in the kilns favourable for certain effects. The experimental firing reached a temperature of about 900°C. In Fukien wood fuel was used for firing the kilns; apparently more would have been required in wet weather, which frequently occurs in the hills where they were situated, and the firing would have been at best as high as 1200°C, for high fired stoneware.[52]

Apart from the very small group of tea-bowls which have been preserved in Buddhist temples in Japan until modern times (Plate 102), all known examples of Chien ware have been salvaged from the discarded saggars, or from the kiln debris. The delicate operation of extracting the bowls from the saggars has generally involved filing off the surplus glaze which had adhered to the mouth, the effect of which operation may be concealed by sheathing the lip in Japan; or possibly by refiring the bowl, in a tricky operation liable to ruin the glaze effect.

There are fine examples in the Baur Foundation as well as in Japan, where a famous oil-spot bowl is still preserved in the Ryuko-in,[53] and another in the Seikadō, Tokyo, with irridescent markings (Plate 102), both showing the ridge below the lip for the fingers of the tea drinker. In the Seikadō, Tokyo, is also a bowl with spreading, out-turned mouth and speckled glaze and with heavy glaze drops above the foot.[54] In the British Museum is a bowl of more elegant profile and with good hare's-fur markings (Colour Plate K). A giant bowl with purplish-black glaze and silvery flecks is in the Freer Gallery of Art, Washington.[55]

[50] Plumer, op. cit., p. 50.
[51] FECB, VII, 1, No. 29, 1955, pp. 19–25.
[52] Plumer, op. cit., p. 50.
[53] STZ, 1955, Vol. 10, Pl. 60.
[54] Ibid., 1955, Vol. 10, Pl. 58.
[55] Freer Gallery of Art, *Masterpieces of Chinese and Japanese Art*, 176, Pl. 43.

The only original and genuine marks on the bases of Chien bowls are numbers and single characters, apparently surnames. Plumer has discussed these and concludes that they have no significance for dating or provenance.[56] He reproduces one inscription with the characters *kung yü* (for Imperial use), but this bowl did not come directly from the waste heaps having been acquired in Fu-chou, and may have been tampered with.[57] On a saggar found by the Chinese archaeologists was an ink inscription giving a date equivalent to 1142.[58] The production is essentially of the Sung period but some kilns may already have started production in the tenth century, when for a brief period, 947–80, the area of Min in which the kilns lay was included within the kingdom of Wu-Yüeh, which also patronized the Yüeh kilns, as we have seen. The Chien kilns may have continued into Yüan, but there is no evidence beyond the end of the thirteenth century for continued working.

The relationship between the Chien wares and the northern wares of Honan is hard to define; both kiln groups were in full operation in the twelfth century, probably reaching a peak about 1200. Although their products can be readily distinguished by a study of the exposed body, the Chien body is of rather coarse grey clay, firing to a dark-brown or near-black; while the glaze is usually darker in the centre of the bowl where it is thickest, paler near the rim where it is thinnest and on the exterior. A characteristic feature of the Chien tea-bowls is the cut-back of the outer profile as it approaches the footrim which is unglazed and recessed, the glaze flow generally stopping short, about the level of the cutback. Some of the special glaze effects are common to both wares, such as the oil-spot and the hare's-fur. Whether these were arrived at empirically at the two kiln groups independently or, more probably, there was some interchange of personnel, especially following the fall of K'aifêng to the Chin Tartars, is likely to remain uncertain. Even if the Chien kilns may have supplied some bowls to the court at Hangchou and were certainly exporting them to Japan, their market was clearly mainly local. Although the northern kilns formed part of a considerable ceramic industry, with exports extending to Korea and South China, there is no evidence of either groups of kilns exporting to South Asia or to the West. It is even suggested that the Chien kilns were actually operated part-time in the winter by the farmers of the area after the close of the harvest and the tea picking.

[56] Plumer, op. cit., Ch. 6, pp. 69–76.
[57] Ibid., p. 77, fig. 50; but others were found at Chiu-chi.
[58] Ibid., p. 78, quoting *Wen-wu*, 1955, No. 3, p. 59 by Sung Pai-yin, on excavations near Shui-chi a town on the Min river.

Chapter 8

KUAN WARE

The official (Kuan) ware of Southern Sung was made at the capital Hangchou in the twelfth to thirteenth centuries, below the Suburban Altar (*Chiao-t'an*) on a ridge south of the city. Here a kiln site was discovered in 1929, remains from which were used to identify a number of pieces preserved intact in collections, Chinese, Japanese and Western, and also conforming to the literary tradition of a ware with 'brown mouth and iron foot'. The body of these pieces is indeed a dark-grey which when exposed in the kiln burns to a deep red-brown approaching black. The clay has been very finely levigated so that it can be used as a very thin support to the thick glaze, which can be seen to have been applied in successive layers, sometimes as many as five, before firing. A broken dish which has passed from the collection of Sir Harry and Lady Garner to the Fitzwilliam Museum (Plate 103), well reveals the relation between the dark body seen as a sandwich between the thick layers of glaze. This relationship evidently encouraged the production of crackle which is commonly found more or less strongly developed on all the products of the Chiao-t'an kiln. The first edition of the *Ko Ku Yao Lun* (1388) mentioned specifically these 'crab's claw' markings, adding that the imitations made at the Lung-ch'üan kilns lacked this crackle. It is due to the tension set up between the glaze and body, with their different co-efficients of expansion, an effect certainly deliberately exploited by the potters.

More recently, exploration of the area has revealed more kilns at Ta-yao and Ch'i-k'ou where wares of this type were made.[1] It is evident that the relationship between Kuan ware and Lung-ch'üan (see Chapter 10) was a close one and the current Chinese view is that the products of both kilns were supplied to the palace for official use. A number of shapes are common to both kilns, but in the Kuan ware there is never any decoration, whereas the Lung-

---

[1] Chin Tsu-ming in *K'ao-ku*, 1962, no. 10, pp. 535–8; Chü Po-chien in *Wen-wu*, 1963, No. 1, pp. 27–35; OCS *Translations*, No. 2, 1968, p. 8.

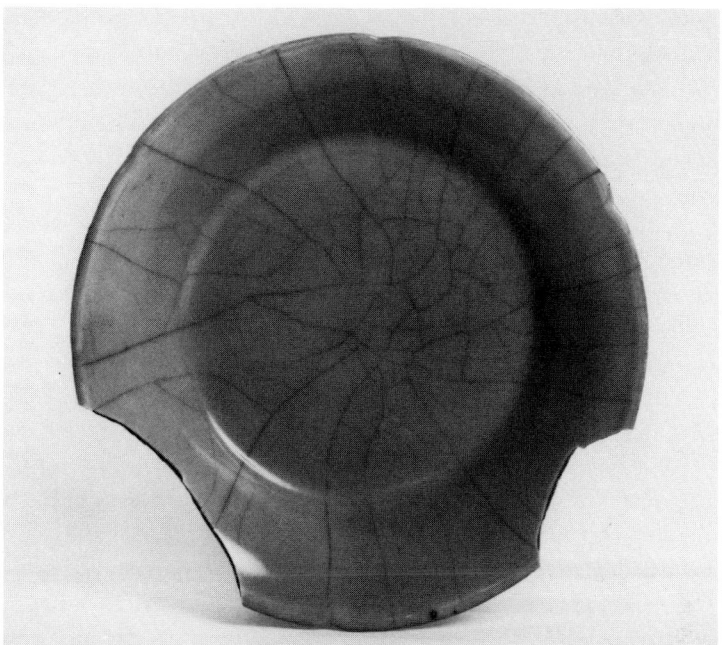

103 DISH with crackled blue-green glaze, broken so as to reveal the relation of body
     to glaze, Kuan ware, Chekiang
     Diameter 18 cm (7.1 in). Southern Sung, 12th century
     Fitzwilliam Museum, Cambridge. See page 132
104 Foliate DISH with crackled blue-green glaze, Kuan ware
     Diameter 22.5 cm (8.8 in). Southern Sung, 12th century
     Metropolitan Museum of Art, Fletcher Fund. See page 134

ch'üan pieces are usually decorated, and crackle is rare and sparse. Kuan ware is scarce, though not so scarce as Ju-yao which was certainly its model. Various shapes of dish are known. In the Fitzwilliam Museum is a dish with foliate out-turned rim and with a bluish-green glaze. A dish with similar foliation but to a flat rim, now bound in copper (Plate 104), is in the Metropolitan Museum. The glaze is paler, a delicate grey-blue. A third Kuan dish with foliate rim, this time curving inwards, is in the Chinese Imperial collection in Taiwan.[2] All three have a wide mesh of crackle in the glaze.

A much more emphatic lobing is seen on a dish in the Percival David Foundation which is octagonal, with each side of bracket profile (Plate 105). Here the crackle is even more widely spread.

In accordance with a deliberate attempt to imitate the Ju-yao of the north, as specified in the account in the *Ko Ku Yao Lun*, we can see the characteristic Ju shape of a narcissus bowl raised on four foliate feet (Plate 106), now in Taiwan, copied from a Ju piece of similar shape also preserved in the same collection, but with a light body (Plate 70).

After the dishes the commonest shapes in the Kuan ware are vases of various forms. The earliest may be the vase of paper-beater shape with flat base and without footrim but with double rings round the neck and one round the shoulder and with a wide crackle in the greyish-blue glaze over a very dark body. A variant on this shape is the octagonal vase on an octagonal high footrim and with dished mouth instead of the gentle turn-out of the Freer vase (Colour Plate L). This has exceptionally thick and flocculent glaze and a closer mesh of crackle, undoubtedly somewhat later and probably of the early thirteenth century.[3] An even closer mesh of crackle covers the vase of unique shape in the Hakone Art Museum (Plate 107), remarkable for its very high, flanged foot, ovoid body and rolled lip. At 36.5 cm (14.4 in) it is the tallest of the group and has a romantic history. For it was unearthed in 1926 in the garden of the Yüan Ming Yüan palace in the Western Hills outside Peking. One can only guess at the story of its burial, perhaps at the time of the destruction of the palace by the Anglo-French punitive expedition in 1860.

A more orthodox shape is the *mei-p'ing* prunus vase in the British Museum from the Eumorfopoulos collection (Plate 108), of typical Southern Sung shape, similar to the *ch'ing-pai* vase in the same collection.[4] The thick glaze covers less completely foot and mouth which consequently show a tinge of the iron-brown body characteristic of this ware. The crackle is sparse but effective in emphasizing the shape and the melting quality of the glaze. Next we may take the small but elegant vase (Colour Plate M) from the Barlow collection, given to the Victoria and Albert Museum in 1967, which also has a blue-grey glaze but with closer crackle. The footrim is high and slightly

[2] ECPP, 1953, Pl. 85a.
[3] TOCS, 32, 1960, no. 159; STZ 1977, Vol. 12, Pls. 6–8.
[4] ECPP, 1953, Pl. 75. TOCS, 33, 1972, no. 120, Pl. 83.

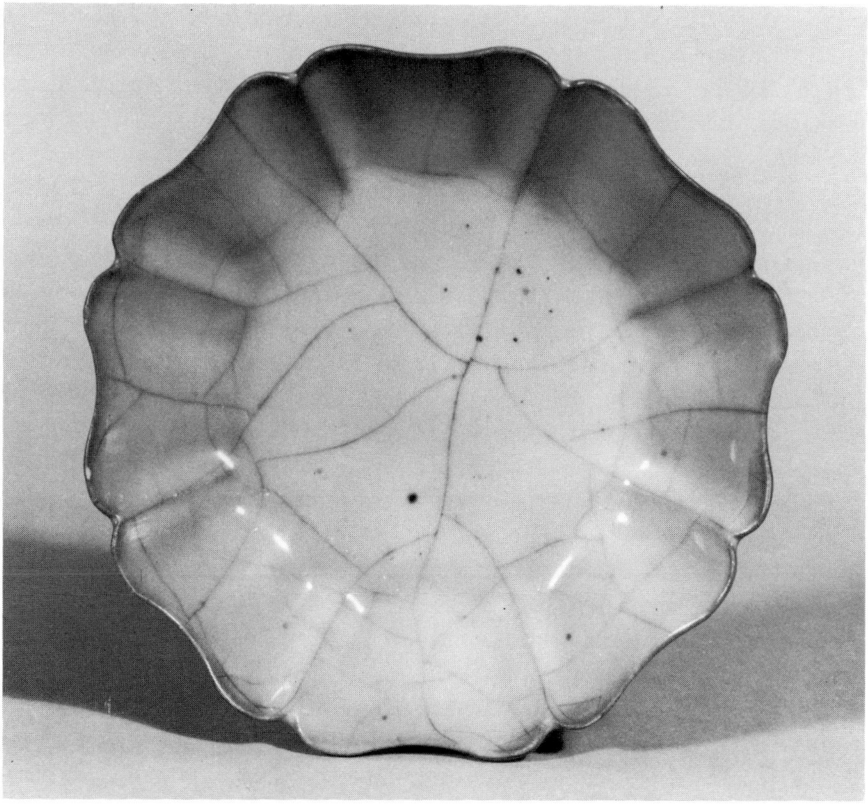

105 Octagonal lobed DISH, Kuan ware
   Diameter 17 cm (6.7 in). Southern Sung, 12th century
   Percival David Foundation of Chinese Art. See page 134
106 NARCISSUS BOWL with crackled blue-green glaze, Kuan ware
   Length 23 cm (9 in). Southern Sung, 12th century
   National Palace Museum, Taiwan. See pages 134, 140

splayed outwards and the lip after turning outwards is finished with a slight
inward turn. A closely similar vase has been found in a tomb dated 1213[5];
and the Barlow vase is no doubt of this period, as is another vase of this shape
formerly in the George de Menasce collection.

Sir Harry Garner discussed the deliberate development of crackle in a paper
given to the Oriental Ceramic Society in 1950, entitled 'Early Chinese
Crackled Porcelain'.[6] He referred to corroborative evidence in the identification of Kuan ware from wasters found in the 1930s in the neighbourhood
of the Chiao-t'an Suburban Altar, as mentioned above. Many of these pieces
reached Japanese and Western collections at that time and do in fact show
the remarkably thin dark-grey body and crackled grey-blue glaze (Plate 109).
But few, if any, are of the quality of the superb pieces preserved in the Imperial
palace collection and elsewhere which had escaped burial and can be assumed
to be indeed of Kuan or official quality. It must be concluded that the Chiao-
t'an kiln also produced wares of lower quality but using the same technique
in the glazing and the control of the kiln. Sir Harry also discussed the claim
by the Japanese for the identification of another superior Kuan ware as that
said to have been made in the Hangchou city at the Hsiu-nei-ssǔ kiln; and
he observed that this claim rests on quite insufficient evidence even for the
existence of such a kiln within the palace precincts. In Bushell's translation
of the *Ko Ku Yao Lun* it was stated that production of the Kuan ware was
'at the Public Works Department'; but Sir Percival David translates this passage 'Kuan ware was made on the orders of the Public Works Department'
(*Hsiu-nei-ssǔ*).[7] This seems to me to be a more correct interpretation of this
passage. In any case the identification by the Japanese of wares of superior
quality with a light body and uncrackled glaze as Kuan seems unjustified.
The group which they have isolated[8] is indeed of superior quality and may
well have been made for use in the palace; but there is no reason why it may
not even so have come from one of the Lung-ch'üan kilns, and these pieces
are here treated with the other products of that group of kilns.

To return to the dark-bodied Kuan ware from the Chiao-t'an kilns: they
fell under the influence of a change in taste from towards the end of Southern

[5] *K'ao-ku*, 1964, No. 5, Pl. 7, fig. 5.
[6] TOCS, 33, 1972, pp. 19–20.
[7] David, op. cit., p. 139.
[8] STZ, 1955, Vol. 10, Pls. 15, 40; F. Koyama, *100 Masterpieces of Chinese Ceramics*, 1960,
Pls. 64–7.

---

107 VASE with crackled blue-green glaze, Kuan ware
       Height 36.5 cm (14.4 in). Southern Sung, 12th century
       Hakone Art Museum, Japan. See page 134
108 *Mei-p'ing* VASE, Kuan ware
       Height 27.4 cm (10.8 in). Southern Sung, 12th century
       British Museum. See page 134

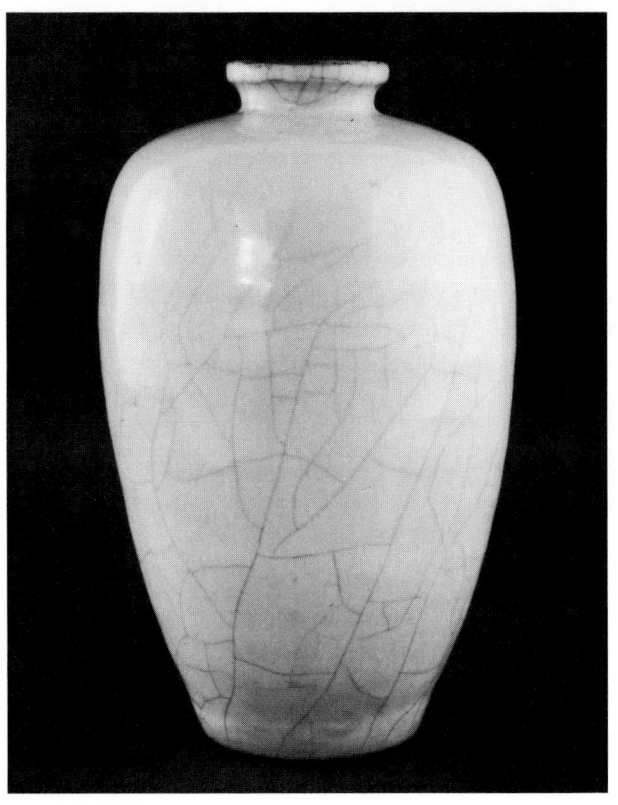

Sung and increasingly under the Yüan dynasty, when a nostalgia became apparent for the shapes of classic vessels in bronze and jade. Under this influence, centred in the court circles for which this kiln worked, the potters began to make such imitations, especially of the bronze *hu* and *ting* and the jade *tsung* traditionally believed to have been used in antiquity for the worship of earth. The shape is that of a truncated cylinder, square in outer section with central hollow circular tube and with grooves at the corners of the outside. Examples of this shape are now found in Lung-ch'üan celadon and in Kuan ware. A noble example of the latter in the Tokyo National Museum (Plate 110) has a fine mesh of stained crackle in the blue-green glaze and is no doubt of early thirteenth-century date. A piece of similar shape is in the Percival David Foundation, slightly larger but less conspicuously crackled.[9] In the Seikadō collection in Tokyo, is an incense burner, of bronze *ting* shape of the tenth century BC, but with decoration reduced to a double string round the shoulder and with a button at the centre of each side. A version of this shape in Chekiang celadon and about half the size was among the pieces recovered from the Sinan wreck.[10]

Two further examples of Sung Kuan-yao adaptations of archaic bronze shapes were in the Alfred Clark collection. One is a small censer based on the bronze *kuei* (Plate 111) and with a pale suffused grey glaze and close crackle of a type traditionally classed in China as *Ko* ware; but having spur-marks both inside and under the foot, it may be rather later than Sung. A finer example of the *kuei* shape is in the Shanghai Municipal Museum,[11] with a very thick glaze and almost no crackle. The second Clark piece[12] is, however, a fine example of Sung Kuan ware, based on the bronze *hu* shape with arrow handles on the short sides, joined by triple ribs and with a further rib at the widest part of the body; the foot is high and slightly splayed outwards. This piece shows signs of having been buried and has developed a secondary crackle on top of the original mesh; it is extensively repaired on either side of the lip. It is now in a Japanese collection.[13]

The wasters actually discovered at the Chiao-t'an kiln site are all fairly small and have a blue-grey glaze, rather than grey-green, covered with a very close mesh of crackle; there is no reason to doubt a South Sung date for them.[14] The bracketed profile of a small dish of this series, given to the British Museum by Mr Riesco (Plate 109), is to be attributed to influence from the north, and it is also found in Lung-ch'üan ware[15] and need not be as late as Yüan, when

[9] Yorke Hardy, op. cit., no. 62; TOCS, 32, 1960, no. 161, Pl. 61.
[10] National Museum of Korea, 1977, Colour Plate 12, and Pl. 21, D. 8.6 cm.
[11] Shanghai Municipal Museum, op. cit., Pl. 35.
[12] Gompertz, 1980, op. cit., Pl. 60; Sotheby Sale 28.3.75, lot 101; *Mayuyama, Seventy Years*, Pl. 466.
[13] STZ, 1977, Vol. 12, Pl. 71.
[14] TOCS, 32, 1960, nos. 165–7, Pl. 63, pp. 22–3.
[15] M. Medley, *Illustrated Catalogue of Celadon Wares*, no. 47, Reg. no. 264, Pl. V.

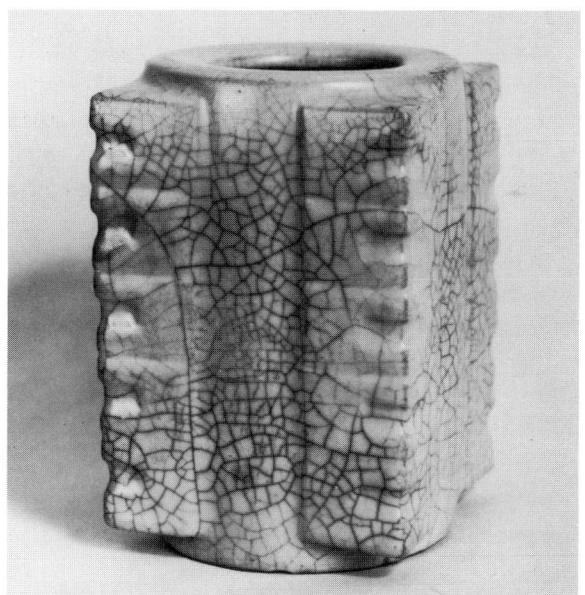

109 DISH with crackled glaze and foliate rim, Kuan ware
Diameter 17 cm (6.7 in). Southern Sung, 12th century
British Museum, gift of Mr and Mrs Riesco. See pages 136, 138
110 VASE in the shape of a jade *tsung*, with crackled glaze, Kuan ware
Height 20.4 cm (8 in). Southern Sung, early 13th century
Tokyo National Museum. See page 138

111 INCENSE BURNER in the form of a bronze *kuei*, Kuan ware
Width 16 cm (6.2 in). Southern Sung, 13th century
Formerly Mr and Mrs Alfred Clark Collection. See page 138

this shape became especially common.[16] These shapes are in fact not included among the celadon wares recovered from the Sinan wreck, except for a modified version of the foliate vase, to which ring handles have now been added.[17] The date for the Kuan wares is therefore probably to be given as early thirteenth century under Southern Sung, just the period of the revived interest in archaic bronze and jade. We can thus regard both types of Chiao-t'an ware as characteristic of sophisticated taste at the Southern Sung capital, Hangchou in the late twelfth and early thirteenth century. As examples of ceramic art they represent the highest point of achievement in virtuoso technique by control of the complete process of production. The number of near-perfect wasters discarded at the kilns also bears witness to the high standard maintained at the Chiao-t'an kilns.

Naturally this high standard is best represented in the palace collections. We have already cited the narcissus bowl (Plate 106) for its resemblance to Ju ware. This piece is also remarkable for having an uncrackled light grey-blue glaze. Two small vases in this collection both with the characteristic crackle are even finer; a flower vase of beaker shape with a flange above the foot has

[16] B. Gray, 'The export of Chinese porcelain to the Islamic World', TOCS, 41, 1975–7, p. 239.
[17] National Museum of Korea, op. cit., fig. 45, STZ, 1977, Vol. 12, fig. 79.

112 Bottle-shaped VASE, Kuan ware
Height 18 cm (7.1 in). Southern Sung, 12th century
Percival David Foundation of Chinese Art. See page 143

113 BOWL with everted lip and crackled sea-green glaze, Kuan ware
    Diameter 15.2 cm (6 in). 12th–13th century
    University of Sussex, Barlow Collection. See page 143
114 SAUCER-DISH with dense crackle of 'Ko' type, Kuan ware
    Diameter 14.8 cm (5.7 in). Southern Sung, 12th–13th century
    Private Collection, Japan. See page 143

a poem by emperor Ch'ien-lung dated 1778 engraved under the foot.[18] A vase of bottle shape with continuous curve from lip to foot and formerly in the palace collection (Plate 112) is now in the Percival David Foundation in London. It is only 18 cm (7.1 in) tall but has a most impressive presence due to its combination of perfect classic shape with romantic pale bluish-grey glaze enhanced by an ice-crackled mesh. Both lip and foot are sheathed in copper bands, perhaps to conceal minute blemishes but the dark body is visible at their edges.

Two well-known small bowls also have copper-sheathed lips. They have in common a shallow and proportionately small foot, but differ in size and glaze colour. The larger is in the Tokyo National Museum and has a dense crackle in the greyish-blue glaze, while the rim is lobed and the sides slightly lower.[19] The second (Plate 113) in the Barlow collection in Sussex University,[20] has a sea-green glaze covering the conical sides and is only 15.2 cm (6 in) in diameter and with a wider stained crackle above a mesh of secondary crazing. Both bowls are worthy products of the Kuan kiln.

Reference was made above to a piece formerly in the Alfred Clark collection as having once been attributed to a Ko kiln.[21] This type was traditionally supposed to have been produced by the elder brother of a pair who operated two kilns in Chekiang at which wares were made with dark rim and iron foot. This tradition, going back at least to the early eighteenth century, was long upheld in the Imperial palace and was consequently accepted as valid in Japan and in some Western circles. In the Percival David Foundation is an incense burner like that in the Clark collection of bronze *kuei* shape and with a similar greyish-white glaze and close mesh of crackle which has been stained to a very dark shade; under the base is incised a poem by emperor Ch'ien-lung dated 1783 in which the vessel is referred to as Ko-yao.[22] However, there is no sound way of distinguishing these pieces of 'Ko type' from the Kuan ware and the whole story seems to have no foundation in historical fact, and there is no reason to believe in the existence of any other separate kiln for this Ko type in Hangchou. A characteristic example of the type in a Japanese collection shows a dense mesh of crackle which has been deliberately enhanced by staining for the agreeable effect (Plate 114). This is a small saucer-dish with narrow flattened rim deriving from a silver shape.

[18] *Chinese Art Treasures*, 1961–2, Pl. 150.
[19] Tokyo National Museum, Exhibition of Far Eastern Ceramics 1970, *China*, Pl. 63; Koyama, op. cit., Pl. 14.
[20] M. Sullivan, *The Barlow Collection; an inaugural lecture*, University of Sussex, 1974, Pl. 20.
[21] Sotheby Sale 25.3.75, lot 98.
[22] S. Yorke Hardy, *Illustrated Catalogue of Tung, Kuan, Chün etc.*, London, 1953, Reg. no. A29, p. 31, Pl. XIII.

Chapter 9

CH'ING-PAI WARES

It is unsatisfactory that we still have to use this descriptive title as a label for the large production at many kilns of this distinctive ware, made over a period of at least three centuries. But, inasmuch as the kilns from which it travelled so widely in the old world were spread over the three provinces of Fukien, Kuang-tung and Kiangsi, and that the largest centre was around Ching-tê-chên, famous as a porcelain centre over a much longer time, there seems to be no satisfactory alternative to the retention of a term which has become established in China and the West alike. Some may still prefer the earlier descriptive term *ying-ch'ing* or cloudy-blue which originated in Japan fifty or sixty years ago; but, as Sir Percival David pointed out in 1955 the term *ch'ing-pai* was in use in China at least as early as the thirteenth century, whereas the use of *ying-ch'ing* was introduced by dealers in this century.[1] *Ch'ing-pai*, literally 'blue-white', well describes the light blue-green glaze of this translucent finely potted ware. Although exported to Korea, there is no reason to think that it was ever produced in a northern kiln and none has been excavated from northern kiln sites.

Production of the ware cannot at present be put back earlier than Northern Sung; but in several eleventh-century dated tombs intact pieces have been found, of which one of the most beautiful is a *mei-p'ing* vase of ovoid shape found in 1952 in a tomb at Nanking dated 1027.[2] It is described as having moulded decoration; but this is clearly a mistake, for, as Wirgin has already pointed out, the peony design is in fact deeply carved.[3] Moulding was not introduced before the Southern Sung period. Here the technique is of carving the dense peony scrolls back to a uniform depth, producing a two-level effect but with rounded contours. A rather later version of this type of vase

[1] Percival David, '*Ying-ch'ing*: a plea for a better term', *Oriental Art*, 1, i, p. 52.
[2] *China's Beauty of 2000 Years*, no. 31, colour plate 2.
[3] Wirgin, *Sung Ceramic Designs*, op. cit., Type Cp 18, p. 58 and Pl. 22a.

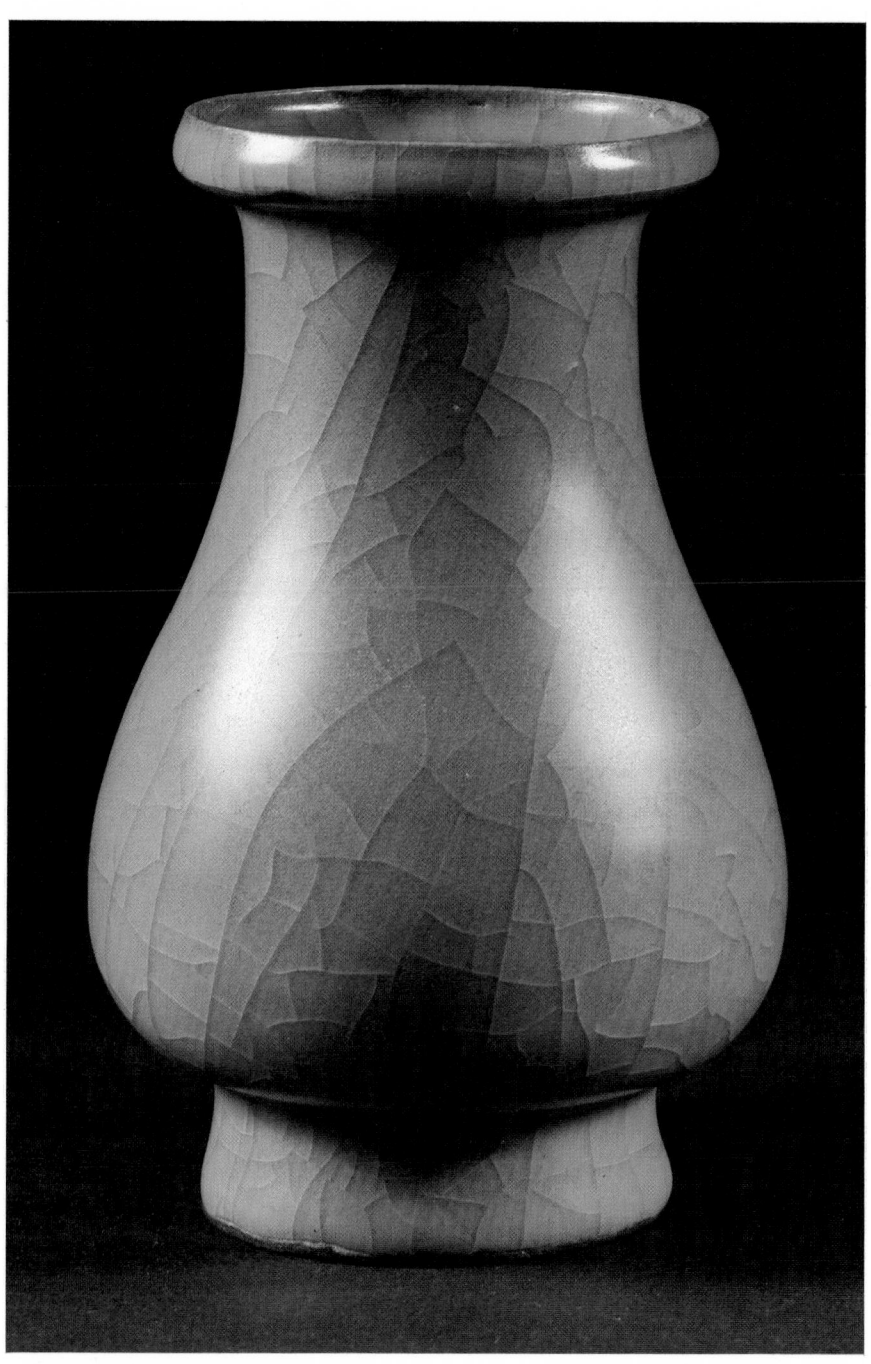

M Kuan-yao VASE
   Height 13.3 cm (5.2 in). Southern Sung, early 13th century
   Victoria and Albert Museum. See page 134

N *Ch'ing-pai* VASE with lobed body
Height 25.4 cm (10 in). Northern Sung, 12th century
British Museum. See page 156

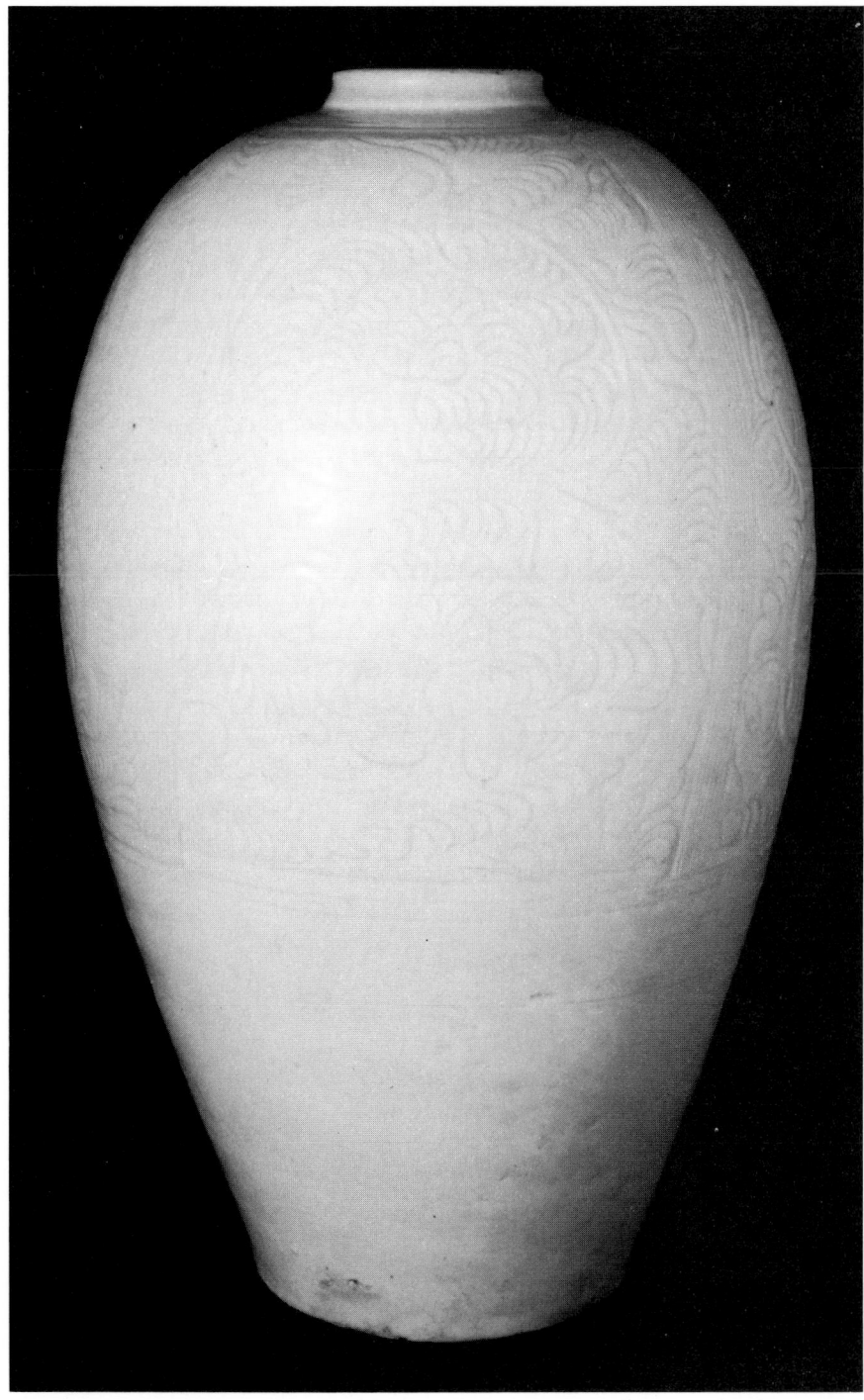

115 *Mei-p'ing* VASE, *Ch'ing-pai* ware
Height 32 cm (12.6 in). Northern Sung, 11th century
British Museum. See page 146

(Plate 115) but with less ovoid body and with shallower carving is in the British Museum collection.[4]

From a tomb dated 1057, excavated in Nanch'êng county, in Kiangsi in 1965, came a wine ewer with lion-handled cover and a hot-water bowl made so that the ewer fits neatly inside, undecorated except for lobing the bowl.[5] This shape was also illustrated by a find from a tomb in Honan dated 1100,[6] already exhibited in the National Historical Museum in Peking in 1957. It continued in production for at least two centuries. A perfect example is in the Idemitsu collection.[7] A more sophisticated form of the shape with carved petals on the shoulder of the ewer and round the tall footrim of the bowl and with trefoil enhancement below the lobes was found at Tê-an in Kiangsi in 1965.[8] A ewer and bowl closely resembling this one is in the British Museum, from the Eumorfopoulos collection,[9] but with petals added also to the cover. A variant form without lobing, but with a running peony scroll round the bowl instead (Plate 116), is in the Hoyt collection in the Boston Museum of Fine Arts. This is no doubt of Southern Sung date. The shape was also copied in Korea in the Koryu celadon of the twelfth century.[10] Here the shoulder forms a more decisive angle with the body of the ewer, thus emphasizing the ultimate derivation of this shape from a metal form.

A further variant form of this type of ewer is found with a more depressed bulbous body, with a flat lid and without the lion finial but retaining the high handle and the strongly curved spout. An example of this type, in a Japanese collection,[11] shows a shallow, floral, carved pattern on the lobed shoulder. Such shallower, more fluid incised decoration is no doubt of Southern Sung date, as is shown on a fully developed *mei-p'ing* vase in the Bristol City Art Gallery,[12] where the peony design is continued to within half an inch of the foot instead of stopping well short of it, as on the ovoid vase from the tomb of 1027. A second example of more conservative shape (Plate 117), with three registers of petals round the body from low down up to the curve of the shoulder, is also in Japan.[13]

Another type of ewer altogether is tall, from 24 to 25 cm (9.5 to 10 in), and with deeply lobed body, long spout, flat cover and otherwise undecorated is probably somewhat earlier. Examples of this type are in Japan[14] and in

[4] TOCS, 38, 1971, no. 120, Pl. 83.
[5] *K'ao-ku*, 1965, no. 11, Pl. 9, 3; Addis, op. cit., 1978, no. 14, p. 22.
[6] At the time of the author's visit.
[7] STZ, 1977, Vol. 12, Pl. 26.
[8] Watson, op. cit., no. 345.
[9] TOCS, 38, 1971, no. 119.
[10] Chewon Kim and G. St. G. M. Gompertz, *The Ceramic Art of Korea*, London, 1961, Pl. 24, dated 11th–12th century.
[11] STZ, 1977, Vol. 12, Pl. 17; *Mayuyama, Seventy Years*, Pl. 420.
[12] TOCS, 32, 1960, no. 208.
[13] *Mayuyama, Seventy Years*, Pl. 421.
[14] Ibid., Pls. 422–4.

116 EWER and BASIN, *Ch'ing-pai* ware
   Ewer height 21.2 cm (8.4 in). Basin height 12.4 cm (5 in). Southern Sung, 12th
   century
   Hoyt Collection, courtesy of the Museum of Fine Arts, Boston. See page 146
117 EWER with carved petals round the body, *Ch'ing-pai* ware
   Height 18 cm (7.1 in). Southern Sung, 12th century
   Private Collection, Japan. See page 146

the British Museum, from the Seligman collection.[15] A fine ewer of this general shape but with wider trumpet mouth and more depressed body is in the Metropolitan Museum of Art, New York.[16] This has a high foot and is undoubtedly of the eleventh century, Northern Sung dynasty date. A white ware ewer of similar shape was found in a Liao tomb of 1080 in Kulun Banner and is now in the Kirin Provincial Museum.[17] The shape no doubt derives from metal, as exemplified in the Pei-huang-shan silver find of ninth- to tenth-century date.[18] When Sir John Addis visited the Ching-tê-chên kiln sites in 1973 he found shards of *ch'ing-pai* ware at Huang-ni-t'ou, undecorated and therefore to be dated to Northern Sung; and at Hu-t'ien, which he believed started in production only under Southern Sung, with added decoration, though he believed that moulded designs started later still, since they were not found here in the first mound. He remarked in his report of this visit, published in the *Transactions of the Oriental Ceramic Society*,[19] on the shallow bases and wide footrings of the pieces collected at this mound, which he contrasted with the high and thin feet of the Northern Sung types found at Huang-ni-t'ou. Moulded designs were found only in the second mound, which is evidently at least mainly of Yüan dynasty date, as is evinced by the presence of tea-bowls of the type found at Chi-chou.

An example of the early type of undecorated *ch'ing-pai* ware is a cup-stand in the Victoria and Albert Museum (Plate 118), from the Eumorfopoulos collection, standing on a high, slightly splayed foot and with an attached lobed saucer of metal shape. The bowl retains connections with T'ang white ware, and it may well date from the tenth century or the very early Sung period. A second piece which depends on form alone for its design is a lampstand in the Eugene Fuller Memorial collection in the Seattle Art Museum (Plate 119). Here the stem is grooved and has a frieze of boldly carved lotus petals at top and bottom as sole decoration. Once attributed to the T'ang dynasty, this also must be no earlier than the tenth century and is probably also Northern Sung. A later form of cup-stand is represented by a pair in the Tokyo National Museum[20] and by a single piece larger and finer, in the

---

[15] TOCS, 32, 1960, no. 211.
[16] Valenstein, op. cit., Pl. 62.
[17] *Wen-wu*, 1973, No. 8, pp. 2–18, Pl. 27.
[18] Hobson, *BMQ*, 1, 1926–7, pp. 18–20; R. S. Jenyns and W. Watson, *Chinese Art; The Minor Arts, Gold, Silver etc.*, London, 1963, Pl. 32.
[19] J. Addis, 'A visit to Ching-tê-chên', TOCS, 41, 1977, p. 6 and Pls. 5 and 9.
[20] STZ, 1977, Vol. 12, Pl. 156.

---

118 CUP and STAND attached, *Ch'ing-pai* ware
       Height 9.5 cm (3.7 in). Northern Sung, 10th–11th century
       Victoria and Albert Museum. See page 148
119 LAMPSTAND, *Ch'ing-pai* ware
       Height 30.5 cm (12 in) 10th–12th century
       Seattle Art Museum. See page 148

Baur Foundation, Geneva (Plate 120). These cup-stands have perforated foot-rims of the stand which is lobed and extends to a flat rim, while the bowl has a lobed and everted lip. A simpler type with lobed rim to the stand and a higher foot is to be seen in an example from the Seligman collection now in the British Museum.[21]

The *ch'ing-pai* ware with incised decoration is well represented by a wine ewer with tall trumpet-shaped neck and flat lid, found in 1963 in a tomb at Ching-tê-chên itself, dated 1173.[22] Here the neck is splayed towards the shoulder as well as towards the mouth, thus giving it a rather heavier appearance, but the incised design of lotus scrolls which covers the whole surface of this vessel, below a triple ring at the level of the attachment of the top of the handle, lightens this effect. The decoration of this piece thus confirms the dating of such decorated pieces to Southern Sung.

Examples of this type of carved naturalistic designs on *ch'ing-pai* wares are illustrated by J. Wirgin.[23] To this group evidently belongs the small kidney-shaped pillow (Plate 121) in the Victoria and Albert Museum,[24] with incised design of boys among blossoms on the upper surface and with moulded phoenix on the side. Another piece of the same group is a cup or jar from the F. Mayer collection with carved lotus round the body.[25] These are no doubt all of Southern Sung date and probably of the thirteenth century. The double-gourd shape is continued at Ching-tê-chên into the Yüan period, but shows a smoother transition between the two gourds and has the handle reshaped as a dragon. Examples of this shape were included among the finds from the Sinan wreck of about 1310.[26] These types are distinct from the well-known ewer in the Musée Guimet which is here assigned to a northern kiln of Ting-yao type.[27]

There are many other shapes produced in the *ch'ing-pai* kilns, but the commonest and that most frequently exported is the small dish. It occurs with many variations in shape and decoration; the rims are frequently lobed and the incised designs are often very cursorily executed, a freedom not necessarily detracting from their charm. In another group the stylized lotus is clearly defined, but, as Wirgin describes it, the design seems to revolve either within a hexagonal rim (Plate 122), or inscribed within a perfect circle.[28] A resemblance has already been noted between lacquer vessels of the Sung period and contemporary porcelain, especially in the case of Ting-yao; but, since lacquer was made only in South China, a comparison with *ch'ing-pai* has greater force

---

[21] Ayers, op. cit., D.223, p. 101, Pl. LXV. BM Reg. no. 1973 7–26.344.
[22] J. Addis, *Chinese Ceramics from Datable Tombs*, no. 18.
[23] Wirgin, *Sung Ceramic Designs*, op. cit., p. 59, Pls. 22–3.
[24] R. L. Hobson, *The Catalogue of the George Eumorfopoulos Collection of Chinese, Corean and Persian Pottery and Porcelain*, 1936, Vol. 3, no. C842.
[25] Wirgin, *Sung Ceramic Designs*, op. cit., Pl. 23b.
[26] National Museum of Korea, op. cit., nos. 182–4.
[27] See above, page 66.
[28] For example the one in the Hakone Museum, STZ, 1955, Vol. 10, Pl. 85.

120 CUP-STAND, *Ch'ing-pai* ware
Diameter 14.5 cm (5.7 in) 12th century
Baur Foundation, Geneva. See page 150

121 PILLOW of kidney shape, *Ch'ing-pai* ware
Length 17.8 cm (7 in). Early 13th century
Victoria and Albert Museum. See page 150

and validity. In 1972 a multilobed *ch'ing-pai* dish was found in a tomb dated 1090 in P'êng-tsê county in Kiangsi;[29] with its sharp distinction between everted rim and flat base, it corresponds closely to lacquer dishes, such as one in the Musée Cernuschi in Paris,[30] said to have come from the site of Chü-lu-hsien inundated in 1108, which is near enough to the date of the tomb find of 1090 to allow of a relationship. A foliate dish in a Japanese private collection[31] is of a similar shape to this piece but with ribbing (Plate 123), which gives it even closer resemblance to the lacquer dishes.

Even commoner are the conical bowls of fine translucent porcelain with incised decoration under the pale-blue glaze. A fine example of this type with unusually carefully designed and executed decoration of boys among stylized vines, is in the Seattle Art Museum (Plate 124). Here the carving stops well short of the rim and must have been laid out with the aid of a stencil or template. Wirgin has identified the plants as peonies,[32] but it seems that the scrolling tendrils indicate the traditional vine growth and that no flowers are intended. The date would be Southern Sung (twelfth century).

The more complex shapes were not so well suited for the export trade but must have been produced for the more sophisticated home market. Among these shapes are cups with fitted stands, and incense burners with pierced covers; of the former examples are in the Victoria and Albert Museum[33] and the Baur Foundation.[34] In the Seikadō in Tokyo is a covered bowl with a saucer of lotus shape (Plate 125). There are also pillows of sculptural form, the most elaborate having as support a pair of interlocked dragons, now in the Palace Museum, Peking.[35] This was found in a Sung tomb in Hupeh province. A pillow of simpler design has the head-rest supported by a lotus flower while providing shade to a reclining girl.[36]

The incense burners with perforated dome covers have moulded decoration and are therefore probably of thirteenth-century date, and are of smaller size.[37] Here should be mentioned a more elaborate type of funerary vase, tall and of baluster shape with elaborate applied moulded ornament including figures of servants, dragons and tigers. They were apparently made in pairs to hold offerings to the dead. The thirteenth century seems to be the period of the full development of this shape. A pair of the type with bird finials, dragons, ducks and deer in relief, as well as figures of serving men applied in the full round, was found in 1965 in a tomb in Kiangsi, dated 1227.[38] A simpler form,

---

[29] Addis, *Chinese Ceramics*, no. 16, p. 25.
[30] TOCS, 32, 1960, no. 11, Pl. 11.
[31] *Mayuyama, Seventy Years*, Pl. 437.
[32] Wirgin, *Sung Ceramic Designs*, op. cit., figs. 17a and b.
[33] Reg. no. C839–1936.
[34] Baur Foundation A120.
[35] *Ku Kung Po-wu-yüan*, 1962, Pl. 35.
[36] Valenstein, op. cit., Pl. 65.
[37] STZ, 1955, Vol. 10, Pl. 7; d'Argencé, op. cit., Pl. XLI.
[38] Addis, *Chinese Ceramics*, no. 23, p. 34.

122 Hexagonal DISH with whirling design, *Ch'ing-pai* ware
   Diameter 19 cm (7.5 in). Southern Sung, 12th century
   Fitzwilliam Museum, Cambridge. See page 150
123 DISH with foliate rim, *Ch'ing-pai* ware
   Diameter 13.3 cm (5.2 in). Early 11th century
   Private Collection, Japan. See page 152

124 BOWL carved with a design of boys among vines, *Ch'ing-pai* ware
Diameter 19.5 cm (7.6 in). 12th century
Seattle Art Museum. See page 152

125 Covered BOWL with SAUCER in the shape of a lotus, *Ch'ing-pai* ware
Diameter 19.5 cm (7.6 in). 12th century
Seikadō Foundation, Tokyo. See page 152

126 Covered BOWL, *Ch'ing-pai* ware
   Height 12.8 cm (5 in). Southern Sung, 12th century
   Hoyt Collection, courtesy of the Museum of Fine Arts, Boston. See page 156
127 Covered BOX with moulded design of phoenixes on the cover, *Ch'ing-pai* ware
   Diameter 9.8 cm (3.9 in). 12th century
   Carl Kempe Foundation, Ekolsund, Sweden. See page 156

with only bird finial and coiled dragon on the shoulder, is in the Barlow collection in Sussex University.[39] This shape is also found in Lung-ch'üan ware and may be of the twelfth century rather than the early thirteenth, though a coarser variety was then exported to Indonesia.[40]

At first sight attributable to the early fourteenth century, because of the relationship of its profile to the Lung-ch'üan vase of 1327 in the Percival David Foundation,[41] is a beautiful *ch'ing-pai* vase in the British Museum, from the Oppenheim collection (Colour Plate N), for it has the same outward flaring trumpet mouth and a similar bulbous body. But this body is fluted, unlike the celadon vase, and the foot is of an elegant petal shape, as in the early wine ewers. Moreover, the shape seems to have influenced that of Korean celadon vases which are datable to the first half of the twelfth century.[42] All of which suggests that the correct date for the British Museum *ch'ing-pai* vase is not later than about 1110 and it is to be attributed to the Northern Sung period, as it was by Wirgin in 1970.[43]

Another shape found in both *ch'ing-pai* and Lung-ch'üan wares is the covered bowl with petal design on both parts (Plate 126); and yet another shape is that of the small round box with slightly domed cover, on which is a moulded design. A favourite motif is a pair of phoenixes with flowers in the intervals (Plate 127). Boxes with moulded decoration of this sort on the cover have been found in several kiln sites in Fukien and these were no doubt the source of the extensive export trade to South-East Asia, Indonesia and the Philippines,[44] and also to the West, where fragments found at Fustat were second only to celadons in quantity for the period to the twelfth century.[45]

Of the Fukien kilns those identified and explored at Tê-hua operated from the Sung dynasty onwards almost entirely for the export market. Of these kiln sites Chou-tou-kung was investigated in 1976 and Pu-tien in 1978.[46] Of the bowls, jars and dishes from these sites the fragments shown in 1980 in the loan exhibition in London and Oxford all showed extensive use of combed ornament as well as carving.[47] The covers of boxes, on the other hand, were decorated with moulded floral motifs, peony or lotus. These too were attributed to a Sung date; but they are probably later, and to be dated to the Yüan dynasty, as Addis observed of the example of this type exported to the

---

[39] Sullivan, op. cit., no. C230, p. 109, Pl. 107.
[40] B. Harrisson, *Oriental Celadon in the Princessehof Ceramic Museum, Leeuwarden*, 1978, no. 55.
[41] M. Medley, *Illustrated Catalogue of Celadon Wares*, Percival David Foundation, 1977, no. 81, Reg. no. 237, Pl. VIII; Medley, *Yüan Porcelain and Stoneware*, Pl. 58.
[42] Kim and Gompertz, op. cit., Pl. 22.
[43] Wirgin, *Sung Ceramic Designs*, op. cit., Pl. 29d.
[44] *Kiln Sites*, nos. 106–9, 154–8, 162.
[45] B. Gyllensvärd, 'Recent finds of Chinese ceramics at Fostat', *Bulletin of The Museum of Far Eastern Antiquities*, 45, 1973.
[46] *Wen-wu*, 1979, Nos. 5 and 12.
[47] *Kiln Sites*, nos. 101–14.

128 BOTTLE excavated at Fustat, white ware, Ching-tê Chên or North China
Height 25.5 cm (10 in). 10th century
Princeton University Art Museum, New Jersey. See page 158

Philippines.[48] But some boxes are earlier, for they have been found on Buddhist sites in Japan which are datable to the twelfth century.[49] The box in the Kempe collection (Plate 127), with moulded design on the lid of a pair of phoenixes and floral scrolls, is different from either of these types, finer and without lobing. This type is probably a product of the Ching-tê-chên kilns and certainly to be dated twelfth century.[50]

We have mentioned the high proportion of *ch'ing-pai* wares among the fragments of Chinese porcelain found at Fustat; among them, however, is one piece that has been reconstituted and is outstanding in quality and of unusual shape. This is a bottle with grooved neck and wide flanged mouth (Plate 128). The body has vertical ribs segmentally placed at the four quarters and the shoulder is high. This vessel had been published by its finder, George Scanlon, as of T'ang date.[51] The dished mouth is indeed evidence for an early date, while the grooved neck connects this vessel with the Seattle candlestick; though this feature continues into Northern Sung, as in the Ting ware *kundika* of about 995.[52] It therefore remains a possibility that this bottle is not from the Kiangsi kilns but from some northern kiln, and that it should be classed as a white ware rather than *ch'ing-pai*; in any case it should be dated to the tenth century.

Among other shapes found in *ch'ing-pai* ware is one of special interest because of its relationship to jade and metal rather than to lacquer. This is a cup on a high splayed foot and with a pair of dragon handles (Plate 129), the heads of which appear above the lip and are consequently unglazed since the cup was fired on the rim. An obvious parallel for the shape is with a group of jade cups, of which two examples were included in the Oriental Ceramic Society jade exhibition in the Victoria and Albert Museum in 1975.[53] In the catalogue these were given the wide range of date 'thirteenth–sixteenth century', while, in the introduction to this section a date of thirteenth–fourteenth century was suggested for the *ch'ing-pai* cups associated with them.[54] One of these two cups once belonged to Cardinal Mazarin who died in 1661, but its previous history is unknown; it is now in the Musée Guimet. Of other similar jade cups the most famous are two in the Iran Bastan Museum, Tehran, from the Ardebil Shrine collection dedicated by Shah 'Abbas I, and said to be 'at least as old as the fifteenth century'.[55] All these cups have dragon handles of the *ch'ih* type with no horns and split double tail. The same feature is to be seen in a single-handled silver cup found with other silver objects in a

[48] TOCS, 37, 1970, pp. 24–5, Pl. 30.
[49] STZ, 1977, Vol. 12, Pls. 271–3.
[50] *Kiln Sites*, no. 236, a waster from the Hu-t'ien kiln.
[51] D. S. Richards, ed, *Islam and the Trade of Asia*, 1970, pp. 81–95.
[52] Watson, op. cit., no. 339.
[53] TOCS, 40, 1976, nos. 325–7.
[54] Ibid., p. 96.
[55] M. Bahrami, 'Chinese porcelain from Ardabil in the Tehran Museum', TOCS, 25, 1949–50, pp. 13–19.

129 CUP with dragon handles, *Ch'ing-pai* ware
  Height 7.7 cm (3 in). Width 10.2 cm (4 in). Southern Sung, 13th century
  University of Sussex, Barlow Collection. See page 158

blue and white *kuan* jar in 1966 at T'ao-hsi in Kiangsu.[56] One piece was
inscribed in Bagspa script and the find therefore tentatively dated to *c.* 1310–
40. The silver dragon cup in general resembles the Ulugh Beg cup of jade
in the British Museum except that in the silver cup the dragon head rises
well above the lip. Although the *ch'ing-pai* cups have recently been dated
c. 1300 by Margaret Medley[57] they were accepted by Wirgin in 1970 as of
Southern Sung date[58] and this seems still acceptable. There can be little doubt
that the origin of the shape was in silver, and the splayed footrim not only
supports this presumption but suggests a T'ang date for the prototype. It
would show yet another instance of the dependency of Sung ceramic forms
on metal prototypes, to which we have several times drawn attention.

[56] Addis, *Chinese Ceramics*, no. 28e, p. 42.
[57] Medley, *The Chinese Potter*, p. 174, fig. 128.
[58] Wirgin, *Sung Ceramic Designs*, op. cit., p. 65, Cp.33, Pl. 28 f–i.

Chapter 10

LUNG-CH'ÜAN WARES

As the Yüeh kilns declined, production began of a celadon ware with similar iron-oxide coloured glaze produced in a reducing atmosphere at new kilns established already in the Five Dynasties period in the Lung-ch'üan district of Chekiang province. The area produced fine porcelain clay, pure white before firing. The 'prunus-green' (*mei-tzŭ-ch'ing*) glaze required three applications after biscuit firing of the body and before the final firing. The Western name of 'celadon' has now been so long and widely established in popular usage that it can be accepted, provided it is used only of the Chekiang wares for which it was first introduced in France in the later seventeenth century from the resemblance of its colour to that of the dress of a classical shepherd named Céladon in a romance by Honoré d'Urfé.

The princes of Wu-Yüeh submitted to the Sung in 978 and this date may be said to mark the end of the Yüeh ware production. Lung-ch'üan was early regarded as one of the classic wares of China; in the first edition of the *Ko Ku Yao Lun* (1388) it is stated that 'those with blue-green colour are valuable, while those with pale green glaze are less so'.[1] This variation is due to kiln action and the situation of each piece in the kiln, as well as the thickness of the glaze applied. Its opacity is caused by a high lime content in the glaze combined with vegetable ash.

Wasters from the Lung-ch'üan kilns came on to the international market in the 1920s and 30s and are to be found in many Western collections, and in Japan; but the actual kilns had to await scientific investigation by official Chinese archaeologists. Between 1956 and 1961 more than two hundred kiln sites were identified in the southern part of Chekiang province, especially around Ta-yao and Chin-ts'un, south of Lung-ch'üan, but also nearer to the city to the east and around An-fu.

The results of these explorations and excavations were published in *Wen-wu*

[1] David, op. cit., p. 142.

O Lung-ch'üan DISH with relief decoration under the glaze and the original metal handles
Diameter 21.5 cm (8.5 in). Southern Sung, 12th–13th century
Percival David Foundation of Chinese Art. See pages 162, 174

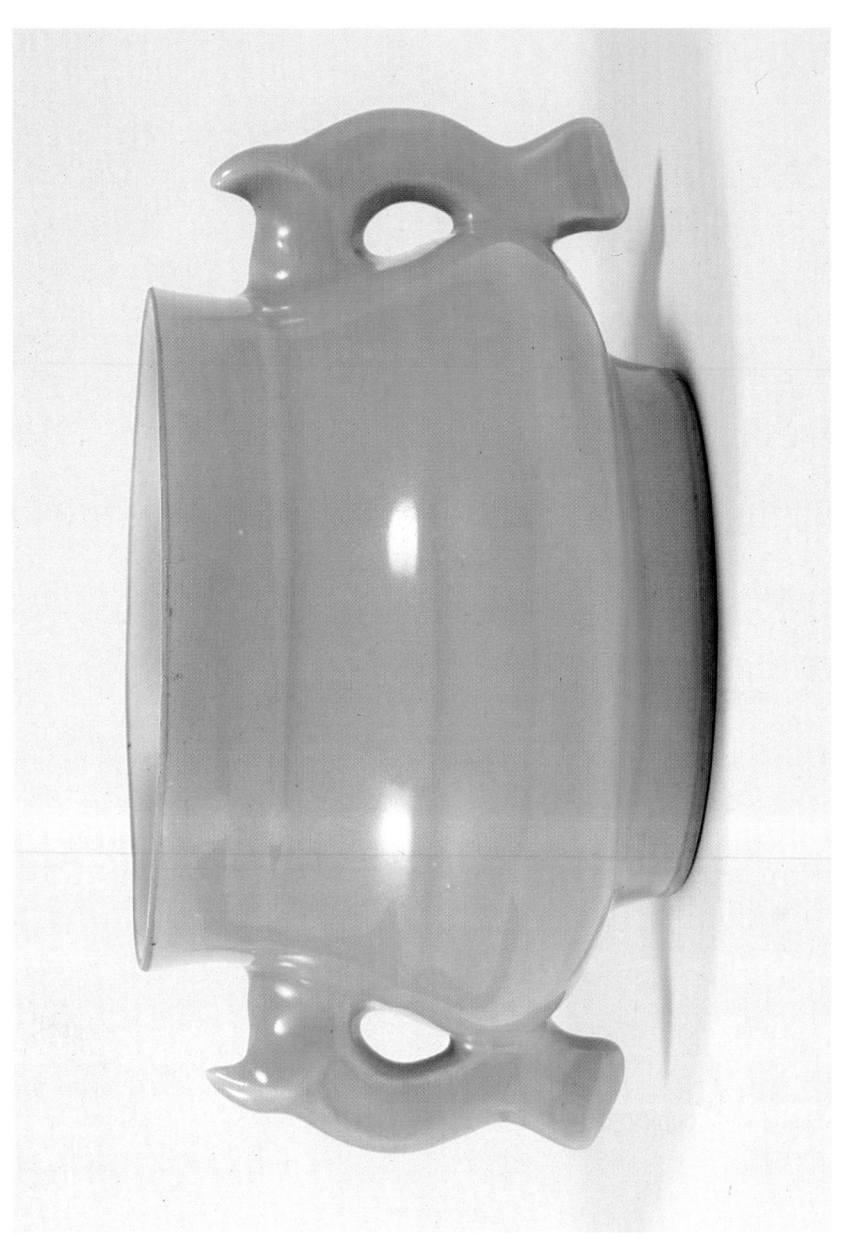

P Lung-chʻüan INCENSE
BURNER of archaic
bronze *kuei* form
Width 18.5 cm (7.2 in).
Southern Sung, 12th–
13th century
Percival David Found-
ation of Chinese Art.
See page 176

130 FUNERARY JAR, Lung-ch'üan ware
   Height 25 cm (9.8 in). Late 10th century
   Formerly Mr and Mrs Alfred Clark Collection. See page 162

(1963, No. 1), a translation of which is No. 2 in the Oriental Ceramic Society's series of *Translations* (1968). In it Chu Po-ch'ien reported the finding of a stratum of kiln waste at both Chin-ts'un and Ta-yao, mostly with carved decoration, carrying on the Yüeh tradition. Finds included a high-shouldered ewer carved with a design of peony scrolls above a frieze of lotus leaves.[2] A covered funeral jar (Plate 130), formerly in the Alfred Clark collection, is decorated in a similar way and may be very early Northern Sung, perhaps before 1000. Since these discoveries another group of early kilns has been found at Chu-chia-ling in Huang-yen, much closer to the Chekiang coast and about half way between Ning-po and Wên-chou; shards from this group were included in the 1980 exhibition in London and Oxford.[3] These too were active under Northern Sung and used a free style of decoration in which combing was used as well as incising. The bases of these vessels are fully glazed but show signs of studs or rings on which they stood in the kiln. They are finer than the products of the Li-shui kilns which lie about half way between Huang-yen and Lung-ch'üan, where the base is bare of glaze and shows signs of having been scraped. As John Ayers pointed out in the catalogue of the Seligman collection,[4] which included several pieces of this type, these kilns seem to have specialized in making funerary vases and evidently for a fairly popular market. They are much less carefully finished than the Clark vase or the best of the Huang-yen pieces, like the so-called 'parrot dish' in the Kiln Sites exhibition.[5] But stylistically the products of both kiln centres represent the transition from the Yüeh-yao tradition of decoration to that of Lung-ch'üan, which increasingly relied upon shape and beauty of glaze for its allure. During the Southern Sung period decoration was kept to a minimum. The pieces from Chin-ts'un and Ta-yao illustrated in the 1963 report show only lotus petals and pairs of fish as decoration.[6]

This latter type was referred to in the first edition of the *Ko Ku Yao Lun*[7] of 1388 as having 'bronze ring handles near the rim'. A basin of this type, complete with bronze rings, is in the Percival David Foundation (Colour Plate O).[8] This has a rather light-green glaze and the foot is burned to the characteristic reddish-brown. The rim is sheathed in copper and the reverse is plain. A fine example of another type of lotus petal appears on a bowl in the British Museum from the Eumorfopoulos collection, on which the petals are arranged naturalistically in three overlapping rings (Plate 131). The more ordinary form on which the petals appear as rays regularly springing from the foot continues into the Yüan and early Ming periods (Plate 132).

---

[2] *Wen-wu*, 1963, No. 1, fig. 8 no. 5; Pl. 1 no. 3; OCS *Translations*, No. 2, 1968.
[3] *Kiln Sites*, nos. 89–92.
[4] Ayers, op. cit., pp. 79–80, note to nos. D155–166.
[5] *Kiln Sites*, no. 92.
[6] *Wen-wu*, 1963, No. 1; *OCS Translations*, No. 2, Pls. IV, V.
[7] David, op. cit., p. 142.
[8] Medley, *Celadon Wares*, no. 54, Reg. no. A221. Formerly Alfred Clark Collection.

131 BOWL with petals carved outside, Lung-ch'üan ware
Diameter 15 cm (6 in). Southern Sung, 12th century
British Museum. See page 162

132 BOWL, formerly covered, Lung-ch'üan ware
Diameter 12.4 cm (4.8 in). Southern Sung, 12th century
Hakone Museum, Japan. See page 162

This kind of petal double-ribbing appears also on covered jars of high quality. A fine quality waster of the type was in the Eumorfopoulos collection and is now in the British Museum;[9] it is crackled and has only a single row of petals and its cover carries a carved lotus flower in low relief. A closely similar jar is in the Barlow collection at Sussex University (Plate 133), also a waster, but with uncrackled glaze. A more sophisticated version of this type of jar (Plate 134) was in the Alfred Clark collection and was given by Mrs Clark to the British Museum in memory of R. L. Hobson, who had helped to form and catalogued their ceramic collection. This has a cover of lotus-leaf shape with wavy rim and subtly modelled ribs on the body. In the Oriental Ceramic Society's 1960 Sung exhibition it was included as an example of Kuan ware;[10] but the body is certainly of Lung-ch'üan type. The quality is, however, outstanding and it may well be that it falls into the category of wares supplied to the court in Hangchou. Its shape continues into the Yüan and early Ming periods but with more sharply defined ribs and less subtle shape, tending to a double, instead of a single, curved profile of the body and a more defined lip. Several of this later type of jar were included among the Sinan shipwreck finds.[11]

Out of the seven thousand or so pieces of porcelain recovered in 1976-7 from the ship sunk off Sinan, no less than five thousand were of celadon ware. The latest coin found in the wreck was of the Chi-ta period of Yüan (1308-11),[12] so that a final date around 1310 to 1330 must be assumed for the cargo. Most of the Lung-ch'üan pieces included are of types that would have been in any case attributed to the Yüan period; but they did include a few types hitherto believed to be Southern Sung, and so accepted in, for instance, Jan Wirgin's book of 1970, and in Volume 12 (1977) in the revised *Sekai Tōji Zenshū* series, on the Sung period. These include the dishes with moulded fish already referred to and, above all, the classic *kinuta* mallet-shaped vases with phoenix or fish handles. In the catalogue of the National Museum of Korea exhibition of Cultural Relics found off Sinan coast in October 1977, these (nos. 297-8, colour plates 3-7) were labelled Southern Sung-Yüan dynasty;[13] while in the text it is stated that 'among the celadons only thirty or forty wares, or one to two per cent of the whole, are believed to be products of Southern Sung Lung-ch'üan kiln according to the conventional opinion'.[14] The account supports this attribution by pointing out that these pieces differ from the rest in body, shape, glaze and the finish of the foot, which is said to show 'traces of forceful cutting after glazing was applied'. The glaze is thick and the colour jade-green.

[9] ECPP, Pl. 89.
[10] TOCS, 32, 1960, no. 158.
[11] National Museum of Korea, op. cit., nos. 63-7 and the group on p. 315.
[12] Ibid., p. 247.
[13] Ibid., nos. 297-8, Colour Plates 3-7.
[14] Ibid., p. 247.

133 BOWL and COVER, Lung-ch'üan ware
Diameter 9.5 cm (3.7 in). Southern Sung, 12th century
Sussex University, Barlow Collection. See page 164
134 JAR with ribbed sides and cover of lotus-leaf shape, Lung-ch'üan ware
Height 12.7 cm (5 in). Southern Sung, 12th century
British Museum, gift of Mrs Alfred Clark. See page 164

The catalogue points out that a few pieces of twelfth-century Koryu celadon were included in the shipment;[15] evidently it included some antiques if the date of 1310–30 is accepted for the wreck. The Lung-ch'üan pieces also might not have been new. In addition, it is evident that these shapes might have been continued into the Yüan period, and there is therefore no need for a revision of the date of all pieces of this shape from Southern Sung to Yüan.

We reproduce three pieces of Lung-ch'üan ware whose shapes can be closely paralleled among Sinan wreck finds. There are two vases of *kinuta* shape: one with phoenix-head handles (Plate 135), the other with fish handles (Plate 136), the first for comparison with the Sinan catalogue, plates 6 and 7, the heights of which are given as 15.5 and 15.7 cm (6.1 and 6.2 in). The Fitzwilliam Museum example is 27.5 cm (10.8 in) in height and appears more slender, while the dished mouth has a more decisive outward turn. A famous vase of this shape in Japan, in the Yomei collection,[16] has a height of 26.5 cm (10.4 in) but has a hole pierced through the comb of the phoenix head, whereas in the Fitzwilliam vase this hole is filled with glaze. Even taller is a vase in Japan known as *Bansei* which is 30.7 cm (12.1 in) high and also has pierced combs.[17]

If we now consider the similar vases with fish handles, and again compare the examples with thicker and denser glaze, which may still be attributed to Southern Sung, with the later types found in the Sinan wreck, we find the criterion of size reversed, the vase in the Victoria and Albert Museum from the Barlow collection being only 16.8 cm (6.6 in) in height[18] whereas the two illustrated in the Korean wreck catalogue[19] are both about 25 cm (9.8 in) tall. A further difference is that these latter vases show the fish attached to the neck of the vase by a lug, while the Barlow vase shows less distinct fish adhering closely to the body, with no horns on their backs. What may be a later version of this type was in the Brodie Lodge collection,[20] where the mouth is more cup-like, the body with sharper angles at the junction with the neck and the handle still more clearly separate. This is 28.4 cm (11.2 in) tall; even taller is the variant in Japan[21] which is 29 cm (11.4 in) in height, has a strongly crackled glaze, and is provided with a flat-topped stopper. Chinese archaeologists say that in their view the flat, horizontal mouth is characteristic of Southern Sung while the Yüan type is dished with significant upward turned lip, as in this piece.

Certainly the tall vase with globular body and three ribs reminiscent of bamboo round the neck in the Percival David Foundation[22] has a horizontal

[15] Ibid., nos. 1–3, all dated to twelfth century.
[16] Gompertz, op. cit., Pl. 80.
[17] STZ, 1977, Vol. 12, Ol. 82.
[18] Sullivan, op. cit., no. C36, p. 89, Pl. 81b.
[19] National Museum of Korea, op. cit., Pls. 4 and 5.
[20] Gompertz, op. cit., Pl. 84a.
[21] *Mayuyama, Seventy Years*, Pl. 475.
[22] Medley, *Celadon Wares*, no. 50, Reg. no. 202, Pl. V.

135 *Kinuta* VASE with phoenix-head handles, Lung-ch'üan ware
Height 27.5 cm (10.8 in). Southern Sung, early 13th century
Fitzwilliam Museum, Cambridge. See page 166

136 *Kinuta* VASE with fish-handles, Lung-ch'üan ware
     Height 16.5 cm (6.5 in). Southern Sung, early 13th century
     Victoria and Albert Museum, Barlow Collection. See page 166

137 VASE with grey-green glaze, Lung-ch'üan ware
     Height 31.7 cm (12.5 in). Southern Sung, 12th century
     Percival David Foundation of Chinese Art. See page 170

mouth with square section (Plate 137), whereas the version of this shape from the Sinan wreck has a dished mouth with upturned lip, as well as a much less full body.[23] A vase of this shape in the Hakone Art Museum[24] is nearer to the Sinan wreck vase and also of the same height, whereas the David Foundation vase is shorter because of the depressed body. It has a beautiful grey-green opaque glaze, thicker than on the later vases, such as the Sinan piece, to judge from the colour plate in the exhibition catalogue.[25]

A third shape represented among the Sinan wreck finds is based on an archaic bronze shape, namely the *tsun*, the wide-mouthed wine-vessel with trumpet neck and bulbous body on a high foot. There are two versions of this shape in the Sinan finds,[26] one with vertical blades on the neck like a *ku*, the other with only moulded relief decoration on the middle section of the body. These are both correctly ascribed in the catalogue to the Yüan period; two similar vases in the Percival David Foundation[27] were still attributed in 1977 to Southern Sung of thirteenth century, though the second is called 'late thirteenth century'.

Yet another bronze shape found among the pieces recovered from the Sinan wreck is the *hu*, with two tubular 'arrow' handles below the neck on the narrow sides of the vessel.[28] We have already called attention to the Kuan-yao Alfred Clark vase of this shape, now in Japan, on which the decoration is confined to three horizontal rings round the neck.[29] The later Lung-ch'üan vase shows two registers of decoration in Warring States style and is probably Yüan, though catalogued as Southern Sung–Yüan. It is worth noting that two bronze vases of this shape were also found in the Sinan wreck.[30]

Finally, there are two types of incense burner based on bronze prototypes: the *li* tripod with hollow legs, and the *ting* with loop handles rising from the lip. The Lung-ch'üan version of the *li* shows the vertical ridges which marked the mould joints in the bronze retained as an aesthetic feature. Nos. 16 and 17 of the 1977 exhibition represent the *li* shape among the Sinan finds. While no. 18 is a variant with dragon handles rising above the lip, no. 16 rather closely resembles two vessels of this *li* shape in the Percival David Foundation[31] where they are both still ascribed to the Southern Sung period. But the finest example of this type in London is that from the Oppenheim collection in the British Museum which has the blue-green glaze known in Japan as *kinuta* type, because of its resemblance to the glaze of the finest mallet-shaped vases. The two incense burners of *ting* shape from the wreck[32] are both attributed to

[23] National Museum of Korea, op. cit., Colour Plate 5, black and white Pl. 15.
[24] *Mayuyama, Seventy Years* Pl. 476.
[25] National Museum of Korea, op. cit., Colour Plate 3.
[26] Ibid., Pls. 24–5 in black and white.
[27] Medley, *Celadon Wares*, nos. 42–3, Reg. nos. 200, 221, Pl. V.
[28] National Museum of Korea, op. cit., no. 6 in colour. No. 14 in black and white.
[29] Gompertz, op. cit., Pl. 60.
[30] National Museum of Korea, op. cit., nos. 287–8.
[31] Medley, *Celadon Wares*, nos. 33–4, Reg. nos. 228, 279, Pl. IV.
[32] National Museum of Korea, op. cit., nos. 21–2 in black and white.

138 INCENSE BURNER of bronze *lien* shape, Lung-ch'üan ware
      Diameter 14.3 cm (5.6 in). Southern Sung, late 12th century
      Percival David Foundation of Chinese Art. See page 172
139 DISH with bracketed rim, Lung-ch'üan ware
      Diameter 17.6 cm (7 in). Southern Sung, late 12th century
      Percival David Foundation of Chinese Art. See page 174

a Kuan style ware because of the dark body and pronounced crackle. This shape does not appear to be represented in Japanese or Western collections; the *ting* vessel excavated at Jui-an in Chekiang and exhibited in Paris and London in 1973[33] is of a different round-belly shape and has a fine uncrackled glaze on a Lung-ch'üan body. In the light of these comparisons it seems unnecessary to upset the received dating of these fine pieces as Southern Sung because of the finds made in the Sinan shipwreck.

The transition from the Sung to the Yüan shape is perhaps most clearly seen in the *lien*-shaped incense burners. There was a number of variant shapes found in the Sinan wreck,[34] among which the three trigrams were the commonest type of decoration by use of moulds. But floral appliqués were also used and some retain the earlier system of horizontal grooves, as on the undoubted Sung pieces, of which there are splendid examples in the Tokyo National Museum and the Percival David Foundation (Plate 138).[35] It will be noted that these two earlier pieces have well-formed lobed feet as compared with the clumsy pedestals on the Sinan types. The glaze also is dense and of finer quality on the Sung pieces. A final example to illustrate the transition from Southern Sung to Yüan will be provided by two *lien* in the former Charles Russell collection[36] and the Sinan wreck[37] on which moulded appliqué flowers are combined with incised or carved stems. The classic example of this type was in the Tenryūji temple in Kyoto and is now in the Hakutsuru Museum and an Important Cultural Property in Japan.[38] The type of pea-green glaze which covers this piece has given its name to a whole class of Lung-ch'üan wares which is now firmly dated to the Yüan dynasty. The criterion, however, is the use of moulded ornament rather than the colour of the glaze. At the same time, the lesson to be drawn from the Sinan wreck finds of celadon is that there was no significant or sudden break at the time of the transfer of power from the Sung to the Yüan dynasty.

In this situation only connoisseurship can be effective in discriminating the Sung wares from the later: a sense of form and feel of the pieces which achieve the pre-eminence of unity of shape and glaze which then reached its highest measure of success, truly a test for sensibility, only to be exercised of course through actual handling. Outside the auction sale room this is not possible, alas, for more than a handful of specialists; the experience might perhaps be extended by readier access to fragments from kiln sites, which are numerous and of less value. A general rule, however, is that the best Lung-ch'üan wares under the Sung have little or no decoration, but restricted usually

[33] Watson, op. cit., no. 336.
[34] National Museum of Korea, op. cit., nos. 79–87.
[35] Medley, *Celadon Wares*, no. 31, Reg. no. 215, Pl. III; Tokyo National Museum, *Chinese Ceramics*, fig. 365; Gompertz, 1980, Pl. 75b.
[36] Gompertz, op. cit., Pl. 88.
[37] National Museum of Korea, op. cit., no. 79.
[38] STZ, 1955, Vol. 10, Pl. 46; Tokyo National Museum exhibition 'Chinese Arts of the Sung and Yüan Periods', 1961, no. 198.

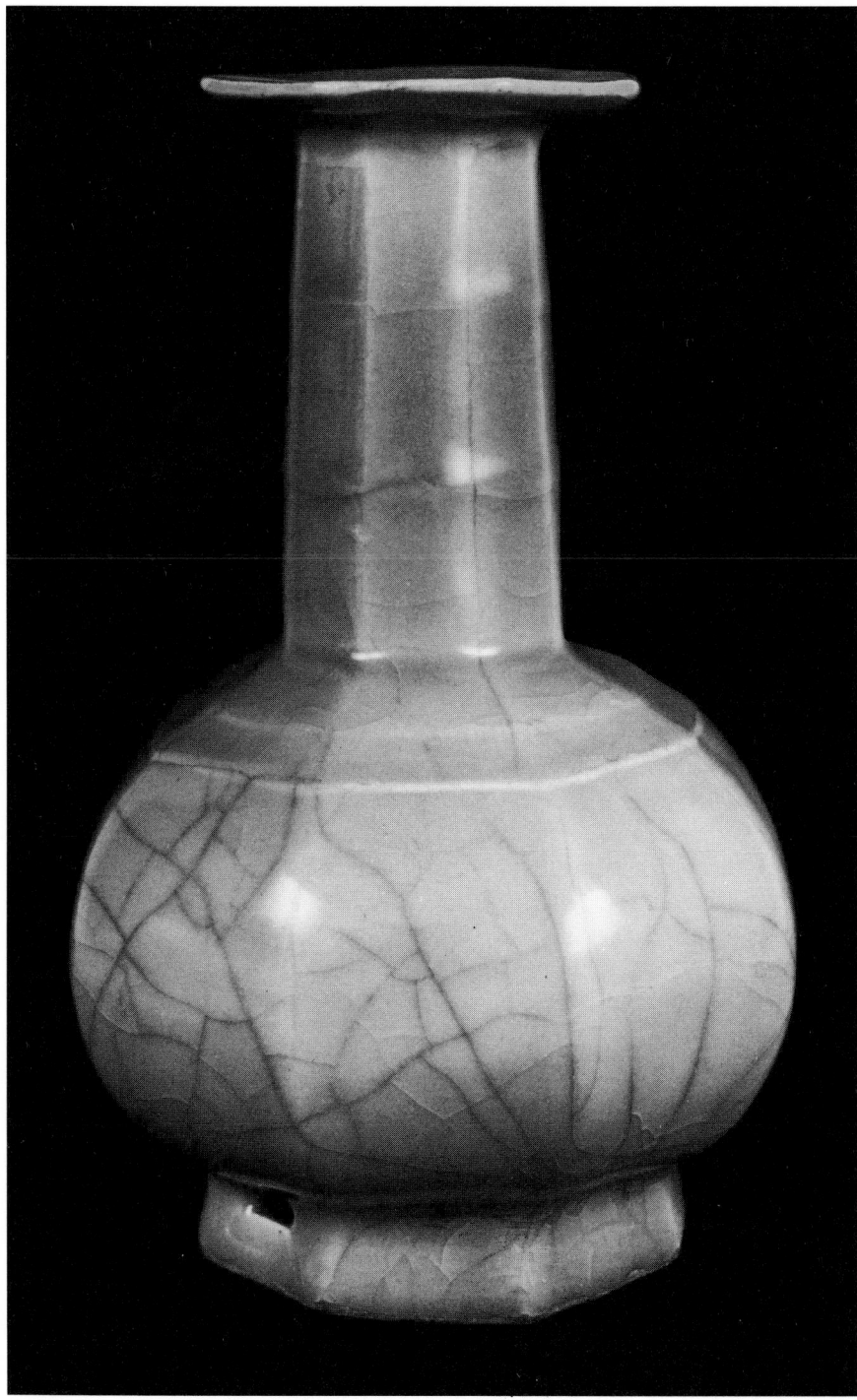

140 Octagonal VASE with crackled glaze, Lung-ch'üan ware
Height 21 cm (8.2 in). Southern Sung, c. 1200
University of Sussex, Barlow Collection. See page 174

to double or triple bands, as we have seen on the *lien* and the vase with depressed body and tall neck.

Metalwork, probably silver, lies behind such shapes as the dish with flat flange like the one formerly in the Alfred Clark collection sold at Sotheby's on 25 March 1975 (lot number 59).[38a] Gold dishes of this shape are in the Kempe collection.[39] The shape may ultimately derive from the Byzantine empire (Cyprus treasure, early seventh century), through Iran.[40] Also deriving from a metal prototype is a dish with bracketed rim in the Percival David Foundation (Plate 139). A similar dish was excavated at Ta-yao;[41] in the report it is called of 'water-chestnut' shape and dated to Southern Sung. Both of these dishes are completely covered with glaze except for the square footrim which has burnt red in the kiln. Grooving is again the sole decoration of another vase of a shape of metal origin, the octagonal vase with flat, wide flanged mouth, a pair of which in the Barlow collection in Sussex University (Plate 140) have a pronounced crackled glaze of exceptional thickness. A curious feature of these vases is the piercing of the high octagonal foot on opposite sides of the rim. This corresponds to usage on the archaic bronze-shape vase and has no function on a ceramic vessel. The ridged collar is also a feature borrowed from a metal prototype and accentuates the angular character of these vases. Both features are also to be noted on a round vase in a Japanese collection[42] with a similar flat flanged mouth. The Kuan-yao version of this shape, with a more depressed body, and less emphatic mouth and footrim, which is not pierced, was formerly in the John Levy collection in London but is now in Japan.[43] This has a closer crackle than the Barlow vases and this is generally so on such pieces of Lung-ch'üan ware as are crackled.

As already emphasized, the finest Southern Sung Lung-ch'üan pieces rely entirely on the quality of shape and glaze for their appeal. An example is the bottle-shaped vase in the Hoyt collection in the Boston Museum of Fine Arts (Plate 141) with its continuous sinuous line from lip to foot and with a profile resembling that of the Ju vase from the Clark collection in the British Museum, but with that greater emphasis on mouth and foot which we have noticed already as a Lung-ch'üan feature. These characteristics are further emphasized under the Yüan dynasty by the spreading of the lip, increased height and slight splaying of the foot.[44]

Another elegant shape is a low cup with a flange handle, probably intended as a brush-washer, once more a shape of metal origin. A perfect example from the Charles Russell collection was included in the Oriental Ceramic Society's celadon exhibition in 1947,[45] and another example, probably a waster

[38a] ECPP, Pl. 73.
[39] TOCS, 32, 1960, nos. 218–9, Pls. 78–9.
[40] *The Arts of Islam*, London, 1976, nos. 159–60; Persia, eleventh century.
[41] *Wen-wu*, 1963, No. 1; OCS *Translations*, No. 2, Pl. IV, 10.
[42] *Mayuyama, Seventy Years*, Pl. 474.
[43] STZ, 1977, Vol. 12, Pls. 67–8.
[44] Medley, *Yüan Porcelain and Stoneware*, Pls. 3, 6a, 25, 50a, 51.
[45] OCS, *Celadon Wares*, 1947, no. 32.

141 Bottle-shaped VASE, Lung-ch'üan ware
     Height 26.5 cm (10.5 in). Southern Sung, 12th century
     Hoyt Collection, courtesy of the Museum of Fine Arts, Boston. See page 174
142 Flanged CUP, Lung-ch'üan ware
     Height 11 cm (4.4 in). Southern Sung, early 13th century
     Percival David Foundation of Chinese Art. See page 176

(Plate 142), is in the Percival David Foundation.[46] This shape is also found in Kuan ware and in Chün-yao. Any of these pieces is worthy to have graced the writing table of a sensitive Sung scholar.

We have already noted above the *kinuta* shape among the Sinan wreck finds, and an example of exceptional quality of this mallet-shaped vase in the Umezawa collection (Plate 143) has led Japanese experts to attribute this and a few other choice pieces to the Hsiu-nei-ssǔ kiln in the palace of Hangchou, modelling itself on the Ju-yao kiln of Northern Sung. They put forward the light colour of the body of these pieces as evidence for this provenance; but, as we have seen, no archaeological evidence is forthcoming to support this claim. We believe that no such kiln ever operated and that these pieces are in fact the finest products of the Lung-ch'üan kilns and may have been supplied from there for palace use. It seems misleading however to grant them the title of Kuan, which is best reserved for the products of the Chiao-t'an kiln described in the last chapter.

Apart from the Umezawa vase, the group includes a tubular flower vase in the Nezu collection and a vase with globular body, tall neck and dished mouth in a Japanese private collection.[47] Hasebe in 1977 admits the first as Lung-ch'üan but still describes the second piece as Kuan.[48] The Nezu vase has a faint crackle but the second vase, like the Umezawa *kinuta* vase, is uncrackled.

Another piece of outstanding quality of glaze and potting is the two-handled incense burner of bronze *kuei* shape in the Percival David Foundation (Colour Plate P). This has a pale opaque blue-grey glaze revealing the light body colour at lip and foot. It is one more piece of evidence for the cult of the antique in the twelfth to thirteenth centuries.

Towards the end of our period there is no doubt that the use of moulds was introduced to aid in mass production. We can instance two types in which moulds were employed. The first is the eight-lobed melon-shaped ewer, only some 12.7 cm (5 in) in diameter, on which the horizontal mark of luting together of the upper and lower sections is clearly visible beneath the glaze. The example illustrated (Plate 144), from the Seligman collection in the British Museum, retains the cover. This is a type exported to the Philippines[49] and probably elsewhere. No doubt the shape continues into the Yüan period.

Likely to be entirely for home consumption is the funerary vase[50] with domed cover surmounted by a bird or animal and with dragon in full relief round the shoulder (Plate 145). This latter element must have been individually modelled and applied by hand, thus giving scope for fantasy. Jan Wirgin

[46] Medley, *Celadon Wares*, no. 39, Reg. no. 212, Pl. IV.
[47] F. Koyama, *Chinese Ceramics: One Hundred Masterpieces from Collections in Japan, England, France and America*, Tokyo, 1960, Pls. 13, 65.
[48] STZ, 1977, Vol. 12, Pls. 79 and 66.
[49] TOCS, 37, 1970, Pl. 24a.
[50] However a funerary vase in the Princessehof Ceramic Museum in Leeuwarden was obtained in Indonesia: B. Harrisson, *Celadon Wares*, 1978, no. 55.

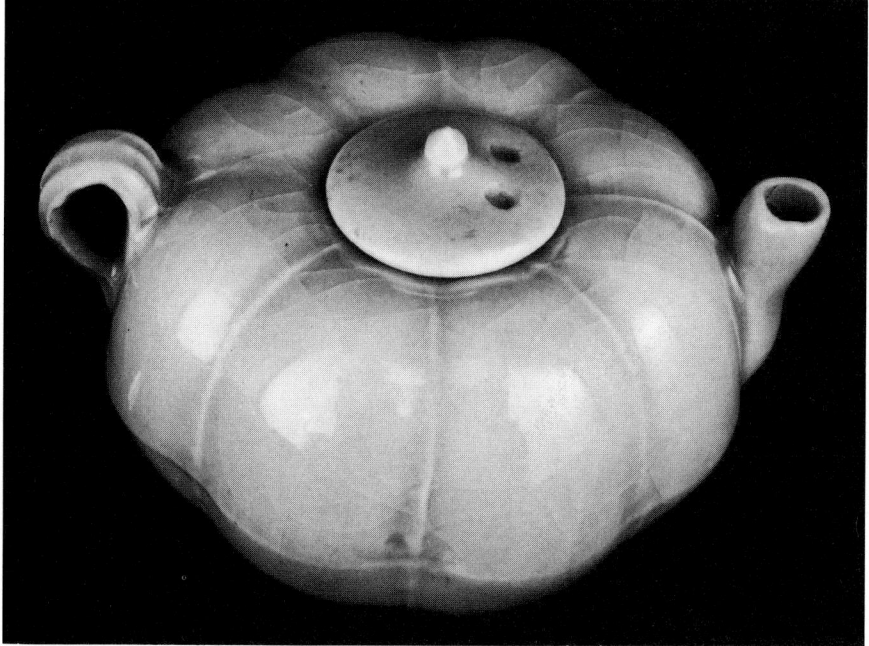

143 *Kinuta*-shaped VASE, Lung-ch'üan ware
Height 25.4 cm (10 in). Southern Sung, 12th–13th century
Umezawa Gallery, Tokyo. See page 176

144 WINE EWER, Lung-ch'üan ware
Diameter 12 cm (4.7 in). Height 7.3 cm (2.9 in). Southern Sung, 13th century
British Museum, Seligman Collection. See page 176

145 FUNERARY JAR, Lung-ch'üan ware
Height 27 cm (10.6 in). Southern Sung, 12th–13th century
Percival David Foundation of Chinese Art. See page 176

illustrates six variant types of these vases,[51] some with ribbed sides and grooved shoulders, some without. The example in the Seattle Art Museum has a thick bluish-green glaze, slightly crackled and is more thickset than the vase in the Alfred Clark example which is barrel shaped.[52] The dragon is also far more eleaborate on the Seattle vase, with four distinct claws.

By the end of the Southern Sung period it is clear that production at the Lung-ch'üan kilns was on a large scale, and that export to oversea markets was of economic importance. This is supported by the evidence of the mass of celadon shards found at Kasado Sengen, the unloading place for Kamakura; and by the predominance of celadon shards in the waste heaps at Fustat, the old city of Cairo. The continuance of this export trade into the fourteenth century is vividly shown by the Sinan wreck. In all these finds the commonest shapes were dishes and bowls. But there was also a demand for small covered boxes in which Lung-ch'üan competed with the *ch'ing-pai* kilns of Ching-tê-chên. One box exported to Japan in the twelfth century, and excavated at the Asuka shrine in Nara,[53] is illustrated by Hasebe; but the finest pieces were probably for the home market, like two of different shapes in the Brodie Lodge collection.[54] These have carved decoration under a *kinuta*-type glaze and carry on the Yüeh tradition. One fine cosmetic box even reached the Philippines;[55] a similar box is in the British Museum. Later these boxes would have moulded decoration and may be dated to Yüan dynasty, as for instance a box in the Royal Ontario Museum.[56]

[51] Wirgin, *Sung Ceramic Designs*, op. cit., Pl. 40a–f.
[52] Sotheby Sale 25.3.75, lot 50.
[53] STZ, 1977, Vol. 12, Pl. 272.
[54] TOCS, 32, 1960, nos. 186, 189, Pl. 65.
[55] TOCS, 37, 1971, Pl. 23c.
[56] The Cleveland Museum of Art, *Chinese Art under the Mongols*, 1968, no. 66.

Chapter 11

TECHNIQUE

While the Chinese kilns under Sung achieved an unrivalled high level of excellence, this was due to progress in the ceramic industry over a long preceding period. Before the Five Dynasties, porcelain, in the Chinese sense of fully fused body and glaze fired at a temperature above 1200°C, had been achieved in both north, with white wares, and in the south at the Yüeh kilns. In both areas also the use of saggars, to protect the vessels from too rapid changes of temperature and from smoke and impurities, had been developed. The Yüeh kilns were the more advanced in variety of shape and decoration and their products travelled widely and were familiar in the north, especially because the princes of Wu-Yüeh who patronized these kilns, sent large quantities of their products as tribute to their northern overlords, the Liao, to whom they were subject for sixty years before their submission to the Sung in 980.

However, kiln practice was different in the north from the south. The northern kiln was relatively small, a built structure of brick plastered with mud, only about 1.15 by 0.85 metres, in a horse-shoe plan with a chimney on the straight side at the back and the firing chamber in front.[1] After the filling of the main kiln-chamber a wall was built to protect it from the full heat of the fire but only up to two-thirds of the height of the chamber, which was probably domed so that the hot draught was deflected from it down to the floor of the main chamber and then through vents at the base of the back wall and out to the chimney, thus giving good draught and circulation. The entrance to the kiln was closed with a stone door after firing ceased so that cooling might be slow and permitting regular oxidation.

A Chün-yao kiln has been investigated, in which the walls were built of

[1] *K'ao-ku*, 1965, No. 8; OCS *Translations*, No. 4, 1968, fig. 4 and p. 8, Pl. 1, reporting on the Ting-yao kiln at Chien-tzŭ Ts'un, a tenth-century wood-fired kiln. However, coal was the more usual fuel under the Northern Sung dynasty. At the Tz'ŭ-chou kilns coal was also the normal fuel. See Mino, *Freedom of Clay*, p. 13.

fire-clay saggars.[2] These protective containers had been invented several centuries earlier;[3] but in the north they were refined to improve the capacity of the kiln and so to increase production and save fuel. In the north, fuel was generally coal, of which there was a plentiful supply; but, with a risk of fiercer heat raised too quickly and from impurities (especially sulphur) affecting the glaze the best Chün was fired with wood. The new type of saggar at the Ting-yao kilns had a stepped profile in section, so that bowls of similar shape but increasing in size might be placed upside down in the saggar, resting on their lips one above the other. This process allowed of the complete glazing of the bowl except for the mouth, which was left unglazed and in consequence rather rough. The practice at the Ting kilns was to sheath the mouth rim, generally in copper but occasionally silver. Other shapes, ewers or bottles, had to be housed singly in protective saggars and were, in consequence, still less common and more expensive. They were usually thrown in sections and these luted together before glazing. The saggars were stacked in the kiln chamber as economically as possible and the sides of the piles sealed together with clay. The firing temperature at these northern kilns seems to have been around 1200–1260°C.

It seems probable that the unglazed vessels were kiln dried at a moderate temperature before the application of the glaze; in the case of Chün-yao, on which glaze was applied thrice, after a first firing at a lower temperature of the unglazed body.[4] It has been established that this ware was normally given three applications of glaze to achieve the suffused lustrous effect after firing; but the body remained relatively thick in relation to the glaze. Even Ju-yao in which the body is relatively thinner, was fired at a temperature slightly below 1200°C; it was left to the southern kilns to experiment with thinner bodies.

Kiln practice in the south was very different. Kilns were usually built up a hillside slope, as they still are in Japan at traditional potteries, partly excavated and partly above ground, built as tunnels and known as 'dragon' kilns, a vivid appellation. One such kiln at Ta-yao in Chekiang,[5] making Lung-ch'üan celadon, was divided into ten or twelve chambers, fed by appertures in the sides so as to hold at least twenty thousand pieces in a single firing. No chimney was required at this type of kiln to increase the down draught, the slope of about sixteen degrees providing sufficient gradient and height. The greatest heat, up to 1280°C, was reached at the top of the dragon kiln and in these upper chambers the finest pieces would be placed for firing.

---

[2] *Wen-wu*, 1964, No. 8; OCS *Translations*, No. 3, 1968, p. 7. For a Yao-chou kiln see Medley, *The Chinese Potter*, p. 117.

[3] Medley, ibid., p. 83; the same author's *T'ang Pottery and Porcelain*, p. 68, citing the finds at Yü-chia-k'ou and Ma-chia-huan near Shou-chou in Anhui of sixth-century material.

[4] Fêng Hsien-ming, *Wen-wu*, 1964, No. 8; OCS *Translations*, No. 3, 1968, p. 11; and *Translations*, No. 8, 1978, p. 11.

[5] *K'ao-ku hsüeh-pao*, 1973, i; OCS *Translations*, No. 7, 1977, pp. 24–8.

The clay here at Ta-yao was sufficiently rich in iron content to achieve the blue-green colour of the finest celadon. Ceramic production reached its highest level of achievement under the Southern Sung, when the use of a lime-alkaline glaze prevented running or the formation of large bubbles, even in a glaze as thick as five applications, between which the vessel was warmed in the coolest part of the kiln. This type of glaze was achieved through the presence in the body of a higher potassium and soda content and by the use of wood fuel at these southern kilns, which naturally required continual stoking during the long firing period. After this was completed, all the fuel holes had to be blocked to control the reduction process which was vital to the achievement of the desired colour. The opacity of the glaze is due to the presence of minute particles of lime (calcium oxide) in suspension. While highly translucent the glaze thus produced a scatter of light, the secret of the *kinuta* quality of the finest Lung-ch'üan celadon pieces. As with Chün ware the glaze was applied in three successive layers after the first biscuit firing, but at the Chekiang kilns a drying off in the kiln between each application of glaze was the rule.

Kiln furniture also underwent further improvement during the Southern Sung period; instead of the container-shaped saggar perfected in the north, a new type was introduced which allowed the stacking of many similar dishes or bowls in a tower-like pile in the kiln. Between each vessel was placed a collar-shaped ring; after the placing of the complete pile in the kiln it was sealed by the application of strips of fire-clay round the exposed circumference. These strips could be knocked off after the firing. Obviously this process demanded much less space and less clay than the traditional saggar; but it must be observed that these saggars could be used many times, whereas the new process was destructive of the clay from each firing.

Individual vessel-shaped saggars were still used for firing the Chien-yao tea-bowls and these were made from coarse clay, wheel-thrown and kiln-baked.[6] After stacking these would be sealed by strips of fire-clay. The glazed bowls were placed in the saggars on a clay button as support; but the glaze stopped well short of the footrim, to prevent it from adhering to the saggar. But, in fact the thick glaze did often run down the sides of the bowls in runnels and attach them to the side walls. Many pieces which grace modern collections had been left in the saggar and thrown aside to be salvaged in this century and detached from the saggar by filing.

As we have seen, *ch'ing-pai* wares were made only in south China, but in several different provinces. It was widely exported; and this would account for the prominence of the Kuang-tung kilns, which would have profited from the use of Canton as a major centre for overseas trade. In Kuang-tung, kilns have been identified and explored at Chao-chou and Hsi-ts'un; but the main centres for production were undoubtedly in Kiangsi, at Nan-fêng and, above

[6] J. M. Plumer, *Temmoku*, 1972, pp. 45 and 55.

all, at Ching-tê-chên. The Nan-fêng wares are of high quality and were fired on the lip, thus permitting a high and finely formed footrim.[7] The body is thin and the shapes include lobed ewers as well as bowls and pillows.

The strength and translucency which characterize the ch'ing-pai wares were achieved through the high felspathic content of the kaolin clay which is named from its source at Kao-ling, the high ridge more than thirty kilometres north-east of Ching-tê-chên. This clay, according to Brankston,[8] consists of 45–50% silica and 30–40% aluminium, with some iron and manganese impurities. Since this clay fuses only at about 1740°C, a fluxing agent is required and this was found in pai-tun-tzŭ (petuntse), a rock which must first be reduced to powder by pulverization and made into bricks for conveyance to the kilns; pai-tun-tzŭ means literally 'little white bricks'. This mixture was ideal for the manufacture of strong white-bodied porcelain; in the ch'ing-pai ware it is so thin as to be highly translucent. The accepted name historically means 'blue-white', as we have seen, and there is indeed a more or less strong tinge of blue in the glaze owing to the iron content of the body and glaze. Ch'ing-pai bowls and dishes were generally fired on the mouth rim, which is consequently bare of glaze; but at the other kilns in Kuang-tung and Kiangsi they were always fired on the foot, which was unglazed and often shows traces of stilts or ring supports.

MOULDS

Both in the north at the Yao-chou and the Ting-yao kilns, and also in the south at the ch'ing-pai kilns, decoration under Northern Sung was carved, incised or combed; only under Chin in the north and Southern Sung in the south did the use of moulds begin,[9] especially for the decoration of saucer-dishes and bowls. In the north this led to a change in the style of decorative design which became much denser and more pictorial. It seems likely that this style of design derived from engraved metalwork, originating in the T'ang period in parcel-gilt silverware. Several fragments of moulds were found in the excavations at the Ting-yao kilns at Chien-tzŭ-ts'un in Hopei in 1961–2 and these were reproduced in the report.[10] Moulds for the decoration of Ting-yao are available for study in some Western collections; they are made of a hard stoneware and crisply carved in intaglio and fortunately bear dates. One in the Percival David Foundation is dated 1184,[11] and two in the British Museum are dated 1189 and 1203. The designs on these moulds are repro-duced by Jan Wirgin[12] who points out that both the 1189 and the 1203 moulds

[7] Kiln Sites, pp. 43–4, entries 214–220 and 222.
[8] A. D. Brankston, Early Ming Wares of Ching-te-chen, Peking, 1938, pp. 63–4.
[9] As noted above moulds were used for box lids at the Yüeh kilns under the T'ang dynasty; Medley, T'ang Pottery and Porcelain, pp. 114–16.
[10] K'ao-ku, 1965, No. 8, Pl. VI and figs. 10 and 12.
[11] Medley, The Chinese Potter, fig. 73, PDF No. 181.
[12] Sung Ceramic Designs, figs. 22a and 23a.

bear *nien hao* of Chin dynasty emperors, which makes it necessary to correct the Northern Sung attributions attached to the Ting-yao kiln finds by the Chinese excavators.[13] In the Yao-chou kilns saggars were employed in the early twelfth century but the bowls were fired on the foot, not on the rim.[14]

In the south at the *ch'ing-pai* kilns moulded decoration of cups and bowls is generally restricted to small central elements, floral or of dragons or phoenix, to which may be added some sketchy incised design outside. Moulds were also used for impressing designs on the covers of porcelain boxes; and this kind of box continues into the Yüan period, but with some decline in quality, perhaps due to mass production for the export market. In the Lung-ch'üan wares the use of moulds did not begin until the Yüan dynasty,[15] when it was used extensively for appliqué motifs, usually left unglazed and so burning red in the kiln. However, some moulded relief was used under the glaze on these wares; but technically this practice differs radically from all-over patterns from moulds in the north, for these dishes were thrown on the wheel and the relief designs of fish or dragons added afterwards before glazing. They thus lead on to the type of biscuit relief described above.

[13] But see now the moulds preserved in China with dates between 1184 and 1206 in *Chūgoku Tōji Zenshū*, Vol. 9, 1981, Pls. 128–33.
[14] Medley, *The Chinese Potter*, p. 116.
[15] Medley, *Yüan Porcelain and Stoneware*, pp. 70–2.

Chapter 12

THE EXPORT OF CHINESE STONEWARES AND PORCELAIN

JAPAN

Under Southern Sung Japanese relations with China, though not official, were 'tolerably close and friendly and allowed of important cultural and mercantile exchanges'.[1] Cargoes carried in Chinese ships maintained this trade, which was continuous and increasing until the triumph of the Bakufu in 1221. There were even some relations between the Sung court and the Taira Kiyomori (1153–81). Later the Shōgun at Kamakura as well as the Daimyō of west Japan carried on a lively trade with China: imports, including especially silks and porcelain, and exports from Japan, gold, timber, lacquer, swords and screens. Many Zen monks arrived in the Chinese ships, bringing porcelain as well as tea, from about 1191, and the influence of Zen Buddhism increased. Consequently it is natural to find among the treasures of Japan's cultural heritage a number of Southern Sung tea-bowls from the Chien and Chi-chou kilns, most of which are now registered as 'national treasures'.[2] Some of these bowls have personal names,[3] especially because of their association with famous tea-masters who valued their qualities of glaze and body and provided silver sheaths for their lips.

Mention has already been made of the great masses of shards of Lung-ch'üan ware found on the beaches below Kamakura,[4] testifying to the level of imports in the twelfth and early thirteenth centuries. Some whole pieces of this ware also have been preserved in Japan, ever since they were imported new in that period. They show that the Japanese appreciated and demanded wares of top quality.

As well as tea-bowls, the Zen monks brought with them to Japan small

---

[1] G. Sansom, *A History of Japan to 1334*, London, 1958, pp. 264, 422–3, 438.
[2] Tokyo National Museum, *Chinese Arts of the Sung and Yüan periods*, 1961, nos. 268–76; *Exhibition of Far Eastern Ceramics*, 1970, nos. 65–70.
[3] STZ, 1977, Vol. 9, Pls. 87–107 and 249–60.
[4] F. Koyama, *Shina seiji shiko*, 1943, cited by Gompertz, op. cit., p. 170.

porcelain boxes for incense pills; *ch'ing-pai* boxes have been excavated from sutra mounds at Buddhist sites in Tanabe, Asuka in Nara prefecture and at the famous Shinto shrine of Itsukushima in Miyajima.[5] At Fukuoka, in the southern island of Kyūshū nearest to the continent, have been excavated Chekiang celadon bowls of the twelfth century;[6] while in Kyoto at the Hoshiji temple site a fine *ch'ing-pai* vase with carved decoration of boys in foliage was excavated.[7] Together these finds testify to the significant level of imports of Chinese porcelain into Japan from south China in the twelfth century, and to their high esteem there, long before the Japanese learned to make porcelain.

KOREA

In Korea by contrast, it was naturally from north China that exported porcelain travelled by sea. When, in the closing years of the Northern Sung dynasty, a Chinese emissary visited the Korean capital, Kaesong, in 1123, he wrote a long report for the emperor, describing in detail Korean society and economy; and this was subsequently published, but without the illustrations which accompanied the original.[8] He found that the Korean celadon had recently much improved in quality of glaze, and added that the various shapes of vessels all copied those of Ting-yao, except for the wine ewers, which shape therefore only he illustrated. We have noted the relationship of the Koryu ewer and basin to the Ting-yao prototype; and in 1976 a joint exhibition was organized by Miss Medley between the Percival David Foundation and the Fitzwilliam Museum especially to demonstrate the relationship of Korean and Chinese ceramics from the tenth to the fourteenth century.[9] Rather curiously, however, in this exhibition it was the incised decoration of Ting-yao rather than the shapes which were shown to have influenced the Koryu wares. On the other hand, the further point made by the Chinese emissary Hsü Ching, that many of the other Korean pieces 'resemble the old "reserved" wares of Yüeh-chou and the new kilns of Ju-chou', was clearly demonstrated at Cambridge by confrontation of spouted funeral vases and bowls with carved lotus petals outside beside the Yüeh-yao prototypes. As to the Ju-yao, the exhibition confirmed visually the previous comparison made by Sir Percival David in 1936[10] and Godfrey Gompertz in 1960.[11] For resemblance is seen not only in glaze but in shape of bottle, cup-stand and dishes, and in kiln practice, even to the spur-marks under the base, showing how the vessel was supported in the kiln, though no Ju piece or fragment has yet been found in Korea.

---

[5] STZ, 1977, Vol. 9, fig. 271–3.
[6] H. Nakayama, *Kōkogaku Zasshi*, XVI, No. 9.
[7] STZ, 1977, Vol. 9, fig. 270.
[8] G. St. G. M. Gompertz, 'Hsü Ching's visit to Korea in 1123', TOCS, 33, 1962.
[9] Medley, *Korean and Chinese Ceramics from the 10th to the 14th century*, 1976.
[10] P. David, 'Commentary of Ju Ware', TOCS, 14, 1936–7, pp. 18–69.
[11] Gompertz, 'Hsü Ching's visit to Korea in 1123'.

Many Sung pieces have been found in Korean tombs of the twelfth century, especially Ting-yao and including the rare so-called red type, sometimes enhanced with gilt floral designs, as described above (page 70). Most of the surviving pieces of this kind now in Japanese collections are said to have come from Korea; and it is even suggested that the gilding may have been added there.[12]

By the mid-twelfth century *ch'ing-pai* wares must have been reaching Korea, for two well-known shapes were copied from these wares in Koryu celadon, namely the ewer and basin *en suite*, and the lobed vase with foliate mouth, which we have seen to go back in China to the eleventh century. This shape is found in Koryu in a vase excavated from a tomb of 1146.[13] It is therefore evident that the fall of the Northern Sung did not put an end to Korean contacts with China. Moreover, another type of ware with iron decoration on a white ground under a greenish glaze, now known to originate in a kiln at Ch'üan-chou in Fukien,[14] has been found in Korea.[15] Tz'ŭ-chou ware also reached Korea; an example of the type of *mei-p'ing* with peonies carved through a black slip is now in the National Museum in Seoul[16] datable to *c.* 1100.

THE PHILIPPINES

Extensive study of Chinese ceramic exports to the Philippines during the past twenty years has provided a secure basis for an assessment of their range and chronology. It is now clear that, while some imports from China were reaching the Philippines as early as the tenth century, from the Yüeh kilns, the total amount arriving throughout the Sung dynasty was very limited and came entirely from south China. Sir John Addis gave the Oriental Ceramic Society in 1968 an excellent survey of our knowledge at that time;[17] and it does not require significant modification today. He concluded that the great increase in the level of imports from China did not begin until the Yüan dynasty, when Chekiang and Kiangsi, and Tê-hua in Fukien, began to cater especially for the Philippine market. Earlier than this, under Southern Sung, there was probably a moderate importation of Chekiang celadons but not in significant quantity. Later there was considerable competition from the kilns of South-East Asia, first from Annam and later from the Sawankhalok kilns of Thailand; but this development falls outside the scope of this volume.

---

[12] Gompertz, 'Gilded wares of Sung and Koryo', *Burlington Magazine*, XCVIII, 1956, pp. 300–8, 401–2.
[13] Chewon Kim and G. Gompertz, *The Ceramic Art of Korea*, 1961, Pl. 22.
[14] *Kiln Sites*, no. 167
[15] STZ, 1977, Vol. 9, Pl. 286.
[16] Ibid., Pl. 288.
[17] J. M. Addis, 'Chinese ceramics found in the Philippines', TOCS, 37, 1967–9, pp. 17–36.

South-East Asia

The existence of an independent pottery tradition in South-East Asia militated against any penetration of this market by Chinese exports. According to Peter Meister[18] there is no evidence to be seen of Chinese influence in Khmer ceramics, either in shape or in glaze. In the last decade of the thirteenth century, after the fall of Sung, Chinese potters and ceramic technicians arrived in Thailand and set up factories, first at Sukhotai and then at Sawankhalok.[19] Subsequently Thai wares were extensively exported to Indonesia. On the other hand, Malaysia, Sarawak and Sumatra lay on the route for exports of Chinese ceramics to the West. Following on exploration by Dr Quaritch Wales, Alistair Lamb[20] investigated sites at Penkalan Bejan, Takuapa and Kataha in the early 1960s and found shards of *Temmoku* type, *ch'ing-pai* boxes and small bottles and some good quality Chekiang celadon of Southern Sung date, together with another type with unglazed foot which must have originated in South-East Asia and not China. Lamb showed that the presence of Islamic pottery and glass fragments at these sites pointed to their being entrepôts for the trade to India and beyond.

Indonesia

The Indonesian market is seen as far more important for Chinese export ceramics. Dr Orsoy de Flines formed a large and representative collection in the museum at Jakarta.[21] The types which predominate are Chekiang celadons, *ch'ing-pai* and south China white wares, many of fine quality. Michael Sullivan in his 'Notes on Chinese Export Wares',[22] based on the public collections in Singapore, considered that most of the *ch'ing-pai* and south China white wares should now be classed as Yüan. Naturally, some examples of these export wares reached Holland, and Barbara Harrisson has reproduced some in her 'Oriental Celadon in the Princessehof Museum at Leeuwarden', including a fine south Chinese bowl with carved lotus design under a grey-green glaze, which may now be tentatively identified as a product of the Fukien kiln at T'ung-an,[23] though superior to the shards from this site. As already remarked, another celadon type found in Indonesia is the funeral vase with dragons round the shoulder from the Lung-ch'üan kilns of Southern Sung date.[24]

---

[18] P. W. Meister, 'Some remarks on South-East Asian Ceramics' in *Legend and Reality; Early Ceramics from South-East Asia*, Cologne, 1977, p. 14.
[19] W. Willetts, *Ceramic Art of Southeast Asia*, Singapore, 1971, p. 16.
[20] T. Harrisson, '"Export ware" found in West Borneo', *Oriental Art*, V, 1959, pp. 40–51; A. Lamb, 'Research at Pengkala, Bujang', *Federal Museum Journal*, NS 6, 1961, pp. 69–88.
[21] E. W. van Orsoy de Flines, *Gids voor de Keramische Verzameling*, Batavia, 1949.
[22] TOCS, 33, 1960–2, pp. 61–77.
[23] Het Princessehof ceramic Museum, Leeuwarden, 1978, no. 15, and *Kiln Sites*, nos. 130–5.
[24] B. Harrisson, op. cit. Nos. 54–5.

SARAWAK

Lying on the direct route to Indonesia was Sarawak, and between 1947 and 1967 'hundreds of thousands of pieces of pre-Ming ceramics' were excavated under the direction of Tom Harrisson.[25] The earliest are Yüeh-type bowls and vases, presumably of tenth to eleventh century date, then many shards of Lung-ch'üan, fish-bowls and mallet-shaped (*kinuta*) vases, some of which are probably Southern Sung, others Yüan. *Ch'ing-pai* wares are also represented in quantity, especially incised bowls on a high foot, and small boxes and also a good ewer. Much rarer are examples of Chien tea-bowls. Many of the finds came from the mouth of the Sarawak river and others from Santubong river; indeed the main sites are all on river estuaries, but some intact pieces were associated with burials in the Niah cave, which seem to extend from the tenth century to the thirteenth.

SUMATRA

It is obvious that the north coast of the great island of Sumatra, which forms the southern side of the straits of Malacca, must have played a part in the export trade between China and the West. But the first attempt at archaeological investigation of this coast was made at Kota Cina by Edward McKinnon in 1972–6.[26] Many coins of Northern Sung date were found and a carbon-14 test on wood-ash yielded a date of 1200 ($\pm$75 years). The ceramic finds were datable between the late twelfth century and the fourteenth. Several types of white ware probably originate from the Tê-hua kilns of Fukien and include both bowls with bare lip and dishes and jars with moulded floral decoration. There were also celadon types with incised lotus design, which once more recall the shards from T'ung-an in Fukien. But I believe that the celadon pieces with moulded four-character good-luck inscriptions, also found in Kedah, to be from South-East Asia, and not from Chekiang. A single shard from the neck of a jar with moulded dragon under a yellow glaze may derive from the Ch'üan-chou kiln at this great Fukien port, as represented by shard no. 172 in the 1980 kiln site exhibition.

SOUTH ASIA AND SRI LANKA

The next entrepôt for the Chinese trade with the West was in Sri Lanka (Ceylon). The oldest centre for this trade seems to have been Mahatittha (modern Mantai), just north of the 'land-bridge' from the island to South India, called Adam's Bridge. This port is established as of the Sassanian period and was

---

[25] C. Zainie, and T. Harrisson, 'Early Chinese stonewares exacavated in Sarawak 1947–67', *Sarawak Museum Journal*, NS, 30, no. 3, 1967, pp. 30–90.
[26] E. P. E. McKinnon, 'Oriental ceramics found in North Sumatra', TOCS, 41, 1975–7, pp. 59–120.

a major place for the trans-shipment of Chinese goods by the ninth century. In 1961-2 William Willetts reported finding both Yüeh-type and early white ware on this site; and later Dr R. S. da Silva carried out a limited excavation[27] which revealed fragments of both Islamic and Chinese wares datable to the ninth/tenth centuries. John Carswell visited this site in 1976 and again in 1979 and plans a major excavation there in association with the Sri Lankan archaeologists, which should throw full light on the history of this port. Meanwhile Carswell has conducted an excavation on another site in this same area, at Vankalai, south of the land-bridge. Here on a beach site he found that the Chinese wares begin only with Southern Sung white ware and celadon mixed with local pottery. He also reported finds of Sung white ware (not Ting-yao however) and Chekiang celadon at Yapahuwa and *ch'ing-pai* boxes at Polannaruwa.

John Carswell also made a survey in 1976 of sites on the west coast of India from Cambay to Quilon, where the literary sources mentioned that there were trading ports. The historic ports of Cambay, Broach, Surat and Goa produced no pre-Ming shards; not surprisingly in areas which have been constantly occupied ever since. Even Calicut, which we know to have been a principal entrepot for the China trade in the fourteenth and fifteenth centuries, yielded no shards. It must be emphasized, however, that this survey represents only superficial study of these sites.[28] It could well be that, in future, evidence may be found by excavation to give body to the literary evidence for the vital role of some of these ports in the east/west trade. We should remember that, while coastal areas were controlled by Muslim rulers, much of the interior, especially in the south, was Hindu and therefore did not represent a major market for Chinese procelain, at least before the fourteenth century. Carswell reported in 1982 that he had located near the mouth of the Tamprapari river the famous port of Kayal (Qa'il), called Cail by Marco Polo who noted the 'rich and noble city' for its trade contacts with the West, Hormuz and Yemen. In a note to Yule's edition of Marco Polo Dr Caldwell described the site, then over a kilometre and a half from the sea, in Tinnevelly district, as covered with 'remains of pottery chiefly Chinese'. John Carswell now writes of 'early Lung-ch'üan', evidently meaning early Southern Sung; for he dates the great period of this port as being after the loss to the Chola of Mantai in 1070, when he believes the entrepôt trade was switched to Kayal on the Malabar coast.[29]

[27] J. Carswell, 'China and Islam in the Maldive Islands', TOCS, 41, 1975–7, p. 124, Pls. 53d and 67b.
[28] J. Carswell, 'China and Islam; a survey of the coast of India and Ceylon', TOCS, 42, 1977–8, pp. 25–58.
[29] F. A. Khan, *Bambhore*, Karachi, 1969.

The Gulf and the Red Sea

The destination for the Chinese overseas trade in the Sung period was the Middle East, by way of the Gulf and the Red Sea ports, serving respectively Iran and Mesopotamia, and Egypt and the Mediterranean area. The boom for this trade in the Gulf was the ninth and tenth centuries; after AD 1000 it was much reduced. The situation is the same for the entrepôt on the Sind coast of Pakistan where Bambhore was a flourishing Muslim settlement whose prosperity began to decline in the eleventh century.[30] But the site is littered with imported pottery, especially Chinese stoneware.

Suhar on the coast of Oman, just outside the straits of Ormuz, enjoyed a rather short spell of prosperity between about 830 and 892, during which time great fortunes were made in the eastern trade financed by a Jewish community but carried by an Arab fleet. Apparently this site has now been swept clean by flood water.[31]

Siraf on the other hand, on the coast of Fars inside the Gulf, has revealed much information as a result of the excavation directed by David Whitehouse for the British Institute of Persian Studies between 1966 and 1973.[32] It must be stressed that here we have good stratigraphic evidence for the chronological sequence of finds, though an absolute chronology is still to be arrived at. However, so far as Chinese ceramics are concerned, it is clear that the earliest stratum is of late T'ang date, early ninth century, represented by black ware and by a type of green and brown splashed ware over a white slip which can be associated with kilns near Ch'ang-sha in Hunan province.[33] White stoneware and Yüeh-type ware, including a bowl with spur-marks which is from Wên-chou in Chekiang, come only from the next phase, not earlier than 850; and white porcelain from a still later phase, probably the tenth century. To this period is also to be attributed the lobed dish with moulded decoration of ducks in flight under a splashed glaze. This is ascribed to a Liao kiln of tenth/eleventh century[34] and to be compared with dishes with moulded decoration under green, yellow and white glaze, exhibited at China House, New York,[35] in 1973, where they were dated about 1090 by reference to pieces recovered from Liao tombs dated that year. Similar pieces are in Japan[36] and

[30] Sir H. Yule, *The Book of Ser Marco Polo*, 1929, Vol. II, pp. 372–3. Private information from John Carswell by letter dated 27.6.82.

[31] J. C. Wilkinson, 'Suhār in the early Islamic period', *South Asian Archaeology*, Naples, 1979, pp. 887–907; A. Williamson, *Sohar and Omani Seafaring in the Indian Ocean*, Muscat, 1973.

[32] D. Whitehouse, 'Preliminary reports on the excavations at Siraf', *Iran*, IX, 1971; X, 1972; XII, 1974.

[33] Medley, *T'ang Pottery and Porcelain*, 1981, pp. 92–6.

[34] B. Gray, 'The export of Chinese porcelain to the Islamic world', TOCS, 41, 1975–7, Pls. 92b and c; a similar dish of Egyptian provenance is in the Meyer collection in Eton College Museum.

[35] Y. Mino, *Ceramics in the Liao Dynasty*, New York, 1973, nos. 22–3.

[36] STZ, 1956, Vol. 11, Pl. 139. *Mayuyama, Seventy Years*, Pl. 325.

one in the Dreyfus collection in London[37] which shows ribbing similar to that on the bowl from Siraf. The white porcelain found there also seems to be from a northern kiln and datable by archaeological evidence to the tenth or early eleventh century; a five-lobed bowl recovered from the palace site[38] resembles the white wares of Liao.

Whitehouse has made clear the immediate impact of these imported Chinese wares on the local ceramic industry in Mesopotamia where glaze and shape were imitated, as well as they could be in lower-fired pottery. Indeed, this fact makes the import of Chinese stoneware and porcelain into the Islamic world far more culturally significant than its import into the economies of Indonesia and South Asia where there was no local imitation.

Imitation in the Islamic lands was of course stimulated by the scarcity and high price of Chinese imports; for, even by taking full advantage of the monsoon pattern, the round trip from Siraf to India alone would take six months, the outward sailing being in summer and the return in the following winter months. But the value of the trade was very great. As late as the twelfth century a merchant shipowner of Siraf, trading to India, called Ramisht, was a millionaire. He died in 1140 after making several endowments of foundations in Mecca.[39] In southern Iran the collapse of Buyid rule about 1055 interrupted internal communications from Siraf and by 1100 the pre-eminence of this great port had gone, having been transferred to the greater security of Kish (Qais) island. However, finds of imported ceramics on this island are at present limited to the Mongol period; and no piece is earlier than the thirteenth century. Indeed overseas trade from the Gulf suffered a period of eclipse after the end of the eleventh century until the Mongols re-established stable conditions. No silver coins were minted in the Gulf area between about 1060 and 1290, a sure indication of economic decline, as Nicholas Lowick has pointed out.[40] By 1330 Kish had been superseded as a trading port by Hormuz island.

Instead, the Far Eastern trade route was switched in the later eleventh century away from the Gulf to the Red Sea ports while the coast of the Yemen provided entrepôt stations. It is also in this connection that the survey of the Maldive islands by John Carswell carried out in 1979[41] should find a place; for they also acted as a station on the route from South India to the Red Sea and East Africa. The inhabitants were Muslim by the mid-twelfth century. The porcelain fragments found there are not older than the thirteenth-century Chekiang celadons. A *ch'ing-pai* box lid has a moulded design on the cover

[37] TOCS, 32, 1960, no. 125, and p. 30 for comments by the author.
[38] TOCS, 41, 1975–7, Pl. 93a.
[39] S. M. Stern, 'Rāmisht of Sirāf, a merchant millionaire of the twelfth century', *Journal of the Royal Asiatic Society*, 1967, pp. 10–14.
[40] N. Lowick, 'Trade patterns on the Persian Gulf in the light of recent coin evidence', *Studies in Honor of George C. Miles*, Beirut, 1974, pp. 319–34.
[41] 'China and Islam in the Maldive Islands', TOCS, 41, 1975–7, pp. 121–98.

and is therefore of Yüan date. We can also estimate the course and categories of Chinese export ceramics at this time from investigations of sites on the Aden litoral and at Aidhab on the Red Sea; but far more significantly at the site of Fustat, the pre-Fatimid capital of Egypt.

Excavations at the Fustat site carried out by George Scanlon between 1964 and 1972 yielded more than three thousand fragments of Chinese ceramics, of which 75% are of Chekiang celadon, according to the analysis by Dr Bo Gyllensvärd published in 1973–5.[42] There is also an earlier group of wares from the Yüeh kilns, all datable to the tenth century; some plain and some incised and some carved in addition. Gyllensvärd attributes less than ten pieces to the Ting-yao kilns, four to Northern celadon, and the white bottle already discussed, with three colour-glazed pieces, to the Liao kilns. The Chekiang celadons extend from Northern Sung to early Ming and they include a high proportion of large bowls and dishes made especially for export to the West; as many as half are stated to be crackled. This condition is perhaps due to burial degeneration. The many blue and white fragments do not concern us. Second in quantity among the fragments after the celadons are the *ch'ing-pai* wares; and here Gyllensvärd found it difficult to draw a line between the Southern Sung and the Yüan periods. He calls attention to lotus bowls of a sugary ware with slightly bluish glaze, suggesting that they might have originated at Chi-chou. It now seems, however, that this ware comes from the kiln at Hsi-ts'un in Kuang-tung, not far from Canton, from where there was a large export trade under the Sung.

The Chinese were building great sea-going junks more than sixty metres long in the twelfth century, before 1178 and probably before 1161 under Southern Sung. By then rutters were recorded; and a map of 'China and the Barbarian countries' was engraved on stone in 1137 and is now preserved in the Pei-lin at Sian.[43] This map shows only China proper, though extraordinarily accurately, and the western regions are only listed in a textual insert. It is, however, proof of the advanced state of cartography in China at that date.

East Africa

Islamic merchants were reaching the east coast of Africa by the ninth century and Muslim colonies were established at several points by the early tenth century, first probably at Manda in Kenya, an offshore island with stone buildings. It supplied mango poles for building to the timberless cities of the Gulf. Here excavation by Neville Chittick between 1965 and 1970 revealed, beside much imported Islamic pottery, some Chinese stoneware of both Yüeh and northern

[42] *Bulletin of the Museum of Far Eastern Antiquities*, Stockholm 45, 1973, pp. 108–10; and 47, 1975, p. 94.
[43] J. Needham, *Science and Civilization in China*, III, pp. 497–590.

white ware, from the tenth to the eleventh centuries. Kilwa, another island colony, much further south beyond Zanzibar off the coast of Tanzania, has been shown to have been a major overseas trading station from about 1200 until the arrival of the Portuguese. Chittick excavated here between 1960 and 1965 and his findings are supported by the sixteenth-century 'Chronicle of Kilwa' in Arabic. By the late twelfth century the power of Kilwa was extensive, based on control of the gold-trade of Zimbabwe. In the thirteenth century the Sultans were striking their own coins; the Husumi palace in Kilwa probably dates from 1191–1215, but the Chinese porcelain found there is not earlier than the thirteenth century.[44] It would all have been carried in Persian or Arab ships; for the first direct contact of China with Africa was not until the voyage of Chêng Ho in 1417–19.

James Kirkman excavated at Malindi on the coast north of Mombasa and revealed columns crowned by Chinese celadon bowls and some *ch'ing-pai* and blue and white porcelain; but I do not accept that any of these are earlier than the later fourteenth century. As to Zimbabwe, it has long been known that shards of celadon were found within the dry-stone walled enclosures. They must have travelled there by the well-established gold route to the coast at Sofala; but they are not earlier than the late twelfth or early thirteenth century, the end of Southern Sung. All these ports had close links with India and it is by trans-shipment from there that all pre-Ming porcelain would have reached East Africa; it was clearly scarce there and valued accordingly for its prestige.

NORTH IRAN

We have not yet considered the finds of Chinese stoneware and porcelain in northern Iran, away from the Gulf. The main site is Nishapur, commercial capital of the powerful Samanid rulers, who traded via the Russian rivers as far as Scandinavia. It was only in 1974 that Charles Wilkinson published a monograph on the ceramic finds there in the Metropolitan Museum excavations of 1935–40.[45] Among the great mass of Islamic pottery there only seventeen Chinese shards were recorded; and one of these (no. 9) is almost certainly an Islamic imitation. Wilkinson dates all these shards to the ninth and tenth centuries. They include Yüeh-type wares, *ch'ing-pai* and two from moulded lead-glazed wares, one from the T'ang kiln at Ch'ang-sha; the other, with a coiled dragon in the centre of a dish, may now be identified as from the Ch'üan-chou kiln in Fukien and dated eleventh century, not ninth. There seems to be no doubt that all these pieces reached Nishapur from Mesopotamia, having made the sea voyage to Basra.

[44] H. N. Chittick, *Kilwa, an Islamic Trading City on the East African Coast*, 1974, Vol. 1, pp. 238–41; Vol. 2, pp. 308–12.
[45] C. K. Wilkinson, *Nishapur: Pottery of the Early Islamic Period*, 1974, p. 254 for the Chinese imported wares.

SUMMARY

Throughout this book the situation of the kiln sites of China in proximity to water transport has been stressed. The same consideration applies to the export trade. The diffusion of Chinese ceramics, which we have outlined and which we have seen to have reached under Sung such large proportions, was entirely by sea. We have seen that great Chinese junks were constructed for long sea voyages as far west as Sri Lanka, where trans-shipment took place to Arab and Persian or coastal Indian ships. At the same time, some Muslim sailors were still making the long voyage to the South China ports. It was only in the early fifteenth century that Chinese ships reached the ports in the Gulf, the Yemen and East Africa.

It was formerly thought that the overland route played an important role in the export trade; but it now seems that the silk route through Central Asia, which had been so active under the later Six Dynasties, Sui and T'ang dynasties, dwindled to insignificance under Sung because of the disturbed conditions along these routes. It was only resumed under the Mongols, at which time alone may it have served as a significant route for ceramic exports. It may be suggested that the fragments of Chinese stoneware found along these routes by explorers, such as Aurel Stein and Kozlov, date only from the thirteenth century, or the fourteenth.

Another conclusion to be drawn from our survey is that excavations in the People's Republic of China have made possible the identification of a large part of the exported ceramics; and that, as a result, the role of south China kilns is now seen to have been predominant even under Northern Sung. Some of these kilns, in Fukien and Kuang-tung for instance, worked almost entirely for export, while the proportion of exports was significant even at Ching-tê-chên from the beginnings of its kilns. By Southern Sung special shapes and sizes were being made expressly to cater to the demand of oversea markets. Quality was well maintained in most of these wares, so that the reputation of Chinese ceramics remained as high at the end of our period as it had been when they first reached the West in the eighth to ninth centuries. The furthest west that so far fragments of Sung wares have been found is Almeria in Andalusia, where fragments of Yüeh ware, datable to the late tenth century, have been discovered, including some inscribed in Kufic script after their arrival there.

BIBLIOGRAPHY

J. M. Addis, 'Chinese porcelain found in the Philippines', TOCS, Vol. 37, 1970

J. M. Addis, 'A visit to Ching-te Chen', TOCS, Vol. 41, 1977

J. M. Addis, *Chinese Ceramics from Datable Tombs*, London, 1978

R. Y. L. d'Argencé, *Chinese Ceramics in the Avery Brundage Collection*, San Francisco, 1967

John Ayers, *The Seligman Collection of Oriental Art*, Vol. 2, *Chinese and Korean Pottery and Porcelain*, London, 1964

John Ayers, *The Baur Collection: Chinese Ceramics*, Vol. 1, Geneva, 1968

Boston Museum of Fine Arts, *The Charles B. Hoyt Collection, Memorial Exhibition*, Boston, 1952

Michel Calmann, *Collection Michel Calmann*, Paris, 1969

John Carswell, 'China and Islam in the Maldive Islands', TOCS, Vol. 42, 1979

John Carswell, 'China and Islam: a Survey of the Coast of India and Ceylon', TOCS, Vol 2, 1979

Sir Percival David, 'A Commentary on Ju Ware', TOCS, Vol. 14, 1936–7

Sir Percival David, *Chinese Connoisseurship: the Ko Ku Yao Lun*, translated and edited with facsimile of the text of 1388, London, 1971

J. J. L. Duyvendak, *China's Discovery of Africa*, London, 1949

Freer Gallery of Art, *Masterpieces of Chinese and Japanese Art*, Washington, 1976

H. Garner, 'Early Chinese Crackled Porcelain', TOCS, Vol. 32, 1959–60

G. M. Gompertz, *Chinese Celadon Wares*, 2nd edition, London, 1980

Basil Gray, *Early Chinese Pottery and Porcelain*, London, 1953

Basil Gray, 'The Export of Chinese Porcelain to India', TOCS, Vol. 36, 1967

Basil Gray, 'The Export of Chinese Porcelain to the Islamic World', TOCS, Vol. 41, 1977

B. Gyllensvärd, *Chinese Gold and Silver in the Carl Kempe Collection*, Stockholm, 1953

B. Gyllensvärd, *Chinese Ceramics in the Carl Kempe Collection*, Stockholm, 1964

B. Gyllensvärd, 'Recent Finds of Chinese Ceramics at Fostat', *Bulletin of the Museum of Far Eastern Antiquities*, Vols. 45, 47, 1973–5

A. L. Hetherington, *The Schiller Collection of Chinese Ceramics*, Bristol, 1948

P. Hughes-Stanton and R. Kerr, *Kiln Sites of Ancient China; recent finds of pottery and porcelain*, an exhibition lent by the People's Republic of China, London, 1980

J. Gordon Lee, 'A Slip-decorated Ting Pillow in Philadelphia and Related Pieces', FECB, XII, 1960

G. Lindberg, 'Hsing-yao and Ting-yao', BMFEA, No. 25, 1953

Hin-cheung Lovell, *Illustrated Catalogue of Ting-yao and Related Wares in the Percival David Foundation*, London, 1964

E. P. E. McKinnon, 'Oriental Ceramics Excavated in North Sumatra', TOCS, Vol. 41, 1977

M. Medley, *Illustrated Catalogue of Celadon Wares*, PDF, London, 1972

M. Medley, *Yüan Porcelain and Stoneware*, London, 1974

M. Medley, *Korean and Chinese Ceramics from the 10th to the 14th Century*, Cambridge, 1976

M. Medley, *The Chinese Potter: a Practical History of Chinese Ceramics*, Oxford, 1976

M. Medley, *Illustrated Catalogue of Ting and Allied Wares*, PDF, London, 1980

Yutaka Mino, 'Tz'ŭ-chou Type Ware Decorated with Incised Patterns on a Stamped "Fish-roe" Ground', *Archives of Asian Art*, XXXII, 1979

Yutaka Mino, *Freedom of Clay and Brush through Seven Centuries in Northern China; Tz'u-chou Type Wares 960–1600*, Indianapolis, 1980

Oriental Ceramic Society, exhibition catalogues:
   a. *Ting, Ying-ch'ing and Tz'u-chou Wares*, 1949
   b. *Ju and Kuan Wares*, 1952
   c. *Chün and Brown Wares*, 1952
   d. *The Arts of the Sung Dynasty*, 1960
   e. *The Ceramic Art of China*, 1971

R. T. Paine, 'Chinese Ceramic Pillows from Collections in Boston and the Vicinity', FECB, VII(3), 1955

Percival David Foundation of Chinese Art, University of London, *A Hundred Masterpieces of Chinese Ceramics from the Percival David Collection*, Tokyo, 1980

J. M. Plumer, 'The Ting-yao Kiln Sites', *Archives of the Chinese Art Society of America*, Vol. 3, 1948–9

J. M. Plumer, *Temmoku: a Study of the Wares of Chien*, Tokyo, 1972

S. Riddell, *Dated Chinese Antiquities, 600–1650*, London, 1979

G. T. Scanlon, 'Egypt and China; Trade and Imitation', *Islam and the Trade of Asia*, Oxford, 1970

M. Sullivan, *Chinese Ceramics, Bronzes and Jades, in the Collection of Sir Alan and Lady Barlow*, London, 1963

M. Tregear, *Chinese Greenwares in the Ashmolean Museum*, Oxford, 1976

H. Trubner, *Asiatic Art in the Seattle Art Museum*, Seattle, 1973

S. G. Valenstein, *A Handbook of Chinese Ceramics*, Metropolitan Museum of Art, New York, 1975

W. Watson, *The Genius of China*, an exhibition of archaeological finds of the People's Republic of China, 1973–4, London, 1973

P. Wheatley, 'Geographical Notes on some Commodities Involved in Sung Maritime Trade', *Journal of the Malay Branch of the Royal Asiatic Society*, Vol. 32, 1959

D. Whitehouse, 'Chinese Stoneware from Siraf; the Earliest Finds', *South Asian Archaeology*, 1973

R. Whitfield, 'Tz'ŭ-chou Pillows with Painted Decoration', PDF, *Colloquies on Art and Archaeology*, No. 5, 1975

J. Wirgin, 'Some Ceramic Wares from Chi-chou', *Bulletin of the Museum of Far Eastern Antiquities*, Vol. 34, Stockholm, 1962

J. Wirgin, 'Sung Ceramic Designs', BMFEA, Vol. 42, Stockholm, 1970

J. Wirgin, 'Sung Ceramic Designs and their Relation to Painting', PDF, *Colloquies on Art and Archaeology in Asia*, No. 5, 1975

JAPANESE

Ataka collection:
    a. *Exhibition of Selected Masterpieces of Old Chinese and Korean Ceramics*, Tokyo, 1970
    b. *Masterpieces of Old Chinese Ceramics*, Tokyo, 1975
    c. *Exhibition of Far Eastern Ceramics*, Tokyo, 1978
China's Beauty of 2,000 Years, exhibition of ceramics and rubbings of inscriptions, Tokyo, 1965
Heibonsha Ceramic Series, Vol. 13, *Tz'ŭ-chou*, 1958; Vol. 26, *Temmoku*, 1962
Fujio Koyama, *The Beauty of Sung Ceramics*, 1959
Fujio Koyama, *Chinese ceramics: one hundred masterpieces selected from collections in Japan, England, France and America*, Tokyo, 1960
Fujio Koyama, 'The Ting-yao Kilns at Chien Tz'ŭ-tsun', *Tōji*, XVIII, 1971
Fujio Koyama, *Post-war Discoveries of T'ang and Sung Kiln Sites*, Tokyo, 1962
F. Koyama, and J. Figgess, *Two Thousand Years of Oriental Ceramics*, Tokyo, 1961
Junkichi Mayuyama, *Chinese Ceramics in the West: a compendium of Chinese ceramic masterpieces in European and American collections*, Tokyo, 1960
Junkichi Mayuyama, *Mayuyama, Seventy Years*, 2 Vols., Tokyo, 1976
Yasuhiko Mayuyama, *Chūgoku Bunbutsu Kemban* (Chinese art tour), Tokyo, 1973
Tsugio Mikami, 'Sung Ceramics and Pottery of the Sung Dynasty', *Kobijutsu*, No. 9, 1955
Sekai Tōji Zenshū (World Ceramics), 1st edition, Vol. 10, Tokyo, 1955; 2nd edition, Vol. 12 by Gakuji Hasebe, Tokyo, 1977
Tokyo National Museum, *Chinese Arts of the Sung and Yuan Periods*, 1961
Tokyo National Museum, *Illustrated Catalogue: Chinese Ceramics*, 1965
Tokyo National Museum, *Exhibition of Far Eastern Ceramics*, 1970
Tokyo National Museum, *Special Exhibition of Chinese Ceramics Excavated in Japan*, 1975

CHINESE

Chao Ju-kua, *Chu-fan chih* (Records of foreign people), 1226; Ch'angsha, 1940; edited and translated by F. Hirth and W. W. Rockhill, St Petersburg, 1911
Chinese Art Treasures, A selected group of objects from the Chinese National Palace Museum and the Chinese Central Museum, Taichung, Taiwan. Exhibited in the USA in 1961–2
Ku Kung Po-Wu-Yüan Ts'ang Tz'u Hsüan Chi, Peking, 1962
Ku Kung Po Wu Yüan Yüankan, Peking, 1980
Porcelain of the National Palace Museum, Taipei, 8 Vols., Hongkong, 1961–2
Shanghai Municipal Museum, *Select Catalogue of Ceramics*, Shanghai, 1979

OCS TRANSLATIONS

  2. 'Lung-ch'üan' (*Wen-wu*, 1963)
  3. 'Lin-ju, Honan; Northern celadon, Chün and Ju wares' (*Wen-wu*, 1964)
  4. 'Ting-yao kiln sites' (*K'ao-ku*, 1965)
  5. 'Tz'ŭ-chou ware kiln sites', Honan (*Wen-wu*, 1964)
  6. 'Yüeh-yao' (*Wen-wu*, 1965)

7. a. 'Chi-chou ware' (*Wen-wu*, 1973)
   b. *Mang-k'ou* (barbed mouth) and *Sê-k'ou* (rough mouth) wares from Northern Sung to Yüan in the north; and Ching-tê-chên, *fu shao* (upside down firing), *K'ao-ku*, 1974
8. 'Development of porcelain' (*Wen-wu*, 1973)
10. 'The extensive international market for Dehua porcelain', *Haiwai Jiaotongshi Yanjiu*, 1980

Sale Catalogues

The Eumorfopoulos Collection, Sotheby, 28–31 May 1940
Mrs Walter Sedgwick, Sotheby, 2 July 1968
George de Menasce, Spink, May 1971
Postan Collection of Early Chinese Ceramics, Bluett and Sons, November 1972
Sir Harry and Lady Garner, Chinese and Japanese Wares, Bluett, May 1973
Mrs Alfred Clark, Sotheby, 25 March 1975
The Malcolm Collection, Sotheby, 29 March 1977

INDEX